Hand of Glory

John Wood

Published in 2015

First Edition

A CIP catalogue record for this title is available from the British Library.

My thanks go to.....

Canon Eric Woods DL, Vicar of Sherborne. It was after a long conversation with Canon Woods touching on the occult, the supernatural and associated topics that I left Sherborne vicarage one evening with the germ of an idea. This idea turned into Hand of Glory.

Many thanks to www.bookcover4u.com for the cover design

Thanks also to Barbara Altman (nee Loveluck) for the photograph.

Many thanks to Susie and Rose of The Doghouse, El Pilar, Benavista for allowing me to turn their splendid pub into a Den of Thieves.

The Hand of Glory chant beginning 'open lock to the dead man's knock' is taken from the work of Richard Harris Barham, cleric, novelist and poet 1788 – 1845. Richard Barham was better known as Thomas Ingoldsby

"Heaven has no rage like love to hatred turned, Nor hell a fury like a woman scorned," spoken by Perez in Act 3, Scene 2," The Mourning Bride (1697) by William Congrave, playwright and poet. (1670 – 1729)

The lyrics to Onward Christian Soldiers are by Sabine Baring-Gould. The music is by Sir Arthur Sullivan 1842 – 1900. Arthur Sullivan is perhaps best known for his collaborations with Sir William Gilbert (Gilbert and Sullivan)

Inspector Loveluck Books

Death will have his day

by

John Wood

A society wedding in Sherborne Abbey is interrupted when the organist is found murdered in the organ loft. The finger of suspicion is pointed at the mysterious 'Lady in Blue'. Inspector Loveluck and his team uncover a huge fraud, involving not only the wealthy members of Sherborne town but also the seemingly harmless but eccentric 'Last of the Summer Wine Investors Club'. When the most prominent member of Sherborne society disappears and Inspector Loveluck's sergeant is kidnapped, the stakes become terrifyingly high. A rollercoaster of events takes them to Spain in the search for the coded diary and the only person who can decode it seems to outsmart Loveluck at every turn.

Hand of Glory

by

John Wood

When three bodies are discovered in hotel bedrooms, Inspector Loveluck begins a complicated investigation which involves pagan rituals and the secrets of a dynasty and its inheritance. When the 'Psychic Fair and Witches Exhibition' rolls into Sherborne bringing Psychics, Witches and thousands of the public in its wake, a story going back twenty five years begins to unfold. Forces from the warring factions of Sherborne Witches and New Forest Witches, whose feuding goes back hundreds of years, line up against each other giving Loveluck new headaches and taking him and his team into unfamiliar territory. This second of the Loveluck mysteries once again pitches the team against clever adversaries who will stop at nothing.

And coming soon .....

Loveluck Investigated
by
John Wood

Inspector Loveluck's wife, Angie, took her own life after several difficult years of marriage. Now, six years later, new evidence has come to light suggesting that it wasn't suicide. It was murder. Loveluck is arrested and has to sit and wait as the investigation runs its course. But Loveluck isn't a man to sit and wait .....

Chapter 1

Smoke.

Smoke rising, swaying, intertwining with itself with hints of colour.

Red from the embers below and yellow from the full moon above.

Vague moving figures are barely discernible behind the smoke, and the chanting is faint.

There is a makeshift circle of twigs and branches and in the centre stands a bowl of saltwater.

It is the full moon.

The moon is the focal point of power upon the earth.

They chant the name of the Goddess of the full moon. Jana.

Ja – na, Ja – na, Ja – na.....

A breeze blows away the smoke and the figures are clearer now in the circle.

A woman places a white shell in the centre of the bowl of saltwater and places nine smaller shells in a crescent shape.

We see five women dancing through the haze. Chanting.

Ja – na, Ja – na, Ja – na .....

Chanting for success in their venture.

These are the witches of the New Forest. Their venture is murder.

A waif like girl swings from the makeshift seat of a long rope attached to the high branch of a tree. She sings a haunting song in a tongue no one else in the group understands. Close by sit four men. The only other members of the group are a man of twenty five summers and a woman of powerful countenance. She holds the power but bows to the leadership of the younger man. She is Nemesis. She is the matriarch.

'I do not trust Winston,' she said softly and slowly.

'No-one trusts Winston,' was his swift reply.

'They don't trust him,' said Nemesis indicating the dancing, chanting witches. 'And they know'

The younger man watched the women swaying to their own chanting. 'Ask them.'

Nemesis walked across to the circle. 'Is the lawyer dead?

The women made a soothing singing noise.

'And is the old woman dead?' They continued the sweet noise. Nemesis smiled in the certain knowledge that the woman was dead.

'And is the imposter dead?' Their soothing sounds echoed 'yes'.

'And is the book-man dead?'

The noises stopped. Silence.

'He lives?'

The women moved into a violent chant. 'Ja-na, Ja – na, Ja – na....'

Nemesis walked swiftly back to her young leader. 'The book-man lives.'

He stood stony faced. 'Then Winston dies.'

'Rufus,' said Nemesis to her young leader. He turned. 'It must be done tonight.'

Rufus nodded. 'Tonight.'

From her swing on the tree the waifish girl began to chant. 'Hand of Glory, Hand of Glory, Hand of Glory.....' The four men sitting on a fallen tree trunk joined the chant. 'Hand of Glory, Hand of Glory...'

And when the Witches of the New Forest joined the chant, Winston's fate was sealed.

The waif-girl fashioned the end of the rope into a perfect noose. Nemesis took a machete from the back of a white pick-up truck and brandished it.

The chanting reached fever pitch. 'Hand of Glory, Hand of Glory, Hand of Glory...' and when Winston came crashing into the small clearing in the woods to collect his pay for completing his commission, one look at the people waiting for him told him they knew the job had not been completed and that his fate was indeed sealed.

Without ceremony he was grabbed by the men of the group, hauled onto the back of the pick-up truck and hanged without fear or favour.

Nemesis took one expert swing of the Machete and held up the prized possession they had been chanting for.

And still the fevered chanting continued. 'Hand of Glory'.

Chapter 2

Inspector Loveluck turned into the rear car park of the Poachers Inn at Piddletrenthide and pulled up behind a police car. He glanced at the long lines of parked cars and turned to his sergeant and said. 'Looks as if the pub is doing a good business.'

'Or was until we showed up,' said Sergeant Sadie Knightly. 'I don`t know which is worst for business. A dead body in one of the bedrooms or a car park full of police cars.'

They climbed out of the car and walked towards a uniformed officer who pointed the way to a row of small chalet style rooms facing onto a swimming pool and a beer garden.

'Room number 7, sir. Dr Ryan and the SOCO team are already there.'

Loveluck and Knightly, having donned protective garments, entered the somewhat crowded room. Loveluck nodded to Dr Ryan and the SOCO team who were going about their respective business.

'What have you got for us?'

'I'm not really sure,' said the doctor. 'The cause of death is fairly clear, but there are some very strange aspects.'

'Strange?'

'Well, if I didn`t know better I would say there might be elements of some kind of ritual being played out.'

'You mean some kind of ceremonial killing?' asked Knightly.

'No. Not ceremonial, but a kind of ritualistic killing. I'll need to run tests, but it could be that the victim was firstly drugged.'

'Nothing very ritualistic about that,' said Loveluck

'Ah, but this man wasn't killed by the drugs. He was garrotted. Strangled from behind by a thin wire. The military use this method of silent killing. It's very effective.' He adjusted his crouching position. 'Come and look at the marks on his throat.'

Loveluck studied the marks then looked around him. 'Any sign of the wire?'

'None,' said the doctor shaking his head.

Knightly knelt next to the doctor. 'They did quite a job on him.'

'He could have been helpless to defend himself but clearly aware of what was going to happen to him,' said Dr Ryan.

'And the hand?' said Loveluck noticing no left hand.

Ryan shrugged. 'The left hand is missing. Cut off fairly cleanly with something very sharp.'

Loveluck left them to it and went outside and beckoned to a uniformed officer. 'What do we know so far?'

'The body was found by the cleaner when she went to do the room at about 12.30 this afternoon, sir. She informed the boss and he called us. The pub's pretty full at the moment, mainly diners and just a few drinkers at the bar. We've asked no one to leave for the time being.'

Loveluck nodded. 'Good. Do you have enough men here?'

'Not for all the interviewing, sir, no.'

'Call for more uniforms.'

'Yes sir.'

'And we'll need somewhere to carry out the interviews. I suppose one of the empty bedrooms will do. Can you find the cleaner and get her to open up Room 8 for us?'

'Yes sir.'

Loveluck turned away and returning to Room 7 was met by Knightly coming out. 'Do you want me to interview the manager, sir? Get a full list of who had booked the room and stayed here for the last week or so. Try and identify the victim.'

'Get anything and everything you can'

Knightly nodded and went in search of the manager.

Loveluck sat at one of the tables in the beer garden. It was as good a place to interview the cleaner as any and he signalled to the police officer as he approached with a woman by his side.

'This is the lady who found the body, sir.'

Loveluck indicated to them both to take a seat and the constable prepared to take notes.

Loveluck smiled at the cleaner. 'And you are?'

'Patsy. Patsy Aspin.'

'What happened this morning when you went to clean Room 7?'

‘Well, it was this afternoon actually. About half past twelve.’ she corrected firmly. ‘I knocked on the door. I always knock 'cos you never know what you’re going to find.’

‘And what did you find?’

‘I've seen some things I can tell you. There was one couple.....I could scarcely believe what they were up to. I didn't know such things were possible.’

‘About this morning,’ said Loveluck.

‘Had to be a pair of circus contortionists, if you ask me.’

‘Mrs Aspin. Let’s stick to the facts please. We don't have much time.’

‘Well,’ she paused for breath and began. ‘Like I said, I knocked on the door and there was no reply. I knocked again just to make sure. You never know they might have gagged themselves or something.’

‘Mrs Aspin!’

‘So then I got my key out and unlocked the door and pushed it open. Then I called out. 'Good morning', I shouted, but there was no reply so I went in. And there he was. On the carpet by the bed. It was horrible. And that wire round his neck. Gruesome.’

Loveluck regarded her for a few seconds. ‘You had quite a good look at the body, Mrs Aspin.’

‘Well, I was.....transfixed,’ she said having searched for the word. ‘I stood there gawping.’

‘I see,’ said Loveluck. ‘And what did you do with the wire?’

‘Eh?’

‘The wire around his neck. What did you do with it?’

‘I didn't do anything with it,’ she blustered. ‘What’re you accusing me of?’

‘The doctor said that there was no sign of the wire. Someone must have taken it, and you were the only person in a position to take it.’

‘It must still be in the room somewhere.’

‘Mrs Aspin. You can tell me now where the wire is or we will search through your belongings and if we find it, and even if we don't, I will charge you with obstructing the police, removing evidence and anything else I can think of.’

He let the silence hang and watched Mrs Aspin consider her options.

‘It's only a bit of wire,’ she said.

Loveluck held out his hand. Sulkily she searched in her bag and handed it over. Mercifully she hadn't cleaned it and Loveluck placed it in an evidence bag.

'Keys,' he said.

Equally sulkily she handed over the keys and Loveluck warned her not to leave the premises.

'How am I supposed to finish my cleaning without my bleedin keys?'

'You'll have to wait until we are finished here, which could be days. Weeks.'

She stood up testily. 'Mr Grayson isn't going to like that. He's got people booked in.'

'Mr Grayson is the manager,' explained the police officer as they crossed back to the row of chalets again.

Loveluck pointed at the chalets. 'One of these can be our interview room. Preferably one without a body.'

'I'll sort it, sir.'

The constable started to leave when Loveluck said. 'Oh. And knock before you go in. There might be some of those circus contortionists in there.'

Dr Ryan came out of the building and joined Loveluck in the beer garden. 'Getting a spot of fresh air?' he asked.

Loveluck nodded. 'I couldn't do your job.'

Dr Ryan shrugged. 'It becomes routine.' Loveluck handed over the evidence bag with the wire in it. 'Where did you get that from?'

'The cleaner. A souvenir collector. Have you any idea when the murder took place?'

Ryan shrugged again. 'Not accurately. If the cleaner starts with Room 7 at 12.30 every afternoon that gives us some kind of time frame. I can say for sure that he was murdered in the last twenty four hours. In reality, I would guess he was murdered last night, around twelve to 18 hours ago. Say nine o'clock last night, give or take a couple of hours.'

Loveluck nodded. 'What did you mean when you said it might have been some kind of ritualistic murder?'

'Just guessing really. But the garrotting is an unusual way to murder a helpless person. It points to some kind of ritual. That and the missing hand. What kind of ritual I can't say. I don't know much about that kind of thing.'

Sergeant Knightly joined them at the table. 'Sorry I took so long sir. Mr Grayson, the manager, fancies himself as a bit of a ladies' man. Anyway, I got what I wanted.'

Dr Ryan smiled and looked on the beautiful face of Sadie Knightly. Mr Grayson wasn't the first man by a long chalk to have been captivated by her

'Pocket contents are available for you I believe, Inspector,' said Dr Ryan. 'Except there aren't any. Pockets empty, no wallet, no keys, no luggage. no nothing.'

Loveluck looked quizzically at the doctor. 'Why would the murderer go to all the trouble to remove everything like that?'

But before there was time to reply a uniformed officer strode smartly to the table and addressed Loveluck. 'I think you had better come, sir. And you too, doctor.'

'Why. What's happened?

'We've got another one, sir. In Room 8'

Chapter 3

Room 8 turned out to be similar to Room 7 in almost every way. Same size, same furniture, same dead body with a thin wire around its neck, same left hand missing. But this time the body was that of a young woman. Loveluck and Dr Ryan exchanged glances and Ryan hustled Loveluck and Knightly out of the room. 'Leave the team to go through things first, Inspector. I'll call you in as soon as possible.'

Loveluck and Knightly stood in the corridor in silence.

'Are you thinking what I'm thinking,' she asked.

Loveluck stared at her, deep in thought. 'Get the keys. All of them. For every damned room in the hotel.'

She returned with the keys and they both waited while she opened the door to Room 9. Knightly went in first and after a few seconds called for Loveluck to enter. She spread her arms wide. 'Nothing'

'Another great first for the Dorset police,' said Loveluck. 'Dorset police inspector manages to find a hotel room without a murdered person in it. This could lead to promotion for us.'

Knightly managed to find a smile. 'It could be a lot worse,' she said.

And how right she was.

Room 10 had another body in it. This time the body of an older woman. Garrotted in the same way. Left hand missing.

Room 11 was also empty but there were small yet clear signs that someone had spent time in the room. The bed seemed to have been laid on but not slept in. Knightly let out a long breath. 'Three rooms with a body in each of them. Two empty rooms. This is grisly '

'Check the bathroom,' said Loveluck.

'You'd better come and look at this, sir,'

'What is it?' He entered the bathroom and found her leaning against the shower wall looking very queasy indeed. In the centre of the shower were the three missing left hands with candles carefully placed between each of the fingers. They were arranged in a triangle and in the centre was a piece of paper with the words

Let those who rest more deeply sleep
Let those awake their vigils keep
Oh, hand of glory, shed thy light
Direct us to our spoil tonight.

Loveluck led her out of the room and they stood by the side of the swimming pool. Dr Ryan came out to talk to them. 'Anything in the other rooms?' he began but stopped when he saw their distressed faces. 'What is it?'

'Room 11. Shower.'

Ryan went inside but he was soon back. 'Leave it to SOCO.'

Loveluck grimaced 'They're welcome to it,'

The questioning of the diners in the Poachers Inn was completed quickly. As Knightly had remarked, 'If I had murdered three people in a pub, I wouldn't go back there for lunch next day when the place was crawling with police'

Questioning of other guests staying at the pub was more difficult as all were out at the time. There were only three guests staying the night of the murders and Loveluck would just have to wait until they returned.

Loveluck was sitting in the beer garden enjoying a cool pint with Inspector Anderson.

'Well. This is a bad deal,' said Anderson. 'I've never come across a case like this before.'

Loveluck nodded. 'It's a strange one all right. Garrotting isn't something you see much of. I don`t suppose you're an expert in the occult and such matters?'

'The wife calls me a pagan from time to time. Not that I know what a pagan is. Don't expect she does either, but that doesn't stop her. Anyway I wouldn't have thought garrotting had much to do with the occult. More the kind of thing they did in the war. Silent murder.'

'It's those severed hands and the candles that give it a strange edge. We need some research doing on all this.

I think your Sergeant Daly might be our man. He's a damned good researcher. Perhaps he could winkle out what all this ritual stuff is about. If indeed it is a ritual murder.'

'There we have a problem,' said Anderson expansively. 'Daly has been complaining about the amount of time he has to spend on the computer doing research. He rightly says that he's a detective sergeant and that he should be out and about, well, being a detective. I don't think he likes being deskbound. And I can't say I blame him.'

Loveluck sighed heavily. 'I'm sure we can work something out.'

Anderson drank deeply of his beer. 'So, what do we know about the murdered three,' he said. 'I am assuming they all have something in common.'

'If they aren't connected with each other in some way, then it means it was a random killing, and I would personally rather wade my way through the black magic than have random murders.'

'Amen to that,' said Anderson enthusiastically.

'But to answer your question,' continued Loveluck and he outlined the severing of the left hand and the placing of the candles between the fingers. 'I don't know who the victims are. Sergeant Knightly is with the manager now getting all the details.'

'Not a pretty case,' said Anderson.

They were joined at the table by Dr Ryan. 'Finished in there?' asked Loveluck.

'Not yet,' he said wearily. 'Just taking a break. What's that you're drinking?'

'Medicine, doctor.'

'A pint of that medicine would go down very nicely. Where's the dispensary?'

'Just through that door over there marked 'bar'.' said Loveluck. 'But here comes the pharmacist himself.'

They turned to see Knightly and Daly leaving the bar followed by the manager, Mr Grayson. 'Can I get you people a drink before we start?' asked Grayson.

Orders were given, the barman sent for and Grayson sat down.

Grayson started immediately. 'I have a very busy lunchtime trade here, Inspector, but I'll give you the facts as clearly as I've managed to get them from my staff.'

'We appreciate your time,'

'Firstly, the booking for all five rooms were made by a Mr John. He paid by credit card and doubtless you can find his details from my records with a little help from his bank.'

Loveluck nodded for him to continue.

'He also booked a table for five people for 8.30 that evening. Last night, that is. He asked to run a tab which he would settle when they left. The rooms were booked for one night.'

'Tell us about the dinner. You said it was booked for 8.30 last night.'

'That's correct. My John himself sat on a bar stool having a drink. Firstly a woman came in. Youngish woman. Twenties. She asked for Mr John and went to join him by the bar.'

'Then an older woman came in. Seventies. Same procedure. Asked for Mr John and when we pointed him out she also went to join him. Then they went to sit at their table.'

Grayson sat silently until Knightly said. 'Then what?'

'They waited and talked a bit. My barman says that the two women seemed to be pushing him for information but he kept putting them off with things like 'Just wait until we're all here. I don't want to keep repeating myself.'

'Did any others arrive?' asked Loveluck.

Grayson shrugged. 'Yes and no. By that I mean that the group stayed at three people and not the booked-for five. So they went to their table and talked and had their meal.'

'So why did you say 'yes and no''

'Because,' said Grayson slowly, 'another man did come in and ask for Mr John. But when the barman pointed him out he didn't go and join him.

This interested Loveluck. 'Can you remember anything about this man?'

Grayson shrugged. 'No, I didn't see him. My barman's the one to ask.'

'You're right. Sergeant Knightly. Go and fetch the barman.'

'Jamie isn't working today,' interrupted Grayson, 'he's back on tomorrow. I think you might like to know that yet another man came in and asked for Mr John. We pointed him out but he didn't go to join him either. Now if you'll excuse me.'

Loveluck nodded and the manager returned to his duties.

'There were a couple of interesting things about the three dead people," said Dr Ryan. 'Nothing I can be sure about until I've had them on the slab, but I think I can say fairly confidently that the first victim was a man of 55 years give or take a few. I think I can also say fairly confidently that he was not a manual worker. His hands were smooth. Probably a professional man. Accountant, lawyer, teacher. Something like that. Well cut suit. Good shoes.'

'And the others?' asked Loveluck.

'The younger of the two women was around 25 years old. Again give or take a couple of years. I'm no great expert on women's fashion but the clothes seemed to come from high street stores. However she wore what seemed to me to be a very expensive necklace and locket.'

'Any picture in it?'

'Yes. A small picture of a man. Might be useful to you.'

Sergeant Knightly stood up. 'I'm no expert on women's fashion either," she said. 'But I'll go and look.'

Dr Ryan nodded. 'I'll come with you in just a minute. But before we go, there was something interesting about the old woman. Hard to pitch an accurate age but around 70. She had very interesting skin. Weather beaten and slightly tanned. Not the kind of skin you get in the UK by and large.'

'You think she could have been a foreigner?' asked Loveluck.

Ryan shrugged. 'Possibly. But more likely to be from somewhere warm, wet and windy. That should leave you some options. There are a few places like that in the UK. Come on Sergeant. Let me see the fashionista at work.'

'So,' Loveluck said to Daly. 'I hear you're bored sitting at a desk all day doing research on the computer,'

'I certainly am.'

'Then you'll look forward to sitting in a bar all evening waiting the return of the other guests who were here when the murders were committed.'

'Aw,' he said in complaint. 'Not on my own. That'll be boring. Can I have someone with me?' He was hoping for Knightly.

'Constable Emmett will be here to keep you company,' said Loveluck inwardly smiling at Daly's crestfallen face.

'As for logistics,' said Loveluck changing the subject. 'The murders may have been committed here but the story lies somewhere else. Where, I don't know, but I'll centre the operation in Sherborne for the time being.'

‘That makes sense,’ said Anderson.

‘Sergeant Knightly will address and update us all tomorrow on what we have learned so far. I’ll delegate the teams.

‘Will I be doing the desk research again?’ asked Daly testily.

‘Yes. I'm afraid so.’

‘Permission to put in for a transfer sir,’ said Daly.

‘Denied,’ said Anderson smiling

‘Actually,’ said Dr Ryan and then paused.

They all looked at him

‘Actually, I know a police officer who would jump at the chance of being involved in the investigation. Even doing deskbound research.’ Ryan looked at them all knowingly. ‘I assume you know the police officer to whom I am referring.’

They all did.

Loveluck broke the silence. ‘Sergeant Pepper is still undergoing therapy. And though she’s back at work doing two and a half days a week I'm not sure she would be up to it.’

‘Everyone here,’ said Ryan, ‘except Sergeant Knightly,’ ‘was present in that field when we dug Sergeant Pepper out of that shallow grave.’

Silence and memories flooded the scene.

‘And none of us will ever forget what she went through and how she was affected by it.’

‘But now she works diligently and well two and a half days a week and, yes, she is still undergoing therapy. And will be for a while.

‘However, in my view, and I am a forensic doctor not a psychiatrist, but in my view if you take her off routine administrative tasks and assign her to this enquiry as a researcher I think it’ll do more for her desire and will to improve than a great deal of therapy.’

Loveluck nodded. ‘Well, it's a thought.’

Dr Ryan said ‘It's more than a thought, it’s a chance...’

‘I will think about it, doctor,’ said Loveluck firmly. ‘Leave it there. Putting aside the possible benefits we must remember that she’s only working half the week. That may not be enough. And I doubt the doctors will agree to her going full time yet.’

Loveluck stood up abruptly to indicate that the conversation and, indeed, the meeting was over. He nodded goodbye to everyone but called Sergeant Knightly over to him.

‘You are happy giving the briefing to the teams tomorrow, aren't you?’

'Yes sir. Completely.'

'It's just that you have discussed all the details with the manager and know more about it than anyone else. Not that that's saying much.'

'Please, sir. Leave it with me. It isn't a problem. I'll have hand outs with all the relevant details available for everyone. I enjoy this kind of task.'

'Good.'

'Just one thing,' said Knightly hesitantly.

'Yes?'

'I'll draw up and write all the hand outs and whatever else is needed, but the routine tasks of photocopying, ringing the scout people and so on I will pass over to administration. If it's all the same to you, sir, I'll give these tasks to Sergeant Pepper.'

'If she's working tomorrow. I don't know her rota.'

'She will be sir.' said Knightly confidently and climbed into the driving seat.

'So. You are driving now, are you?' he said with a smile.

'Yes, sir. Hang onto your hat. You know I'm a bit of a speed merchant.'

Chapter 4

The following morning Sergeant Janine Pepper was at the police station by eight o'clock. The desk sergeant looked up in surprise. 'I didn't expect to see you in today,' he said. 'You do know it's Saturday, don't you? And according to my rota you aren't due in again until Monday.'

'Yes, I know,' she replied. 'But something has come up and I'm needed.' How good those words sounded to her. To be needed. Of course she had no idea if she was needed or not, but the short and cryptic message from Sergeant Sadie Knightly saying 'Be in work by eight tomorrow morning.' had been enough for her.

She'd heard the station gossip about the murders in the Poachers Inn but details were very sketchy indeed. Whatever Knightly wanted it was bound to be more exciting than the last three weeks spent as an administrative assistant.

Glad to be back at work though she was, she knew that she was never cut out to be a secretary or gopher in an office.

'Good morning,' rang the cheery voice of Sergeant Knightly.

Both the station sergeant and Janine Pepper answered her. They both looked at her eagerly but for different reasons.

'OK. Sergeant. I don't have much time. You must have heard something about the murders yesterday.'

'Gossip. Not much else.'

'Well. I want you to duplicate these handouts for the police teams working on the case. If you have time to, let's say, glance over them then you will know as much as anyone else in the Dorset police force.'

Pepper smiled excitedly. 'Something to get my teeth into at last.'

'Never mind that,' said Knightly. 'The fact is that the team will want someone who can handle the research into a number of things. When you have read the briefing hand outs you'll probably get the gist of what I mean.'

'Oh, I'll read them.'

'Whether or not you get brought into the team as a research assistant, and it'll be nothing more from what I gather, depends on Inspector Loveluck. I have no authority in this matter. But if you happen to have some knowledge of what we need, then it'll help sway him.'

'What kind of things? Give me a clue,' said Pepper.

'Just read the notes and use your brain. Oh. And you might see words like Black Magic, Satanism, Paganism and other isms. Ignore them. People are using words they don't understand. Just read the notes and find out what we need to know. Right. I have a briefing to give in thirty minutes or so. Get copying,'

'Hell's Bells. What are we involved in here?' asked Pepper.

'That,' said Knightly smiling her sweetest smile, 'is what we want you to find out.'

As Knightly stood back and admired her own handiwork she gave herself a pat on the back. 'Pretty damned good Sadie.' She was in the old scout hut and was admiring the boards she had erected. The names of the victims, place of residence and age were displayed prominently as blanks. There was a sketch of the rooms at the Poachers Inn and a guide to who died where. Photographs would have to wait until family and friends had been visited.

She had one photograph, though. Taken by the SOCO team and emailed through to her that morning.

'Looks very impressive,' said one of the officers who had helped her with the display.

'It does, doesn't it?' she said. She looked at the words which were written largest. 'HOW ARE THESE THREE VICTIMS CONNECTED?'

'Wow,' said a voice from behind them. 'This looks good'

Knightly turned to see Sergeant Pepper. 'You like it then?'

'Terrific,' said Pepper. 'Here are all the handouts, diagrams and photos you wanted. All present and correct.'

'Just time for a cuppa before people start arriving,' she said. 'Care to join me?'

And she was still there when Loveluck arrived. 'Hello,' he said to Pepper with a smile. 'What are you doing here?'

'Just delivering the paperwork for the meeting sir.'

The room was beginning to fill and they took their positions in front of the information boards.

‘Good morning,’ said Loveluck calling the meeting to order. ‘I expect most if not all of you know something about why we are here. The murders at the Poachers Inn. I know that quite a few of you were out there and the rest of you will have picked up information from other officers. Not to mention a great deal of misinformation and tittle-tattle.

‘To start things off, Sergeant Knightly will outline what we know so far, which isn't much, and what we are planning to do today. I know today’s Saturday, but we can't sit around doing nothing until Monday.

‘Sergeant. All yours.’

Sergeant Knightly strode to the front of the information boards like she had been doing it all her life and began laying out the bare bones of the case. When the murders happened. How many people murdered and the location, the Poachers Inn which several of them knew already.

‘Sergeant Pepper will pass round the room plans showing who was killed where.’

There was a pause as Pepper went round with the room plans, a task which was lengthened by the number of people saying how pleased they were to see her back.

‘Right,’ said Knightly. ‘I hope the plan is fairly self explanatory. ‘You also have a list of who was in which room, and what little we know about them. The list reads

‘Room 7 Middle aged man, probably professional. Mr John
‘Room 8 Young girl, maybe in her twenties
‘Room 9
‘Room 10 Older lady, maybe early seventies
‘Room 11

I would dearly love to know who were in Rooms 9 and 11.’

‘Yes, constable.’ she said pointing to an officer with his hand up.

‘I've heard, and it may just be tittle tattle, but I've heard that the murders were done in a, well, strange way. Is that true?’

‘Yes it is, and I'll be coming to that in a moment. Just sticking with the victims for a moment, we have no names for any of them except Mr John and that may not be his real name. Any means of identification was removed so we’ll be scanning all missing persons reports and wait for the forensic reports to see if they throw any light on the matter.’

‘Yes,’ she said to another officer with his hand up.

'They must have been on the hotel register.'

'Correct. But not so. We are hoping to get a lead from the bill for the rooms which was paid for by credit card.'

She let them converse for a minute before continuing explain the details of the murders and how they were done.

'Finally, all victims had had their left hands severed. Neatly.' Then she nodded to Pepper. 'The photos please, sergeant.'

Pepper went round handing out the photos of the three hands with the candles between the fingers.

'This is how we found the hands.'

With that she sat down so that the officers could talk amongst themselves for a while.

Loveluck stood up and said. 'All right, the team leaders know what their duties are and will brief their teams accordingly.

'The priorities are to find the connection between these victims.

'To track down whoever was in Rooms 9 and 11 because we believe that people from the same group were booked into those rooms.

'We need to check restaurant bookings at the Poachers Inn to track down whoever else was in the building at the time of the murders. Of course, the murderer may just have pulled into the car park and committed the murders one by one and then left. Still, it all has to be done. Good luck.'

Loveluck joined Knightly, Anderson and Pepper over a drink. 'Well done Knightly. And you Pepper. I must say you're looking well.'

'I feel it, sir'

'How's the therapy going?'

'Physically I'm as fit, if not fitter, than ever. Psychologically I think my therapists are pleased with my progress. But,' she added reluctantly, 'I know there are a few issues. Mainly to do with mood swings and anger but these are improving all the time.'

Loveluck put his hand on her shoulder. 'Take all the time you need. We'll be waiting for you.'

'If there's anything you want me to do for the team, say, with administration or perhaps research of any kind I would be really thrilled to help.' She exchanged a swift glance with Knightly which Loveluck noticed.

‘I don't know what you two have cooked up between you,’ he said ‘but we’ll need some research and administrative help. And Sergeant Daly is fed up doing it, so.....’ He let the sentence hang.

‘I will co ordinate with Sergeant Pepper,’ said Knightly. ‘If that's all right with you.’

‘Yes,’ he said with a smile. ‘That's fine by me. Just don’t overdo it.’

‘It’ll give my Sergeant Daly a chance to get out and do some detective work, said Anderson. ‘How are we splitting up the investigation, Jack?’

‘What I thought we might do is this. I want Knightly to tie up all loose ends at the Poachers Inn. And pin the manager down. What's his name?’

‘Mr Grayson.’ said Knightly.

‘You think he knows a lot more than he is telling, don't you.’

Knightly mused. ‘I don't know how much he knows, but I do know he has been lying about leaving everything to his staff. He might just not want to get involved or he may have something to hide. I'll see what I can get out of him. And I’ll chase up the people in Rooms 9 and 11’

‘Yes. Do that. And speak to the cleaner again. And all the staff. See what you can get out of them. If they were a group, someone must have noticed something’

‘Meanwhile, Inspector Anderson and his team can try and track down and interview anyone and everyone who was here last night. Diners, drinkers, guests. Everyone.’

‘Right,’ said Anderson. ‘Where's Daly? By the time we’ve finished with this lot he’ll be begging to go back onto desk research.’

‘I’m going back to the Poachers Inn to have another chat with Mr Grayson,’ said Knightly.

‘I’ll come and join you for lunch,’ said Loveluck. ‘At about one o’clock.’

In fact it wasn’t Loveluck who joined Knightly for lunch, but Inspector Anderson and Knightly who joined Inspector Loveluck for afternoon tea at the Three Wishes Cafe.

Anderson and Knightly entered the Three Wishes and glanced around but couldn’t see him.

‘Are you looking for Inspector Loveluck, dearie?’ asked a lady from behind the counter.

'Yes.'

'You'll find him in the back garden. Loves our back garden does Inspector Loveluck. Says it's nice and peaceful and helps him think. Such a nice gentlemen is Inspector Loveluck. Just up there, through to the back, dearie,' she said to Anderson.

'I didn't even know you had a back garden.'

'Oh yes. Loves our back garden does the Inspector. Such a polite gentleman.'

'Come on dearie,' said Knightly with a grin. 'Let's go and find that nice polite Inspector Loveluck.'

They walked through the cafe into what was indeed a very charming back garden and found Loveluck sitting at a table studying the menu.

'Nice spot you have here,' said Anderson. 'Come here often?'

'I've been here a couple of times. That's all.'

The waitress arrived to take the orders. Anderson and Knightly ordered cream teas. 'Same for you?' said Knightly to Loveluck.

'Oh no,' interrupted the waitress. 'I think I know what the Inspector wants. Smoked salmon with free range scrambled eggs and a grilled muffin followed by three balls of ice cream. Vanilla, choc-chip and raspberry ripple Am I right, Inspector?'

Loveluck nodded uncomfortably as Inspector Anderson smiled and said 'Just been here a couple of times?'

'I think I should name this meal after you, Inspector,' she went on. 'Inspector Loveluck's favourite I shall call it.'

'How about 'Three Balls Loveluck's favourite?'' suggested Anderson but she had toddled off, out of earshot.

'Right,' said Loveluck. 'Sorry I had to change the arrangements, but glad you're here. I just wanted to make sure we are all up to date and, er.... Well, to be frank, to have a few words without Sergeant Pepper here.'

Anderson and Knightly exchanged interested glances.

'Nothing much from forensics yet. Causes of death all confirmed as garrotting but anything else will have to wait for results of tests. Basically, we have nothing to go on.'

'What about the severed hands and the candles between the fingers?' said Knightly. That's odd and it must mean something.'

'Perhaps Pepper will come up with something,' suggested Anderson. 'She's up and running this week, isn't she?'

Knightly shrugged. ‘Yes and no. She is only working two and a half days a week officially whilst she continues her therapy but she’s started coming in in her own time. And it’s been noticed.’

Loveluck nodded thoughtfully. ‘Let’s deal with the Pepper thing right now. I’d like to get her back on the team in one capacity or another. And the sooner the better. I don’t see much point having her in Admin when she’s at our meetings and researching into the case.

‘The trouble is,’ said Anderson, ‘you know Sergeant Pepper. Keen to get in the midst of things. Into the limelight. She’ll need monitoring carefully.’

‘And,’ added Knightly, ‘if she’s having temper problems we can’t risk having her going ballistic with members of the public.’

All three sat in silence, Anderson and Knightly eating scones with cream and jam whilst Loveluck nibbled on his muffin.

‘What I have decided to do is this. I want to bring her back onto the team in a non-detective capacity. The doctors wouldn’t allow that anyway. But I’ll have to draw up a very tight list of duties for her. Keep her well away from the public until the doctors tell us she’s fit for full duties. If she ever is.’

‘And you want us to help?’ asked Knightly.

‘Yes. Keep her busy with detective related admin work. Keep an eye out for her going off on her own. We all know how capable she is of that.’

‘Sounds a bit like spying on her,’ said Knightly with a touch of distaste.

‘It’s protecting her and helping her slowly back into her proper job,’ said Loveluck forcefully. And if you can’t sign up to that Sergeant Knightly, you’re not the officer I thought you were.’

Knightly looked down and said softly. ‘Sorry boss.’

‘And we’ll keep this arrangement until the doctors give the all clear for her to return to her full detective duties.’

‘If she ever is,’ repeated Anderson slowly.

And on that sombre note they finished their meals and sat silently in the late summer sunlight.

Chapter 5

Loveluck took the call from Daly in his office. 'We have news from the bank about the murdered man Mr John, sir'

'Good. What is it?'

'It seems that Mr John is in fact called John Small. He is a solicitor with an office in Lymington in Hampshire.'

'Got any phone number for the office?'

'No phone number sir, but an address. It's 16a, The Angel Courtyard, Lymington. It's just off the high street behind The Angel Hotel.'

Loveluck jotted down the details. 'Thank you Sergeant Daley. Do you know where Sergeant Knightly is?'

'No sir. No idea.'

Loveluck rang off and then punched in Knightly's number. 'Yes sir. You wanted me?'

'Where are you?'

'At the Poachers Inn. The barman who was here last night comes on duty in 15 minutes. I'm going to interview him.'

'I'll be right with you, Sergeant. Don't start without me. Give me 20 minutes.'

In a clearing in a wood at Wootton Bridge in the New Forest, a ceremony was taking place. A hand, a left hand, was in a pickling jar and a small gathering of people were watching the grisly sight with fascination.

Nearby a shallow, wide stream of sparkling clear water, ankle deep at most ran quickly over the tiny feet of the waif Kayra who was humming happily.

'How long before it's ready?' asked Rufus.

Nemesis shrugged. 'It'll be ready when 'tis ready. The Hand of Glory cannot be hurried.' She watched Rufus turn irritably away, his steady blue eyes, long hair and tight lips looking angrily magnificent. 'Too charismatic for his own good,' she thought to herself. 'By far'.

A voice carried across the air. They turned to see Kayra skipping through the water and then onto the grass towards them. For once, she was singing in English.

Let those who rest more deeply sleep
Let those awake their vigils keep,
Oh, hand of glory, shed thy light,
Direct us to our spoil tonight.

'Where did you learn that song, Kayra?' asked Nemesis.

Kayra hummed the tune and looked wistfully into Rufus' eyes. 'I've always known it.' Then she sang in her strange unidentified language again and skipped back to the water.

'Where did you find her?' asked Nemesis.

'I didn't,' said Rufus. 'She found me.'

Inspector Loveluck entered the bar of The Poachers Inn to find Sergeant Knightly sipping a fruit juice and reading the paper. 'Good morning, sir. This is Jamie the barman.'

Loveluck nodded and sat on a barstool. 'I understand you spoke to the three people who were murdered.'

Jamie stood silent and defensive. Loveluck cast a questioning glance at Knightly who said, 'Jamie is concerned about talking to the police because he's scared that the murderer will come for him if he does.'

'Is that correct?'

Jamie nodded. 'Three people have already been murdered. I don't want to be the fourth.'

'But you've already spoken to the manager. And he's spoken to us so we know the gist of it anyway.'

'Then you won't need any more from me, will you?'

Loveluck regarded him closely. A scared young man with some, but not much, reason to be so. 'Withholding evidence from the police is a serious offence. Particularly in a multiple murder case. We might even consider that you're helping a murderer avoid arrest. There could be a suspicion of this being an inside job with you as the inside man. You could be charged with being an accomplice to murder. That could mean a life sentence.'

'You can't pin this murder on me,' whined Jamie. 'I had nothing to do with it.'

'Maybe not. But we know you were a witness and a very valuable witness. If you don't help the police then you're helping the murderer. Simple logic'

Jamie prevaricated and beads of sweat stood out on his brow. A very scared young man indeed. 'All right, he said. 'But not here.'

'Then where? asked Knightly.

'Do you know the Brace of Pheasants at Plush? It's just up the road.'

'I know it,' said Loveluck.

'Tomorrow lunchtime. One o'clock. In the bar. It's my day off.'

Loveluck nodded and stood up to leave. 'Until tomorrow.'

As they left the bar Loveluck said. 'We're going to Lymington. I'll drop my car off at my place. It's just in the next valley. We'll go in yours.'

The drive to Lymington went swiftly. Knightly was chatty and Loveluck was silent but it seemed to suit them both. And Knightly drove rather faster than Loveluck or the law preferred.

'Do the Hampshire police know we are coming onto their patch?'

Loveluck glanced at her. 'No. We're only going to investigate the background of someone murdered in Dorset. No crime has been committed in Hampshire.'

'And what if we discover that a crime has been committed in Hampshire?'

'We cross that bridge when we come to it.'

Lymington is a pretty, small town in Hampshire on the edge of the New Forest and on the River Solent. From the harbour you can see the Isle of Wight and also take a ferry across to the Island. Loveluck and Knightly walked down the high street looking for the Angel Hotel. 'It's a long street,' said Knightly. 'I'll ask someone. Excuse me, sir. I'm looking for the Angel Courtyard by the Angel Hotel. Do you know it?'

'Certainly do, young lady. I have a shop in the Angel Courtyard. Are you looking for anyone in particular?'

‘Yes we are. Number 16a. A solicitor. Mr John Small. Do you know him?’

The man shrugged. ‘John Small? Only to nod and say good morning to. Considers himself a bit too precious to get involved with the shop keepers. But harmless enough, I’d say.’

‘Is his office easy to find?’

‘Not too bad. If you carry on down here for about a hundred yards you’ll come to the Angel pub on the left. The Angel and Blue Pig they call themselves these days. Anyway, turn left into the Angel courtyard and go straight past the pub’

‘That’ll be the day,’ mumbled Knightly.

‘The pub has a sort of beer garden and you go straight past that too.’

‘And pigs might fly.’ She mumbled again.

‘Keep walking until you get to a sort of car park. It isn’t far. Then turn back on yourself and you’ll see a white building with steps going up diagonally. At the top are numbers 16a and 17.’

They strode on down the high street. ‘It reminds me of Sherborne in some ways. Very pretty. Much newer than Sherborne. But it does have a harbour.’ Knightly prattled on in this way as they walked and eventually arrived at the Angel.

‘And now,’ said Loveluck pointedly, ‘we are going to walk past the pub as the man said, and past the beer garden. Notice any pigs flying, Sergeant?’

‘No sir.’

‘After we’ve been to the office you can tell me why you are so keen to get yourself onto traffic duty.’

‘Yes sir.   Sorry sir.’

They followed the man’s instructions, turned back on themselves and there was the white building and there were the stairs going up the wall in a diagonal fashion with a white handrail leading them to two small doors at the top. They climbed the stairs and there they found a sign saying ‘John Small. Solicitor at law’

Knightly knocked on the door which opened to her touch. She exchanged glances with Loveluck. He motioned her to silence and she gently pushed the door open. They entered what would have been a small reception area which was empty. Knightly went on to a connecting door which again opened to her soft push. She entered the main office which was a complete shambles. Furniture and papers everywhere.

Loveluck silently motioned her towards a further door in the room. She stepped across briskly but silently and went in fast and hard. 'Police.'

Then she popped her head round the door and smiled at Loveluck. 'All empty sir. Small kitchen and a toilet. Both empty.'

'Seems someone got here before us. I wonder what they were looking for?'

'I wonder if they found it,' said Knightly. 'I suppose that a crime has now been committed in Hampshire. Are we contacting the Hampshire police?'

'What crime?' asked Loveluck.

Knightly smiled. 'I was thinking about breaking and entering?' She waved her hand across the mess of furniture and papers on the floor of the office.

'I don't see any evidence of breaking and entering,' he said. I see evidence of an untidy secretary and an unusual arrangement of furniture, but breaking and entering? I'm not sure.'

'If you say so, sir.'

'I do, Sergeant. I want to learn a little more about Mr John Small before we hand this over to Hampshire police. Like what kind of cases did he work on? Where does he live? Does he have family?'

Knightly looked at him, then her eyes looked past him to the door. He turned.

'And what the hell do you think you are doing?'

They both stared at the woman standing in the doorway. A tall, well built woman. 'Well? What the hell do you think you're doing? And what's this mess?'

'Police,' said Knightly showing her identification. 'We are investigating the death of Mr John Small. Who are you?'

'Death?'

'Yes. John Small was murdered two days ago in a pub near Sherborne. Who are you?'

The woman stared at her defiantly for a moment as though in consideration of whether to answer or not. 'I'm Samantha. I'm the secretary. People call me Sammy.'

Loveluck had been regarding her steadily throughout this conversation. Tall, strapping lass. Probably in her forties. Put her in a suit of men's clothes and she might pass for a man. But the curves were definitely female. 'Can I see his appointments book?'

She shrugged. 'My office is mainly for show. The drawers and cupboards are empty. He has a few very secret clients. Even I don't know who they are. There is a diary kept for appointments but he fills it in. I keep the diary but he fills it in.'

'Can we see it, Sammy?' asked Loveluck.

She shrugged and took it from her bag. 'I never leave it in the office. Strict instructions.'

Loveluck leafed through the pages. Appointments made in the usual way but no names of people. He looked for the entry for the night of the murders.

It read; RJ514 meeting for five at the Poachers Inn, Piddletrenthide, Dorset. 20.30

'Can I keep this?' he asked.

'Sure.'

'And do you have a spare key? We'll need to come back.'

She nodded and handed over a key.

'I'll also need his home address. And phone number.'

She duly jotted them down and Loveluck and Knightly went back down the stairs and headed for the Angel. 'Fancy lunch?' he asked.

Back at the solicitor's office, Sammy called a number. A smile crossed her face as she said softly. 'They went for it hook, line and sinker.'

Chapter 6

The Last of the Summer Wine Rambling Club were strolling through the woods near Middlemarsh on the Sherborne to Dorchester road. Their destination was the Hunter's Moon pub in Middlemarsh and a fine, solid lunch to reward their ramble. The President of the club, George, was leading at a gentle pace. Most of the members of the club, but not all, were of a certain age where rambling had to be done at a gentle pace.

'Nearly there', shouted George. 'Another ten minutes should do it.'

'I need a pee,' said Lily Bryant. 'And I need it now.'

George leaned on his stick and said. 'OK. Two minutes rest.' He might well have saved his breath as everyone had already sat on the ground and Lily had gone into the bushes. They lay back and mused on a fine ramble on a fine day and with a fine lunch just down the road.

But the silence was broken by a piercing scream from the bushes where Lily had gone.

'Lily,' shouted George. 'Lily. Are you all right?'

Lily`s daughter Anna ran into the bushes. 'Mum. What is it?'

Lily was looking upwards and Anna followed her gaze. Hanging from a branch was a man with his left hand severed.

'Can we come in?' asked George.

'Yes. I'm decent.'

They all went into the clearing by the bushes and looked up at the body. It was a strange, eerie sight and the fine day seemed to render it more gruesome than it already was.

'I'd better call the police,' said George preparing to tap 999 onto his phone.

'Not now,' said Lily urgently.

'Why ever not?'

‘George. It’s only three months since I was arrested for the murder of the Sherborne Abbey organist. I think that Jack Loveluck will find it mighty odd that here I am again at the scene of another murder. I don′t want to go through all that again.’

‘We can′t just walk away and leave him hanging there,’ George argued. ‘If Jack Loveluck found out that *that* had happened he really would start to get suspicious. And anyway, all the charges were dropped.’

Lily pointed up at the hanging man. ‘That....thing isn′t going anywhere. Just leave it until we are back in Sherborne. Come on. Let’s have some lunch.’

‘I don’t think it’s right,’ said George.

‘All right,’ said Lily. ‘Just leave it until after lunch. And don’t say that I was here. Got that everyone. I wasn’t here. Right?’

They all mumbled agreement and then passed on to the road and to the Hunter’s Moon, some appetites not as strong as they had been.

Loveluck and Knightly sat in the beer garden of The Angel studying the menu. ‘It doesn’t appear to have the Loveluck special,’ said Knightly.

‘Just order and keep your smart remarks to yourself. In fact when you go in to order the food, ask where this address of John Small’s is. I think we could do with a map of Lymington.’

‘There`s a Waterstones bookshop right next door to the pub. I noticed it when we came in. I’ll nip in there and get a map.’

Loveluck sipped his beer and looked at the address. Lentune Cottage, Quay Road, Lymington. A few minutes later he was looking at the map. ‘Seems like it’s just down the road,’ said Loveluck. Down the High Street, then Quay Hill. At the bottom of Quay Hill, turn right and you come into Quay Road. That’s our job after lunch. Then back to Sherborne.’

‘But first, here comes lunch. And very fine it looks too. Tuck in, sir.’

Inspector Anderson and Sergeant Daly trampled through the undergrowth as they followed a uniformed officer. ‘Don′t they have paths in these places?’

Daly smiled. ‘It’s back to nature, sir. Breathe in the sweet air. Enjoy the beauty that nature gives us.’

It was at this point that they spotted the hanging body. 'Is that what you mean by the beauty that nature gives us?'

They walked around the body, noticing the missing left hand and the clean sever.

'We left him hanging up sir,' said a uniformed officer. 'We thought you might like to see him in situ, so to speak.'

'Quite right, officer. Has the doctor been sent for?'

'Dr Ryan's on his way.'

'I wonder why they only cut off his left hand. It can't have been to stop us getting his identity from fingerprints. His right hand will give a lovely set.' Anderson continued to muse as he again slowly circled the body. He looked up at the long rope and the rather well made noose. 'It certainly isn't suicide. This is murder, pure and simple.'

Loveluck and Knightly strolled to the bottom of Lymington High Street and onto Quay Hill which was cobbled. They followed the cobbled narrow road as it turned right and they passed through a number of small artisan shops. 'This is so sweet,' said Knightly. 'What a cute place.'

Loveluck nodded. 'Very much an old part of the town.'

They walked on until they reached the harbour and Quay Road. 'This is lovely,' said Knightly in full tourist mode. 'Look at the boats.'

They strolled slowly on. 'That's it,' said Loveluck. 'Lentune Cottage.'

They stopped before a small, white cottage with a fence enclosing a path leading to a back garden..

'Nice little place. And it overlooks the harbour.'

'Actually sir, it overlooks the car park.'

Loveluck nodded sadly. 'If you had any soul, sergeant, you wouldn't see the car park, only the harbour.'

'But I am a detective sergeant and I have been trained to see what's there, not what I want to see. And what I see is a car park.'

'Wrong. What you see is a car park *and* the harbour.'

'Indeed I do, sir' replied Knightly with a smile. 'And if I turn around I see Lentune Cottage where the late Mr John Small lived. Shall I try the door?'

And as she tried the door it opened. 'Very careless of Mr Small not to lock his door.'

But as they entered they saw once again overturned furniture, papers strewn all over the place and on the mirror in lipstick was the single word. 'JAKOB'

'Seems they got here before us again, sir. Or perhaps he got here before us again. Jakob, that is.'

Loveluck walked slowly round the small room and then through all the rooms of the cottage. All rooms had been given the same treatment.

'Do you think a crime has been committed yet, sir? Or is this just another 'unusual furniture arrangement'?'

They went back downstairs.

Loveluck stared in puzzlement around the room. 'There's something not right about this.'

'In what way?'

'Well. Take that small table for example.'

Knightly looked at the table overturned and lying on its side. 'What about it?'

'What do you think was on it?'

Knightly looked around. 'Probably those photographs.' She carefully picked up three photographs in stand-up frames. They were photos of a group of men. One on a bicycle ride, two others on beach trips.

Loveluck picked up a small notebook and flicked through the pages, 'This could be interesting.' He nodded thoughtfully. 'I agree about the photographs.. So why knock the table over?'

Knightly thought for a moment and said. 'Why not?'

Loveluck smiled broadly. 'What a brilliant answer. 'Why not?' You are an angel.' And with that he walked out of the cottage.

Knightly caught a glimpse of herself in a mirror, shrugged at her image and said; 'So that's what angels look like.'

'Knightly!' bellowed a voice from the street.

She gave herself a last smile and wink in the mirror. 'Coming, sir'.

In the woods near Middlemarsh the Scene of Crimes Officers had arrived as had Dr Ryan. The body had been cut down and Dr Ryan was giving it a preliminary examination.

'Anything yet, Doctor?' asked Inspector Anderson.

Dr Ryan shrugged. 'Male. Aged around forty. Died of strangulation from being hanged. Left hand severed neatly. Not done by any medical instrument. It was probably a very sharp implement of some kind. Butcher´s chopper or a machete. Something like that. It was severed after death.'

'Any idea when?'

'I would say he's been here for a couple of days. I can give you more when I have him on the slab.'

Anderson approached a scene of crimes officer. 'Anything yet?'

'Well, assuming the scene of the crime hasn´t been contaminated, and I am assuming it hasn´t as it wasn't reported until today, then I can make a couple of possible conclusions. Firstly, a group of people were here recently.'

'The body was reported by a rambling club,' said Anderson.

'I know that, but one group of people were here for some time. Not the rambling club. A different group. There was also a vehicle here. The tracks are clearly visible. In fact I can show you where the vehicle was parked and where it was moved to.'

The officer showed Anderson the route. 'You can see, Inspector, that it stopped here for a while and the track indentations are deeper.'

Anderson looked down, then up. They were exactly underneath the hanging rope. 'You think he was hanged off the vehicle.'

'Yes. And then the vehicle was driven away with several people in it.'

Anderson looked down at the tyre marks again. 'Can you identify the vehicle from these marks?'

'I can identify the tyres easily enough back at the lab. The vehicle must have been big enough to carry a number of people. Maybe eight or ten. And of the right shape to stand a number of people as they prepared an unwilling victim for the hanging.'

Anderson nodded. 'Are we looking for a lorry or a pick-up truck?'

The SOCO officer nodded. 'I would say a pick-up truck. And working on that assumption we can search for any evidence around here and on the way out of the woods. And now I must get back to my work Inspector.'

'Yes of course. Thanks for your help.' He turned to leave but was restrained by the SOCO officer.

'Just a moment. Let´s see what this is.'

Another SOCO officer was running towards them. 'I thought you might want to see this, sir.'

He handed over the small white piece of evidence. 'Where did you find it?'

'Near where the vehicle was parked. I reckon it must have scraped against a tree. I also reckon it must have been a pretty old vehicle. Anyway, it's paint and it's white.'

The officer showed the paint scraping to Anderson. 'If my officer is right, and on first glance I'm inclined to think he is, then this scraping of paint could tell us a great deal about the vehicle.'

'Could it tell you the make? The year?'

The SOCO officer laughed. 'All in good time, Inspector. We need to find more evidence and get it back to the lab before I can tell you anything definite.'

Sergeant Pepper walked from Sherborne police station to Sherborne Abbey. A short walk and as she walked across the Church Green she thought of all the events that had taken place since the murder of the organist some months earlier and the tangled investigation it had led to. Not least her own kidnap and burial alive out at Lake Farm.

All water under the bridge now. Except for the mental scars it had left.

She entered the abbey and was approached by a gentleman helper. 'Welcome to the Abbey,' he said offering her a guide to the building. 'Is it your first time here?

She smiled. 'I have been here many, many times. I'm actually looking for the vicar, Toby Austin. Is he around?'

'I haven't seen him this morning. Have you tried the vicarage? The large building just across the green. Set back a little.'

'No. No I haven't. I'll try there. Thanks.'

'I can't promise he'll be there,' he said but she was already making for the door.

Sherborne vicarage is a fairly imposing building and Pepper strolled to the door ever so slightly in awe. She rang the bell and a lady answered. 'I'd like to speak to the Reverend Toby Austin,' she said brightly.

'The vicar is busy at the moment. Do you have an appointment?

'No I haven't, but I think he may be able to help me. The name is Pepper. Detective Sergeant Pepper. He knows me.' She showed her identification which the lady scrutinised.

'I know your name. You were mixed up with that organist murder, weren't you?'

'I was one of the investigating officers if that's what you mean. And like the vicar, I'm very busy. So?'

The lady took the hint and disappeared into the house and soon Pepper heard the familiar sound of Rev Toby Austin shouting as he flapped his way to the door. 'Janine ! Janine Pepper ! How lovely to see you again. It must have been months. How are you? What a terrible ordeal it must have been for you. Come in and sit down, sit down. Tell me all about it. No. No. I'm sure you don't want to talk about it.'

Pepper smiled a very fond smile. Still the same old Toby. Enthusiastic, talkative, flapping around. 'It does my heart good to see you again, Toby.'

'Good Lord. Don't let the widow Albright hear you say that. A fine woman, as you know, but a little prone to the green-eyed monster.'

Pepper laughed. 'The good widow Albright still on the scene is she?'

'Golly yes. Still alive and kicking.'

'And still singing?' asked Pepper mischievously referring to an evening when the good Widow Albright, well into her cups, sang Eskimo Nell all the way down the high street with the poor vicar pushing her in a wheeled computer chair. 'Did she lose any money in the scam?'

'None. The source of her money was legitimate. In fact she made a profit out of it.'

They continued to talk about old times for a while before Pepper approached the business in mind.

'Toby,' she said seriously. 'I need a little help with something. I'm not sure if you are the man for it but I think I might be tinkering on the edges of the occult. As part of an investigation that is. Do you know anything about that kind of thing?'

He stood up from his desk and waved his arm about the small office. All walls were covered from floor to ceiling in books. See this lot? Many things are covered by the books in this room. Many, many religious tomes, of course, but also other things. Now I don´t know what you mean by 'tinkering on the edges of the occult' but,' and here he hesitated. 'the thing is, Janine, I do have a certain feel for things which might be described as mystical. I'm not saying I am a mystic or anything like that, but I do have certain....powers, if that's the right word. Still, before we go into all that, what has happened that you need to learn about the occult?'

And now Pepper let it all out. She knew that Loveluck would be furious if he ever found out that she was giving the vicar details of the investigation and she knew he would be even more furious if he found out she was interviewing people against express orders to the contrary. She told the vicar about the three bodies they had found in The Poachers Inn. She told him about the garrotting of the three victims. She told him about the candles wedged between the fingers of the victims, pointing upwards. Then she was quiet.

The Rev Toby Austin sat in thought for a considerable time. Eventually he said. 'Candles, of course, have been used in ceremonies since time began and most so called occult groups are spin-offs from different religious groups. The ties between the occult and religion have always been very close. Candles wedges between fingers have also featured often. Were the candles lit, by the way?'

Pepper shook her head. 'No.'

'It certainly is of great interest to me. Can you give me a little time to look into it? I'm very busy with vicaring at the moment but I'll look into it for you, Janine. Do keep me updated with any new developments.'

Giving promises to keep him fully updated she left the vicarage and went to sit on a bench on Church Green. She felt very pleased with herself but oh so aware that Loveluck must never find out about what she was up to. But then again, it was only research she was doing, she argued to herself, and wasn't that what she was supposed to be doing?

Chapter 7

Detective Inspector Jack Loveluck sat at his favourite table in the Three Wishes garden and prepared to begin his late breakfast. The Three Balls Loveluck Special, as Anderson would have it. Hardly had the first piece of smoked salmon touched his lips when a bright and cheery voice called out 'so this is where you sneak off to, you cunning old dog. And very nice too.'

Loveluck had his eyes closed to better savour the tastes but he didn't need to open them to know who had just arrived.

'Olwen Evans, I presume.'

'Right first time. What a splendid detective you are.'

'Ace crime reporter of the Western Gazette and first rate pain in the butt.'

'Right again, my little chickadee. And not to forget, occasional lover of one Detective Inspector Jack Loveluck.'

'How could I ever forget,' he said unenthusiastically. 'How did you find me?'

'Easy. I sat outside the Sherborne police station until you appeared, and followed you here.'

He opened his eyes and stared at the woman before him. Olwen Evans. Reporter at the Western Gazette and self-styled ace crime reporter. In fact, no longer self-styled as the paper now officially billed her as ace crime reporter.

'Do you like what you see?' she asked doing a twirl. 'The last hurrah of the summer fashion before the broody browns of autumn appear.' She was of medium height, slim, aged early forties with a shock of curly hair and a slightly raddled face. And very feisty. The original intrepid reporter who let nothing get in the way of a hot story. Including morals.

‘So come on, Jack. Brass up like a gent and give me the lowdown on the murders at the Poachers Inn. Three murders I understand.’

‘Your information is correct as always.’

‘So who are they? Family? Friends? Gang warfare?’

Loveluck shrugged. ‘No idea. We have no clue who they are yet.’

‘Oh yeah, buddy,’ she said in her best Brooklyn voice. ‘So what took you and the unbelievably gorgeous and very irritating Sergeant sexy Sadie Knightly off to Lymington yesterday?’

‘How on earth....’ began Loveluck but finished the sentence with a shrug.

‘Ace crime reporters cannot reveal their sources.’

‘Anyway,’ continued Loveluck, ‘Sergeant Knightly says you are her role model. I thought that that would put her in your good books.’

‘Well, it does of course. But she’s too beautiful by half. Girls with cheekbones like hers should be banned. So what were you doing in Lymington if not chasing up a clue about one of the murdered three?’

Loveluck took a mouthful of his meal.

‘I can help you Jack. I have a friend used to work on the Lymington Times. He still has lots of contacts there. And you know we work well together.’

She let him consider this for the time it took him to eat another mouthful. ‘Just give me their names and I’ll put the wheels in motion.’

‘Not a hope.’

‘OK. Then I can’t help you.’

Loveluck considered his options and then said; ‘There were three people murdered as you clearly already know, but only one of them has so far been identified. We have no idea yet who the other two are.’

‘Give me the name of the one you know.’

‘You can’t mention his name in the Gazette,’ said Loveluck firmly. ‘Not just yet. You still have a very good lead story.’

Now it was Olwen’s turn to consider her options. ‘All right. I’ll hold back on the name for a day or two.’

‘Until I say,’ said Loveluck firmly.

‘Whatever.’

‘OK. The name is John Small. He’s a solicitor.’ He gave her the home and office addresses for Small. ‘Both his office and home have been turned over in a search for something. See if you can find anything on his secretary as well. A woman called Samantha. Calls herself Sammy. I′ll be giving the same information to the Hampshire police so we can see if your versions agree at all.'

'The press will prove better than the police. You wait and see. As I've told you before, Jack. This pen is mightier than that truncheon.' Then in one swift motion she polished off the remains of Loveluck's breakfast. 'Gotta go. Got some digging to do.'

He watched her bounce off towards the cafe door, giving him a cheery wave as she went.

Loveluck entered the Sherborne police station and was immediately hailed by the officer on reception. 'Inspector Anderson would like to see you as soon as possible, sir. I believe he is in his office.' Loveluck turned in the direction of Anderson's office, knocked and entered.

'Ah. Good morning, Jack. Have you heard about the Middlemarsh hanging yet?'

Loveluck shook his head. 'No. Do you mean our Middlemarsh on the Dorchester Road?'

'That's the one. We've found a corpse hanging from a tree.'

'Not pretty. Where exactly was he. Is it a he?' Anderson nodded. 'Where exactly was he found?'

'In some woods on the Sherborne to Dorchester road, only a short hop from the Hunter's Moon pub. There was evidence of a group of people gathered there and a vehicle. SOCO think it might be some kind of pick-up truck. They found some white paint scrapings so they might be able to work their magic on that and come up with something for us.'

'Good. I wish you the best of luck with it.'

'That's not the real reason I asked to see you, Jack. You see, the thing is, Dr Ryan thinks he was murdered a couple of days ago. Preliminary findings, you understand. He wouldn't commit himself, but he reckons it was done on Thursday night.'

Anderson let the conversation pause and watched Loveluck to see what he was making of the information. Loveluck thought briefly and said, 'Am I to assume that you are drawing some kind of conclusion about the hanging in the woods and the murders at the Poachers Inn?'

'Not particularly drawing any conclusions, but the woods and the Poachers Inn are what, three or four miles apart? It's a possibility.'

Loveluck shrugged. 'Well. I suppose.'

Anderson drew his chair much closer to Loveluck's and they sat close together, face to face. 'And what if I further told you that his left hand had been severed.'

Loveluck reacted sharply to this. 'Then you would interest me strangely, Michael Anderson.'

'I thought that might be the case,' said Anderson. 'And there's more.'

'Tell on, my theatrical friend and Inspector.'

'The body was discovered by the members of a rambling club.'

Loveluck inwardly groaned and it showed on his face. 'Please don´t tell me it`s that lot. I couldn't bear it.'

'Well,' said Anderson, 'I won´t tell you. I won´t tell you that the name of the person who rang the police was George...' Loveluck groaned. 'And I won´t tell you that George said that he would be in the Crown this lunchtime if I wanted to talk to him. Which I do.'

Loveluck shook his head. 'How do they do it? How do that set of eccentric old dodderers seem to get involved with everything. The Last of the Summer Wine Rambling Club, I suppose?'

'The very same set of eccentric old dodderers. I am going to interview George in about an hour. Do you want to come?'

'I can't. I have an interview to do with the barman of the Poachers Inn. We're meeting him at the Brace of Pheasants. Which reminds me. Have you seen Knightly?'

'Yes. She flew out of here like a bat out of hell about half an hour before you arrived.'

'Did she say where she was going?' asked Loveluck.

'Yes. She said she was going to follow a lead up in Lymington and could you do the interview yourself.' Anderson smiled.

'She said that, did she,' said Loveluck. 'Did she mention anything about her phone not working?'

'Not a thing.'

'Then that young lady is going to have some explaining to do. Have you got time to show me the hanging site?'

'Just about. George can wait. I´m sure he'll find something to do in the Crown.'

The two men stood up. 'Are you going to phone Knightly?' asked Anderson.

'No. Let's see how long it takes her to decide that she should contact me.'

Anderson gave a quick smile which showed how he relished the fireworks to come.

The hanging site, when they arrived, was still a police scene with the SOCO squad still investigating. Anderson approached the lead SOCO officer. 'Good morning. I suppose you know Inspector Loveluck.'

'Of course. Worked many a crime scene together, Jack and I. Hello Jack.'

Loveluck nodded. 'Finding anything interesting?'

'A veritable cornucopia of evidence. I think I can tell you pretty much everything that happened the night of the hanging. Though maybe not in the correct order. Come and sit down a minute.' He led them over to a tree which had been cut down and the trunk made a very fine bench indeed.

'If Inspector Anderson won´t mind me repeating a few things he already knows...' Anderson waved his assent and the SOCO officer went on. 'I'll tell it in the order I think it happened which may not be entirely correct, and I'll bring in other evidence we haven't had time to get into the lab yet. A bit like Dr Ryan offering his opinion on a dead body shortly after finding it. He gives you his first impressions but covers himself entirely in case later evidence shows up a different story. In the same way, I'll give you my early impressions of what happened whilst covering myself if things look a little different when we have all the evidence in the lab.'

'We understand entirely.'

'All right, then. These are my early impressions. Firstly, there was a group of people arrived here in a white pick-up truck.'

'You're certain of that?' asked Anderson.

'Yes. Since yesterday we have found another piece of evidence. When the truck scraped the tree a piece of the bodywork fell off. It was rusted and the truck must have been pretty old, but that small piece of metal could tell us a lot more about the van. Paint and metal can be very informative. But that's for later in the lab. They parked the van over here,' he said getting to his feet and carefully taking them on a circuitous path to the spot to avoid contaminating any further possible evidence. It was parked just here. The indents in the ground were clear to our team. We will be getting results of the tyres very soon.'

He walked them to where the rope still hung from the tree. 'It had rained quite steadily over the last few days and that helped a lot with footprints. And the footprints were very interesting. I'm afraid I can't give you a one-legged man like Sherlock Holmes might have done but I can give you something which I consider just as interesting.'

He waited for effect.

'And what did you find that was so interesting?' said Loveluck to break the silence.

'Several of the group, and I estimate the group to be about 8 strong or thereabouts, were barefoot. Pretty unusual late in the evening. And how, I hear you thinking, do I know it was late in the evening?'

'Tell us.'

'The candles.

'Candles?' said Anderson. 'Are we moving into fingerprint territory here?'

'Could be. They were ordinary commercial nightlights but there could be fingerprints.'

Anderson grinned broadly. 'They're handing it to us on a plate. Hardly professionals.'

Loveluck mused. It did seem that they had indeed left them clues enough for the dimmest of cops to find them. Anderson thought they were lucky but Loveluck didn't believe in that kind of luck.

'Staying on the subject of footprints, the ones that weren't barefoot were wearing some kind of footwear with no proper soles.'

'Like slippers, you mean?'

'Possibly. But I would go for something a bit more substantial for night wear in the woods.'

'Like what?'

The SOCO leader gave them an old fashioned smile. 'Like moccasins.'

Anderson laughed. 'Sounds like you're describing an Indian encampment. Any wig-wams?'

'Is there any more?' asked Loveluck.

'One major find since yesterday and that is a car abandoned on the edge of the woods.'

'Cars get abandoned all the time like that.'

'Ah yes. But in this case there is a clear track running from the car to this clearing. Like someone walked, or probably ran, through the undergrowth leaving a clear track. I have the car number for you,

Inspector,' he said to Anderson. 'I'd rather you didn't go to the car until my boys have been over it. But I'll ask you one thing. Who came by car to this place but didn't leave here?'

They thought this over for a few seconds, then all three, in unison, looked up at the rope still hanging from the tree.

Anderson smiled again. 'Handed to us on a plate,' he said with great satisfaction and walked away towards his car.

Loveluck and the SOCO officer exchanged knowing glances. 'How much of this is red herring,' asked Loveluck.

'You tell me. You're the detective. I just give you the evidence.'

Sergeant Sadie Knightly sped along the A31 towards Lymington. She knew that Loveluck would give her a real rollocking when she returned but she had this hunch. A hunch backed up with a vague memory and a lot of hope. Not much at all, when she began to think of it seriously but it was something she had to check on, and she knew that Loveluck would be against her going to Lymington again on such a flimsy premise.

The hood of her sports car was open and her fair hair flowed behind her as the breeze hit her face. This is how she liked to live life. On the edge. With that she pushed her foot a little further on the throttle and glided past several cars. She wondered if Loveluck still thought of her as an angel.

Loveluck was sitting at the bar of the Brace of Pheasants at Plush and his thoughts of Knightly were a long way from angelic. He was sitting alone. The barman Jamie had not turned up yet and he was a troubled man. Sergeant Knightly off on a lead follow-up without word or permission. A hanging crime scene which seemed too good to be true and now a witness who didn't look like showing up.

He ordered another pint and rang the Poachers Inn and asked for Jamie's phone number. He got no reply from the mobile and rang the Poachers again to ask for Jamie's home number. This time he got Jamie's mother who told him that Jamie had left an hour ago to meet Inspector Loveluck and that he would call in at the Poachers Inn along the way.

Loveluck put his phone on the bar and considered the possibilities. Perhaps Jamie had got cold feet. Loveluck hoped this was the case because the alternative didn't bear thinking about. That Jamie was right all along and was the next in line to be murdered. And had been.

Sergeant Knightly parked in a car park behind the Angel and walked back through the Angel Courtyard. She saw the diagonal steps with their wooded handrail and ran up them two at a time, entering the office without knocking. Sitting at the desk was Sam reading a magazine.

'What brings you back' she said.

'You, partly. You see, I want to know more about Mr Small.'

'I can't really tell you much about him. What do you want to know?'

'You said before that he had a few secret clients. What did you mean by a few and what did you mean by secret?'

Samantha closed her magazine and sat back in her chair. 'I told you before, this reception area is really just for show. Mr Small handled everything. I would occasionally get phone calls but I passed them straight onto Mr Small.'

'And the names of the secret clients?'

'I have no idea.'

'I don't believe you.'

'You can believe what you like. Mr Small dealt with everything. I was reasonably well paid to be a kind of pretend receptionist and I was being paid to keep my nose out of things. Now and then people would turn up at the office. Proper people if you know what I mean. People who wanted legal help. For divorces, house conveyancing. That kind of thing.'

'What did you do with those?'

'I sent them away. I told them that Mr Small was working on very important matters and was fully booked.'

Knightly walked round the room picking her way through the debris still lying on the floor. 'Why don't you tidy this lot up?'

'I can't without Mr Small's permission.'

'Sam. Mr Small is dead. Tidy up. Go home.'

'What about my pay for the month?'

'How does he normally pay you?'

'Direct into my bank account.'

'Then it will probably go directly into your bank account this month. And maybe next month too as there is no one to cancel the payment order. Money for nothing.' This seemed to cheer her up. 'Will you come to Sherborne to identify the body? We don't know anyone else who knew him.'

Sam shrugged. 'I might. Will you send a car for me?'

'I'll do better than that Sam. I'll come myself. Monday at two in the afternoon suit you?'

'Why not?'

'I'll pick you up at this office,' Knightly smiled and went into the larger office. John Small's office. This too was still in a complete mess. 'OK Sammy. You can leave me alone in here. I may be quite a time.'

'Do you want a cup of tea?'

'What a good idea. Thanks.'

Knightly went down on her hands and knees and began sifting through the mess of files and papers. She methodically began at one end and worked her way across the room. Samantha came through with her tea. 'Milk, no sugar.'

Knightly smiled. 'yes. How did you know?'

Sam looked Knightly up and down and said. 'Obvious'

Knightly continued with her search of the papers on the floor and in the desk drawers and cupboards. Two things struck her as strange. One was that all the cases were for completed work of a trivial nature and the other was that they were all at least five years old.

She called out to Sammy. 'How long have you worked for Mr Small, Samantha?'

'Ever since he opened this office.'

'And when was that?'

Sam appeared at the door. 'About a year ago.'

'Is that all?'

'Yes. He came down from Dorset way. Somewhere in the sticks. I can't remember where. Anything else 'cos I want to nip out to the cafe for a coffee.'

'No. I won't be here that long. I'll close the door behind me for what it's worth.'

Sammy left and Knightly continued with the search on her hands and knees. None of the cases in the files related to the time Small had been in Lymington, and as she began to read the detail on one or two of the documents it was clear that they all referred to cases in Dorset.

As she read with interest she was suddenly aware of a presence in the room. No noise, no motion. Just awareness that she was not alone. She continued to read and to shuffle her position into one where she could move easily. Then she sprang to her feet and turned.

‘POLICE. DO NOT MOVE’

She was face to face with two slightly bemused men. ‘Well, now,’ said one of the men. ‘We are police too. And what’s more, we don’t recognise you.’

Knightly visibly relaxed. ‘Detective Sergeant Sadie Knightly. Dorset police.’ And she showed her identification.

‘And what, pray, are the Dorset police doing here in little old Lymington?’

‘Investigating a murder which took place in little old Sherborne in Dorset. And the man who owns this solicitor practice was one of the people murdered.’

‘One of them?’

‘Yes. It was a triple murder.’

‘Well, then, Sergeant Knightly. If you want to come investigating in Hampshire perhaps you would be good enough to contact the Hampshire police before you do. I’m sure we can be a great deal of help to you. Perhaps we could help you find your way back to Sherborne, for example.’

‘Very kind, but no need thank you. I’m going to be a tourist in your town and have lunch somewhere pleasant. What did you say your name was, constable?’

‘I didn’t. But I am Detective Sergeant Wilson and this is Detective Constable Pike.’

‘Good day, gentlemen,’ she said as she brushed past them and went out of the office and down the stairs breathing a huge sigh of relief as she went.

And then she ran.

Out to the high street past The Angel, down the high street and onto the cobbles, sharp right and continuing along the cobbles dodging past holidaymakers and gossiping traders. Straight on she ran alongside the harbour until she came to Lentune Cottage where the door opened to her touch and also to her immense relief.

She imagined that the Hampshire police officers wouldn’t be too far behind and that her time was very limited.

But as she entered the sitting room she was stunned to find it completely neat and tidy with everything in its place. No sign of the shambles of the previous day. She thought for a moment she might be in the wrong cottage but the table with the three pictures on it was still there.

She took the photographs and slipped them into her pocket, and began to look around for the other thing she wanted.

'Do you want a cup of tea?'

A look of confusion passed over her face. 'Sammy?'

'Yes, dear. Milk no sugar?'

'Perfect.' Knightly continued to look until she sensed Samantha standing in the doorway.

'You won't find it dearie. Not if you look all day.'

'Where is it,' said Knightly in a challenging manner.

'Nowhere you're going to find it.'

'What are you doing here, anyway,' demanded Knightly.

'I might ask you the same thing. I do some housekeeping for Mr Small.'

'Mr Small is dead.'

'Even so, got to keep the house clean.'

'You're crazy,' said Knightly.

'Crazy I might be. But I've got what you want. I don't know why you didn't take it yesterday. I see you've taken the photos this time.'

'Give me the notebook.'

'What's it worth?'

'Give me the notebook,' snapped Knightly. 'Or I'll arrest you.'

Sam laughed out loud. 'Those nice Hampshire policemen will be here any minute and I think they'll let me go again. And this little book stays with me,' she said holding the book just out of Knightly's reach. 'I think you'd better go.'

Then Knightly made a spring for the notebook, snatched it and ran from the house, back along the quay and up the cobbles all the way to her car. She sat in her seat, engine roaring, heart pounding. Then she swung the car round, tyres squealing, and out of the car park and on the road back to Sherborne.

Meanwhile in Lentune Cottage, Sam picked up her phone and dialled. She spoke just four words. 'It went like clockwork.'

Chapter 8

Loveluck drained his pint and was about to leave the Brace of Pheasants when Jamie the barman came in. He looked swiftly around him then ambled over to Loveluck at the bar.

'You're nearly two hours late.'

'Yeah, sorry about that. I got busy.'

'What do you mean 'you got busy'. We had an appointment for one o'clock. Where've you been?'

'I forgot today was Saturday. I always help out on a bloke's garden on a Saturday. Bit of extra money for me.'

'Why didn't you ring me?'

'Sorry I didn't think. Look do you want to talk about what happened that night in the Poachers or what?'

Loveluck sighed. 'All right. Let's start.'

'Before we do, can I have a pint? It's hard work gardening. Thirsty work'

A pint was reluctantly ordered. 'Anything else?' asked Loveluck, 'or can we begin?'

Jamie shrugged. 'Sure. Ready when you are.'

'I've been ready for two hours.. OK. Tell me from the start.'

'Right. I've been thinking about this so I can probably tell it pretty quick.'

'Even quicker if you make a start.'

'I was working the bar that night. The two girls were doing food orders and filling in helping on the bar if it got busy. Get the idea?'

'Yes,' said Loveluck patiently. 'I'm managing to follow you so far.'

'Let me know if I'm going too fast for you.'

'Just get on with it.'

'Anyway this guy comes in. Smartly dressed. Suit and tie and all that. He comes up to me and says that he is Mr John and that he would like a half of lager. So I gets him a half of lager and ask if he would like anything else.'

'Can we skip the niceties, if you don't mind.'

'Ah,' said Jamie with a hint of triumph in his voice. 'But you would miss some good bits if I did because then he said that he was waiting for some guests to join him and he had told them to come to the bar and ask for Mr John.' Here he paused for effect but a glance at Loveluck's face encouraged him to continue pronto.

'Then a youngish woman came up.', but Loveluck stopped him with a wave of his hand.

'Tell me more about Mr John. What he looked like, what he spoke like. Was he nervous? Anything like that.'

Jamie thought this over. 'Well. You've seen his body so I suppose you know what he looked like. But he was a bit of a fussy bloke. Bit of an old woman, if you get what I mean. He had some papers with him and a note book and he kept looking at his watch and jotting things down like he was timing something. Or timing the people who came to join him.'

'What did he speak like?'

'Very precise. He was very precise. Spoke a bit slowly but very clearly.'

'So you could hear all he said?' asked Loveluck with the beginnings of a rush of interest surging through him.

'Well I could if I hadn't got anything else to do except sit around ear wigging. But I was working the bar and it gets busy. I heard bits, it's true.'

'Go on,' said Loveluck.

'So. He sits at the bar with his lager looking at his watch and all that when this woman comes in. Sort of youngish if you know what I mean.'

'How young?'

Jamie shrugged. 'I dunno. Older than my sister. And she's twenty.

Jamie could only have been nineteen or so and a girl of twenty five would have seemed old to him. 'Tell me about the girl.'

'She was a bit pissed off. She kept saying things like 'Am I the only one here? I've got better things to do than this and things like that. And he kept trying to calm her down saying things like, 'don't worry Lina. The rest will be here. There's something in this for you.'

'Lina,' said Loveluck abruptly. 'He called her Lina? Are you sure?'

'Course I'm sure.'

'It's an unusual name. It couldn't have been Tina?

'No,' said Jamie with feeling. 'It was Lina. My ears do work, you know.'

'Yes. You ear wigged very well.'

Jamie gave him a sour look. 'Do you want me to carry on?'

'Last orders please,' came the call from the barmaid. 'Any more for anymore?'

'Pint for me,' said Jamie sharply.

'Half for me,' said Loveluck wistfully. 'Then what happened?'

'Keeping with the younger woman for a mo,' said Jamie, 'she came up to me and asked for Mr John and I pointed him out and she went to join him. The rest I've told you.'

'What did Lina speak like?

'Posh. At least fairly posh. She spoke nicely. Not that forced, false posh like some of the hooray Henrys and Henriettas we get down the Poachers.'

'Educated background, you mean.'

'Yes. Nice girl, but a bit pissed off as I said. Then the older woman came in and asked for Mr John so I pointed him out and she stood there a while and looked at them both. Especially the girl.

'You mean she looked at the girl. Do you think she knew her?'

'I don't know if she knew her or not. I don't think so. They didn't say much. But the old woman might not have been as old as she looked. I mean, she had a wrinkled and leathery face like the wind and the weather had been working on it. A bit like the old fisherman you see at the seaside. And she had a yokel type voice.'

'Yokel type voice?'

You know. All Oo R like the Wurzels. Except it weren't Dorset or from anywhere round here.'

'The Wurzels were a Somerset band I think,' said Loveluck.

She might have been from the Somerset coast. I don't know. But not a Dorset yokel.'

'But she went to join Mr John and Lina at the bar.'

‘Yes she did. And she started giving Mr John a hard time about not everyone having turned up yet and how she had come a long way and was tired and stuff like that.’

‘Did he call her by her name?’

‘Yes he did but I can’t remember it. I think it was foreign.’ Then Jamie looked as though a light has just started to shine in his brain. ‘Perhaps she was foreign. Not a yokel at all. Yes, she was speaking English but with a strong accent. She really could have been foreign.’

‘You’re doing really well, Jamie. What happened next?’

‘Then a man came in and asked for Mr John. I pointed him out like before but he didn’t go to join him’

‘Tell me about him’

‘Well, he was nervous. That’s for sure. Drank three brandies in no time. And he kept looking at his watch as well. Fidgety.’

‘Description?’

Jamie blew out his cheeks. ‘That’s tough. Because just as he came in that large group of diners arrived and started buying drinks. Kept me pretty busy. But he was quite old. About your age.’

‘What?’

‘I mean he was about your age, whatever age that is. Probably quite young.’ But the damage was done and Loveluck was gently seething inside. ‘He had a rug. That’s one thing I can be sure of. And an awful rug it was too.’

‘A rug? What are you talking about?’

‘A rug. You know. Hairpiece. Wig. Call it what you will. And it must have been a cheap one because it fooled nobody. Everyone was pointing at it and laughing behind their hands.’

‘What did he speak like?’

Jamie shrugged. ‘He only said Brandy and Soda three times and he sounded normal but nervous.’

‘Time gentlemen please’ shouted the barmaid.

‘Just a few more minutes,’ said Loveluck.

‘Be quick then. I’ve got things to do this afternoon.’

Loveluck said swiftly. ‘Another man came in. Tell me about him.’

‘Yes. He came in and asked for Mr John. I pointed him out as I had done with the rest and he sat out of sight of them.’

‘How did he speak?’

‘Short, clipped. Didn’t look at me. He kept looking round the pub as though searching for someone.’

‘Anything memorable about his appearance? A rug or anything?’

‘Short hair. Could be military. Certainly very fit looking and not someone I would like to get on the wrong side of. Maybe the same age as the girl. Very focussed. A watchful man.’

‘What did he drink?’

‘Water.’

They walked out to the car park together and separated with a brief wave and Loveluck hoped that a watchful man wasn’t watching Jamie right then.

Loveluck drove to Sherborne police station and walked in. ‘Is Inspector Anderson around?

‘Gone home, sir. It is Saturday afternoon.’

‘Anyone else around?’

‘No sir. Except perhaps Sergeant Daly. I know there was something he wanted to finish off but I think that’s all.’

‘No sign of Sergeant Knightly?’

‘Not since she left for Lymington this lunchtime.’

‘Lymington? Are you sure she went to Lymington?’

‘Yes sir. At least that’s what she said.

Loveluck shook his head and strolled slowly to his car. He drove home to Cerne Abbas, parked outside the Royal Oak and walked the few yards to his home. He showered and changed, all the time thinking about the mass of information that had come in and wondering how much of it he could trust. He was more than a little concerned about Sergeant Sadie Knightly. Always a dynamic and sometimes bombastic officer, she was none the less reliable and this absenting herself without consulting him was a new side of her he didn’t want to see develop.

He walked across the road to the Royal Oak and entered. It was too early to be really busy but he knew it would be packed with customers before long. Archie caught his eye and indicated a pint waiting for him. Loveluck walked over. ‘Very efficient, Archie. Cheers.’

‘It’s in for you. Secret admirer over there.’ Loveluck followed his gaze and saw a very familiar profile. He smiled. ‘Thanks, Archie’

Loveluck edged his way to the table and sat down. ‘Good evening sergeant.’

‘Good evening, sir. I ordered you rump steak rare. With chips and peas. Archie said you liked that.’

'Yes I do. And for you?'

'The same, sir. I love rare steak.'

They sat in an awkward silence for a spell, neither one looking at the other. Loveluck eventually broke the silence. 'Enjoy your trip to the seaside?'

'Yes thank you sir,' she muttered softly.

'Speak up Knightly.'

'Yes thank you sir.' She barked out 'Very much sir. Have much to tell you sir.'

'And it had better be good.' He replied slightly tartly.

Dinner and wine arrived and they set about it with gusto, both hungry and both in need of something to do to cover the awkwardness.

'I'm sorry I didn't tell you directly that I was going to Lymington, sir' she suddenly burst out.

'Or indirectly.'

'The thing is I had an idea about those photographs and I remember you saying that the note book was interesting so I thought I had better go and get them.' It sounded thin and she knew it. 'But I saw Samantha at the office. She still goes in even though he's dead. She wants to collect her pay. I think she'll carry on going into the office as long as the standing order at his bank continues to pay her. Which could be years.'

'Sounds like easy money.'

'I also told her I was going to collect her from the office on Monday afternoon and bring her in to identify John Small. As far as I know we don't have anyone else who knows him.'

'Why didn't you tell me you were going to Lymington?'

'I don't know. Some sort of brainstorm.'

'Well I know. You wanted to go and chase up your leads and you thought that I would make you come to interview Jamie the barman with me. Which I would. Lymington could have waited.'

They sat in silence for a while.

'There's something else I should tell you,' she said softly.

'About the two Hampshire policemen?'

'Oh. You seem to know all about it.'

'Not all about it, but some police keep in touch with each other. And this is not the first time you have got above yourself recently. You are here as a temporary replacement for Sergeant Pepper. Temporary replacements are easily found.'

Knightly sighed deeply. 'It's not *that* important.'

'Yes it is.'

'You don't think I'm competent to go interviewing on my own, do you?'

'Of course I do.'

She blinked. 'Really?'

'Of course. You are, in my opinion, a very highly competent officer.'

She thought it over for a few seconds. 'So, you're just miffed because I didn't tell you? I didn't go along with protocol?'

'Nothing to do with it.'

She shrugged. 'Then what?'

Loveluck mulled it over for a few seconds, then looked at her deeply. 'You're quite a sportswoman, aren't you?'

'Yes, sir. I'm keen on a number of sports.'

'And do you number skiing amongst them?'

'Yes, sir. I love skiing.'

Loveluck sat back in his chair. 'Do you ever ski off-piste?'

She nodded. 'Sometimes.'

'Off-piste skiing can be very dangerous, can't it?'

'Yes, sir. It can be very dangerous.'

'So, tell me. When you ski off-piste do you leave the details behind at the ski centre of where you will be skiing and what time you expect to be back?'

'Of course.'

'Why?'

'Why?' she repeated.

'That's what I said. Why?'

'Well, so that if you have some kind of accident and you don't return the rescue teams can come looking for you with some idea of where you are. People who climb mountains do the same thing for the same reason.'

'Exactly,' said Loveluck. 'So yesterday when you went to Lymington you did, in fact, go off-piste without telling anyone.'

Knightly understood the parallel completely.

'And when I pulled you over the coals for not telling me where you were going, was it because I didn't think you were competent?'

'No sir.'

'Or was it because I was miffed because you hadn't told me?'

'No, sir.'

'Then why do you think I was angry?'

‘Because you were concerned about my safety and welfare.’

‘Exactly. And more than that, as your superior officer I’m responsible for your safety and welfare. Do you understand?’

‘Yes, sir. Can I just say how sorry I am? I really didn’t think. I won’t go off-piste again without telling you. Ever.’

‘Good. Now let’s finish these excellent rump steaks and have another glass of wine.’ He started to pour two large glasses of red. ‘As it’s Sunday tomorrow and as we both live in Cerne Abbas and only a short walk away from this pub I think we can safely....’

‘Get piste?’ she suggested

Loveluck smiled and called a waitress. ‘More wine, please.

Chapter 9

Sunday lunchtime found Inspector Loveluck back at the scene of the crime at the Poachers Inn. He was standing by the swimming pool looking across at the row of chalet rooms where the dead had been found. Rooms 7 to 11 were in an L-shape along one side and one edge of the pool. Room 11 was on the edge and the others along the side. He walked a slow lap of the pool and came to a halt outside room 9 which was roughly halfway along the length of the pool.

He stood with his back to room 9 and the pool in front of him and surveyed all he could see in a huge arc from left to right. To his left was a terrace which stood at a higher level than the garden level he was at. Some people were sitting outside to eat, drink and enjoy the sun. They would have a good view of the pool and rooms from there. There were also some rooms on the terrace but probably without much of a sighting of the death rooms.

Directly in front of him was a long terrace of rooms in two flights. The ones at floor level might have a view of the death rooms, but the ones above them would have a perfect view. He scanned along the terrace. Outside stairs up to maybe six or seven rooms on the first floor. He very badly wanted to know who had been in those rooms on the night of the murders.

'Fancy a swim' came a voice as two hands pushed him towards the water, then pulled him back.

Loveluck turned to see Olwen Evans and said irritably, 'Don't do that. You could have pushed me in.'

'Stop being grumpy. You can swim, can't you? Anyway, which are the grisly rooms? Show me round.'

Together they did a lap of the pool. 'Mr Small was found in room 7.'

'How was he killed?'

'Garrotted.'

'That's nasty.'

‘And unusual. In the next room was....’

‘Just garrotted?’ asked Olwen

‘Isn’t that enough?’

‘Not if what I heard is true.’

Loveluck sighed. ‘And what has the Western Gazette’s ace crime reported heard now? And how do you get to hear it so fast?’

‘You know I’m going to find out sooner or later, probably sooner than you, so you might as well tell me.’

Loveluck moved on ignoring her. ‘In room 8 was a girl of 25 or thereabouts. We don’t know anything about her.’

‘Sergeant Knightly does.’

‘What!’

‘She gave me a complete rundown on her wardrobe. And a right jumble it was too. From cheap tack to high street norm to very flashy expensive. That girl has a story to tell.’

‘Had a story to tell.’

‘It’s not been told yet. And I intend to tell it.’

Loveluck pushed on. Room 9 empty. It was booked but not used.

‘Room 10 had an elderly woman in it. Garrotted, like the others. Room 11 was empty. Again it had been booked but not used. At least, the bed had been lain on but not slept in.’

‘He did it. Room 11 did it. The mysterious man in room 11,’ she said dramatically. ‘You wait and see. Room 11 did it.’

Loveluck smiled. ‘Let’s get a drink and you can tell me all about Mr John Small.’

They took their drinks on the terrace overlooking the garden. Loveluck’s head still felt a little groggy from the previous night’s meal with Sergeant Knightly, though it would take a very optimistic police inspector indeed to try and convince anyone it was the meal that made his head feel groggy.

‘Cheers,’ said Olwen brightly. ‘Or should that be ‘hair of the dog.’’

Inspector Loveluck brushed her comments aside with a wave of his glass. ‘Tell me what you learned about John Small.’

Olwen pushed her curly locks back, took out a note book and some computer print outs and said. ‘Not a lot.’

‘You as well.’

‘Yes. He didn’t show up on the radar in Lymington until about a year ago. Mark, that’s my reporter friend, says that there is little known or said about him. He didn’t hang out with the legal crowd at all. Didn't belong to anything you might have expected. Rotary club, round table, that sort of thing. Had an office in the Angel Courtyard in Lymington but didn't get involved with anyone there. None of the shopkeepers seem to have known much about him. Bit of a dead loss all round.'

'Nothing at all, then' said Loveluck with a sigh.

'Not really. It seems he did spend some time with his secretary, Samantha Alcock. They would drink in the Gordleton Mill on the edge of the New Forest. Posh joint by all accounts. Spent a couple of months as almost regulars and then,' she snapped her fingers, 'gone' otherwise very little is known.'

Loveluck played with his drink, making circles with the base of his glass and forming wet patterns on the table.

'Well, there are a couple of things. I don't think they are of any importance, but they make my reporter's nose twitch. Like, why were they at the Gordleton Mill so often and then suddenly never there again? Something was happening there or in the area. Reporter's nose twitching. What were they there for? What were they up to?'

'Sounds plausible,' said Loveluck.

'Another thing. My pal Mark.'

'The reporter,' added Loveluck.

'The very same. He really couldn't find any more of Mr Small in the Lymington and New Forest area, so he dug backwards. Tried to find out what he had been up to before he pitched up in Lymington a year ago.'

'And'

'Nothing.

'He trawled through all the usual solicitor records but found nothing. He spread his net not only further back in time but wider in area. Pushed down to Christchurch and then Bournemouth. Nothing. He really couldn't give anymore time to it so he took a bit of a gamble and, figuratively, stuck a pin in a map. By which I mean he said to himself 'which small area can I intelligently search.' And the answer he came up with was?'

Loveluck shrugged. 'Was where?'

'He asked himself 'Where was he killed?' Answer 'Sherborne''

Loveluck felt a quiver of excitement. 'What did he find?'

Olwen proudly took out a sheet of paper. She handed it to him. 'Twenty five years ago there was a solicitors firm in Sherborne called

'Bassington, Small and Peacock'. And the Small was a Mr John Small.'

Loveluck grinned broadly.

'Lunch' said Olwen, 'is on you.'

They whiled the time away waiting for lunch to arrive chatting over a range of subjects. They touched on the subject of marriage.

'Have you ever been married?' asked Loveluck.

'Me? Yes I have. Just once.'

'Did it last long?'

Olwen looked wistful. 'I got married young. He was a teacher. Lovely man. I got a job as a secretary at a local paper and I suppose that's where the trouble began.'

'How do you mean?'

'Well, although I was a secretary I used to see the reporters coming and going and they seemed so exciting to me. Off to dig out a scoop. Front page story.' She laughed. 'I suppose most of them were going to interview Mr and Mrs Bloggs on their fiftieth wedding anniversary or something similar. But I'd got the bug. And sometimes at weekends they would invite me out with them when they went out for a drink. It was heaven for me. There I was with all these hard bitten reporters. And they enjoyed a drink or two and I just went along with it. It was a fabulous new world to me.'

Loveluck smiled. 'I can imagine you as a young secretary getting caught up in all that.'

Olwen smiled. 'And there were men, too. Our group of girls would get chatting to men. And so would I. And after a few drinks, well, I ended up in more men's cars with my feet on the dashboard than I care to remember.' She laughed. 'God I was a randy little tart. Great fun though.'

'Can't have been much good for the marriage.'

Olwen shrugged. 'The marriage was pretty well over by then. I'd seen a whole new world that I wanted to be a part of. I got a job as a cub reporter at the Western Gazette, moved to Yeovil and that was that.'

'And now you are Olwen Evans, ace crime reporter of the Western Gazette.'

'Yes. A serious and successful journalist.'

Loveluck smiled. 'Still a bit of a tart,'

She laughed. 'I'll always be that. I'm not a young girl anymore, but still sassy and sexy enough to pull successful men.'

Their memories both went back to a night some three months earlier they had spent together.

Suddenly Olwen pointed. 'Now if you want your women young, gorgeous and sexy beyond belief, here comes the one for you.'

He turned to see Sergeant Sadie Knightly approaching. 'Good morning,' she called cheerily. It only seems a few hours since we parted. Thank you for a lovely night, sir.'

Olwen's eyes opened wide with interest and she smiled. Loveluck peered at his shoes.

'Pepper is fetching the drinks. We've been out running together this morning.'

'Inspector Loveluck and I have been out running together as well. Running a few ideas past each other.'

Sergeant Pepper joined them and was surprised to find Loveluck and Olwen there. 'Quite a gathering,' she said. 'Sadie and I have been out running.'

'Yes. She said'

'And we decided to come here for lunch. I wanted to see the scene of the crime. Just out of interest.'

'It's down there,' said Knightly pointing towards the pool and rooms a level below them. We'll go down and have a look after lunch.' Then she turned to Loveluck. 'One thing I forgot to tell you yesterday, sir.' Then she stopped and looked at Olwen.

Loveluck intervened. 'We're having a meeting tomorrow. You, me and Inspector Anderson. Share information, catch up and try to see if we can weave together some kind of theory as to what happened. Best to save all the detail until then.'

'Don't forget my snippet of information,' said Olwen. Then she turned to Pepper and Knightly. 'You see I've turned up the fact that John Small was a partner in a law firm in Sherborne. Twenty five years ago. A long time ago, I know, but a connection all the same.'

'And I know he had an office in Weymouth about three years ago,' said Knightly.

Loveluck chimed in. 'That just gives us twenty two years to fill in.'

'Will we have all the forensic results tomorrow, sir?'

'I don't know'

‘No, we won’t,’ said Pepper. ‘I mean, you won’t. Dr Ryan will present a report which may or may not be complete. The SOCO team well have a preliminary report available for you, but there is so much evidence, some of which needs more research with truck manufacturers that a final report could be a while in coming.’

They looked at her in surprise. Pepper shrugged. ‘I’m working in admin. Reports are admin. They come my way.’

Loveluck and Olwen’s meals arrived and Pepper and Knightly left them to eat and walked down the steps to the level of the garden, pool and rooms. They trod much the same ground as Loveluck had done earlier and he could see Pepper plying Knightly with all kind of questions. Olwen watched them as she ate. ‘I feel sorry for her.’

Loveluck followed her gaze. ‘You mean Sergeant Pepper?’

Olwen mused awhile. ‘Actually, I think I mean Detective Sergeant Pepper. Because a detective is what she is. Just watch her.’

‘I spend a lot of time watching her, but she is still undergoing treatment. She can’t go back to detective work until she is given the all clear.’

‘And I think we all know that that might be never. I understand she is having anger problems.’

‘Among other things, but as far as we are concerned the anger problems are the main ones. We can’t have her losing it when interviewing the public.’

‘She’s angry, Jack.’

‘I know she is, but...’

‘Do you know what anger is? Real anger?’

Loveluck turned away to watch the two sergeants by the pool.

‘Because she has every right to be angry. She was buried alive, for Christ’s sake, by that vile bastard Tony Tillotson. The same bastard who whipped me. Remember?’

‘Tillotson is in Prison.’

‘Buried alive for thirty six hours. Freezing in that horrible field, going half crazy. And when they dug her out.’ She stopped. Lost for words. ‘You remember what she looked like. Shaking, blabbering, fear of evil in her eyes. It was only four months ago. She’s a detective, Jack. Not an administrator. Just like I was a journalist, not a secretary.’

Loveluck pushed the remains of his Caesar Salad away. ‘It was a terrifying experience for her. And that’s why we have to give her time to recover. Leave it to the doctors, Olwen. I'm a copper, you're a journalist, and they are doctors.'

They stood up to leave. 'I've got a confession to make,' she said.

'Go and see the Reverend Toby Austin. That's his line of business.'

'No. I've done something that is as bad as anything I can imagine. It's on my mind night and day.'

He looked at her more carefully. 'Are you serious?'

'Yes I am, Jack. Deadly serious.'

He turned to leave. 'Go see the vicar of Sherborne. Talk to Toby. I don't do confessions. Unless you are confessing to a crime, of course, in which case it *is* my job to listen. I assume you aren't confessing to a crime.'

She hesitated. 'I'm not sure.'

'Talk to Toby. Moral issues are his line, not mine.' And with that he walked back into the pub and out of the front door.

Chapter 10

At nine o'clock sharp on Monday morning Inspector Loveluck, Inspector Anderson and Sergeant Knightly assembled in Anderson's office at Sherborne police station. They had each a collection of files with them which they had all read and, in theory, all three should know the progress made by the other two.

'Right' said Loveluck. 'I think we all have busy days today so let's press on.'

'Who's going to start?' asked Knightly.

'I think the first thing to do is to decide whether we think we are dealing with two crimes here or one.'

'The two crimes being?' asked Knightly.

'The murders at the Poachers Inn and the hanging in the woods near the Hunter's Moon,' said Anderson. 'I personally think they are linked. And I think so because of......'

'Can we,' said Loveluck loudly, 'save out conclusions until *after* we have discussed the evidence? And seen the forensic reports? It is the way round we are supposed to do things.'

'Of course you're right,' said Anderson. 'And let's do things as they happened. The first thing was the murder at the Poachers Inn. Jack, do you want to start us off?'

Loveluck nodded, arranged his papers and was just about to begin when the door burst open and Sergeant Pepper came bustling in. 'Morning everyone. I hope I'm not disturbing you but I know how you all like to have a drink at these meetings.'

Loveluck sighed and sat back in his seat.

'Tea for Inspector Loveluck. Just how he likes it. And tea for Sergeant Knightly, just how she likes it. And coffee for Inspector Anderson just how he likes it.' She smiled and bustled out of the room.

There was a short silence. Loveluck and Anderson exchanged glances. 'She wants to be involved. Should we invite her to stay?' asked Knightly.

Loveluck shook his head. ‘We can’t let her force her way back in. We have a plan for her reintroduction to detective work and it depends on the doctors’ reports. We go along with that. We involve her in administration so she keeps loosely in touch, but that’s all.’

Anderson nodded in agreement.

‘Right.’ Loveluck rearranged his papers and prepared to speak when the door opened and Pepper once again bustled in.

‘Sorry. I forgot the biscuits. All your favourites.’ Then she sat down, opened a notebook and said. ‘Have I missed anything?’

‘Sergeant Pepper,’ said Loveluck patiently. ‘Shouldn’t you be doing administrative work?’

‘Yes, sir.’

‘Well? Why aren’t you?’

Pepper looked surprised. ‘But I am, sir. I am here to make notes of the meeting. And these notes will be used to draw up minutes of the meeting so we all know what we agreed on, what actions were decided upon and any other important matters. Chief Inspector John Waddington said he had wanted properly minuted records of meetings for years.’

‘You’ve spoken to the Chief Inspector?’ said Anderson.

‘In my role as temporary administrator I’ve been researching for the job, for though I am in fact a detective sergeant I do, nevertheless, want to do my temporary job as well as I can. That’s why I put a couple of suggestions to the Chief Inspector. He was quite pleased.’

Loveluck and Anderson exchanged questioning glances and Knightly stared fixedly at her notes.

‘In which case,’ said Loveluck with controlled patience, ‘you must sit there quietly and take your notes.’

Pepper shut her mouth tightly and nodded.

‘As Sergeant Knightly wasn’t at the interview with Jamie the barman from the Poachers,’ here Loveluck paused and Knightly continued to stare at her notes. ‘I will précis what happened at that interview. I learned nothing new about Mr John Small except that he spoke slowly and precisely. We already knew that he had a solicitor’s office in Lymington by the New Forest where he also had a small cottage on the quay.’

‘By the car park,’ added Knightly and wished she hadn’t.

‘We know that his office and home have both been turned over. We also learned that the office was pretty much a front, though a front for what we don’t know. His secretary, the strange Samantha Alcock, call me Sammy, says Mr Small handled a small number of secret clients and that the rest was a sham. Including her. And just for good measure she was also his housekeeper.'

Loveluck paused and put down his notes. 'Sergeant Knightly has paid a further visit to Lymington and perhaps she would be good enough to report now.'

'I went to the office and again saw Samantha, call me Sammy, Alcock. She was quite chatty. There were a couple of things from the office I wanted to see again but as I was searching I was disturbed by two Hampshire police officers. They made me feel a bit uncomfortable so I said my hello and goodbye and left.'

'One of the officers concerned,' said Loveluck, 'told me you were last seen running hell for leather through the Angel Courtyard. He assumed you were going to Mr Small's cottage and would happily have given you a lift as he was driving Sammy home.'

Knightly pursed her lips and nodded in understanding. 'That's how she got there.'

'Anyway, I got what I wanted. Three photographs and a small notebook, none of which I have had the time to study yet.

'I have also learned,' continued Loveluck, 'from a different source that twenty five years ago in Sherborne there was a law firm called Bassington, Small and Peacock. And that the Small was in fact Mr John Small.

Anderson tapped his pencil on his notes. 'Twenty five years ago, Jack? We are dealing with a crime that happened four *days* ago. Do you really think it can have any bearing?'

Loveluck shrugged. 'Who knows, but it links him to Sherborne. And as he is our only real lead we have to follow it up.'

'Moving on, but staying with the Poachers Inn murders, there are a few other interesting facts. Firstly the young woman who was murdered was called Lina. Spelt Lena or Lina. I am spelling it L I N A for the time being. That should bring some results as we look at missing persons now we have a name.'

'Any questions so far?'

'Did you get all this off Jamie the barman?'

'Yes. He was a very good witness. Lousy timekeeper but a good witness.'

'Finding Lina could be a great breakthrough,' said Pepper. 'Ooops, sorry. Just thinking out loud.'

Loveluck went on to describe how Jamie had described the older woman as not perhaps as old as he first thought, but certainly weather beaten. 'Jamie also said that she had a funny name. He couldn't remember it but he thought it might have been foreign. He described her speaking voice as perhaps a broad accent but not from these parts. A bit like the Wurzels who I think were from Somerset. He also thought that perhaps she was foreign and spoke English with a foreign accent.'

Knightly shrugged. 'Interesting but not very helpful.'

'No. The progress is with Lina'

'Anymore?' asked Anderson.

'Yes. The two men who arrived but didn't speak to Mr Small. One of them was nervous and drank three brandies in short time, whilst the other was Mr Cool and drank only water. He thought that Mr Cool might have been military. Clipped speech, short hair, very fit looking. It's a possibility. And he seemed to be looking for someone. Anyway, that is the state of things at the Poachers except to say that there are some rooms in the beer garden at first floor level which would have a great view of the pool and all the death rooms. In fact of the whole garden area. We need to know who, if anyone, was staying in those rooms.'

'Some interesting snippets there that might be important.'

'That's it for me,' said Loveluck.

Anderson moved straight in. 'OK. The hanging in the woods. There is a mass of evidence and forensics, and a mass more to come so I won't bore you with going through all that. I'll just point out some of the major things. Firstly, the murders at the Poachers Inn and the hanging in the woods took place on the same night at roughly the same time as far as we can tell. Secondly, the three victims in the Poachers had their left hands cut off as did the hanged man. I don't think I need to labour the point to say that I believe the two events are connected.'

'I think we can take that as a working assumption,' said Loveluck warily.

'Other main points. There was a group there in the woods that night. Seems they wore moccasins. That seems to me like it should be a really important fact but I can't for the life in me think why. The group didn't seem to make much effort to cover their tracks. In fact there seems to be almost an intentional glut of evidence.

'One thing that was found at the site was a car. The car was registered in the name of a Mr Winston Gale of Winchester. There is no Mr Winston Gale at the address the car is registered at and there never has been. So explain that one. We are actively looking for Mr Gale but I fancy that he was the only person not to leave the scene of the hanging. And he didn't leave it because he was the man hanging there.

'There is loads of minute detail but you can save that for a bit of bedtime reading.'

Loveluck began to put his papers into his brief case. 'Any questions, comments, theories?'

There was no response. 'All right. Inspector Anderson, you have your work cut out with the hanging case. And finding out who the moccasin tribe are. And how Winston Gale was connected to the tribe and to the Poachers Inn three. Is Sergeant Daly available to assist you?'

'Yes, thanks to Pepper here doing so much research herself.'

'Thanks, Sergeant. You are doing a great job.'

Pepper looked slightly miffed. 'Doesn't anyone want to know what progress my researches have made?'

'Oh sorry, sergeant. Yes of course we do.'

'I haven't had much time because of my admin duties here,' she said pointedly. 'But I have been doing some background research and I am beginning to get the feel of the whole occult subject. I hope to be able to report some concrete findings soon.'

'Good,' said Anderson somewhat patronisingly. 'I'm sure it will be a great help.'

'Sergeant Knightly will be helping me try and track down John Small and his Sherborne connection of twenty five years ago.'

'I don't think there is much more to be gained from the Lymington, New Forest connection,' said Knightly.

'Oh no,' said Loveluck suddenly. 'There is one thing I forgot to mention. Olwen Evans told me that John Small and Samantha, call me Sammy, Alcock spent about two months as regulars at a place called the,' here he searched around for a piece of paper. 'Yes. The Gordleton Mill, near Lymington. Up market place by all accounts. Then suddenly after two months, they stopped going there.'

'And?'

'Well, and nothing. It's strange and it is in the New Forest. Maybe something was going on there.'

Knightly shrugged. 'Maybe they enjoyed going there and then lost interest in the place. Or got banned. It doesn't seem a very choice lead to me.'

'Either way, I want you to go and look the place over and ask questions.'

'Off-piste?'

'Keep me informed. This lunchtime I want us to go back to the Poachers and have a closer look at the guest list. Particularly people staying in the first floor terrace opposite the death rooms.'

'Is it all right if I go to the New Forest pub, the something or other mill, on Wednesday?'

'I don't see why not. Any special reason?'

'I don't want to go doing that kind of thing on my own. A single woman stands out a bit. On Wednesday I can take a friend.'

'Don't get a member of the public into danger.'

'We're only going for a meal. And there's no chance of that.'

'Then there's no problem. Confirm the date with me.'

'Of course, sir.'

The meeting broke up and they all dispersed.

Loveluck strolled slowly through the police station towards the door. He stopped at the station officer's desk. 'Morning sir.'

'Good morning. Can you tell me if Sergeant Pepper is here on Wednesdays?'

'Yes sir she is. But only in the mornings.'

Loveluck smiled and went on his way into the dull, grey morning.

Wootton Bridge in the New Forest crosses Avon Water and it was in this water that Kayra was paddling now. The tiny waif-like girl was singing in her usual strange tongue and wore the peaceful, beatific countenance that was always with her, A garland of self dressed flowers were in her hair and she skipped through the water at complete peace with this world and possibly several other worlds as well.

In a clearing by this beauty spot sat Rufus on a fallen log and it was clear that he was not at peace with the world. His handsome features and robin's egg blue eyes were disturbed. His mouth was set tight and he was taking small twigs and breaking them into smaller pieces before discarding them with an irritable flick of the wrist.

One of his young followers sat beside him on the log.

'Be at peace, Rufus. We must wait.'

'Wait?' Rufus replied sharply. 'Wait for what? For the book man to come for us?'

'Why call him the book man? We know his name. It's Jakob.'

'I don't like him having a name. I preferred it when he was anonymous.'

'What is it between you two? The rest of us know nothing. We've helped with the murder of three people and yet you tell us nothing. We need to know what's going on.'

Rufus stared him firmly in the eye. 'Bartholomew. Do you doubt me? Are you questioning me?'

'No Master.'

'I think you mean yes, master. You do doubt me.'

Their eyes met and the unspoken threat was clear. Bartholomew walked away wishing he could have cut his tongue out rather than anger Rufus.

Rufus stood up and walked to the water's edge and watched Kayra singing and existing beautifully. He slipped off his moccasins and walked through the shallow water. 'What is it you're singing?'

'A song of a maiden who loved a man but he loved another.'

He smiled. 'You don't seem very upset that she lost her lover.'

She smiled wistfully. 'No. I am pleased she lost her lover. Other people's sadness makes me happy.' She skipped a few yards through the water and then turned. 'Will you kill Bartholomew? You must, you know. He can't be trusted.' And then she was into another song that Rufus didn't understand.

Inspector Loveluck entered the bar of the Digby Tap and spoke to the landlord. 'Has Chris Williams been in?'

'Not yet. You two aren't going to start fighting, are you Inspector?'

Loveluck chuckled. 'We're the very best of friends.' In fact Loveluck and Williams had a somewhat prickly relationship that policemen and solicitors sometimes do in small towns. 'I'll have a pint of Doom and whatever Chris wants.'

Loveluck went to sit in a pew seat facing the bar and scanned the room around him. It was a little early for a lot of customers but those who were there passed the time with a fine drink and reading the magazines and the walls. The walls were full of reading matter and photographs.

The solicitor came in quickly through the doorway, spotted Loveluck and moved straight to him. 'Sorry to keep you waiting Jack.' He shrugged. 'A client. Is that for me?'

He took his pint and had a refreshing mouthful. 'Now, what can I do for you?'

'Probably very little. I am trying to trace a law firm that had an office in the town twenty five years ago. I've never heard of them.'

'What were they called?'

'Bassington, Small and Peacock.'

The solicitor reacted with a knowing look.

'Do I assume you know them?'

'Certainly I know them. Why are you interested in them?'

'The name of the law firm has cropped up in the course of an investigation and I'm trying to find out a bit more about them.'

The solicitor sipped on his beer. 'They were a funny sort of outfit. Ted Bassington was a good chap and held it all together. Small was a borderline crook and Peacock was off his rocker. Or perhaps I should say 'borderline bonkers''

Loveluck reacted accordingly and asked. 'Tell me about the Small part of the business.'

Williams thought for a moment. 'Alfred Small. Nasty piece of work.'

'Alfred Small? Ah. Might have the wrong Small.'

'No. He was certainly called Alfred Small. Wouldn't trust him an inch.'

Loveluck was downcast. 'We are after a Mr John Small.'

'Oh yes'' said Chris Williams brightly. 'The son. Took over briefly when the old man died. I'd forgotten about him.'

'What was he like?'

'John Small? Boastful. And sly. He would come in this bar, actually, and chat with us. Always seemed to be on the make. Looking for the main chance. Insinuating that he might have a nice little contract where he could make plenty of money. Hit the jackpot, he used to say. He talked like that. I don't suppose he ever did. He wasn't a very good lawyer. Too lazy and after the easy money. Why? What's he done?'

'Well. He's got himself murdered.'

'Really? John Small murdered? Perhaps he did hit the jackpot after all.'

Loveluck shifted his position and drew a little nearer to Williams. 'I really want to find out more about this John Small. Is there anyone, anyone at all, who might know something?'

'The best person to speak to would be Ted Bassington.'

'Is he still alive?'

'Yes. He only retired a couple of years ago.'

'That's fantastic. Does he get in here?'

'You mean the Tap?'

'Yes.'

'No. Never comes here.'

Loveluck was disappointed. 'Have you got his address?'

'I have it written down somewhere but I'll have to send it on to you. But I can give you the name of his local pub.'

'Terrific.'

'The Doghouse.'

Loveluck thought a while. 'Doghouse? I'm not sure I know that one.'

Chris Williams smiled. 'I'm not surprised. It's on the Costa del Sol in Spain.'

When they left the Digby Tap Williams gave Loveluck the email address of Ted Bassington which he had found on his phone and the promise of any further help should he need it. He also promised to ask around about John Small.

Knightly, Loveluck knew, was back at the Poachers Inn asking about guests who might have had rooms with a view of the murder scene.

Loveluck strolled up Cheap Street to the Three Wishes Cafe to enjoy a spirits lifting tea and bite to eat. The waitress saw him enter and called out to the kitchen. 'Inspector Loveluck Special with tea in the back garden please.'

He stared in amazement and said. 'Do they really know what that order means?'

'I think all our customers know what it means. It's our most popular dish.'

Feeling somewhat pleased with himself he strolled into the garden with a smug smile on his face. 'What a strange world'

Chapter 11

Sergeant Sadie Knightly was waiting at the door of the Poachers Inn when they opened. She had already done a tour of the back garden, the pool and the death rooms and the rooms opposite. She went with Mr Grayson to see the rooms. 'I'm really interested in rooms twelve to eighteen,' she said. I'd like to look round the rooms and know who was in them. I mean staying in them.'

'I've printed that information off for you,' he said and handed her a print out. You can see that only two were occupied.'

She looked at the sheet of paper. 'Can I keep this?'

'Of course.'

'I see that rooms 15 and 17 were occupied. I'd like to go inside them both but I fancy that number 15 is the one I'm really interested in.'

'It seems you're in luck. The lady in room 15 is still here. She leaves tomorrow. The gentleman from room 17 has left but you have his contact details there.'

'The lady occupant of this room' and here she checked her list, 'is a Mrs Preston. Is she here now?

'No. Mrs Preston is an elderly lady with family in the area. Her routine is usually the same every day. Breakfast at the usual time, then out to sightsee or visit family, then back at five in the evening for a cocktail and then a lie down before dinner. Early dinner around 7.30 and maybe have a cocktail on the terrace and an early night.'

Knightly laughed. 'Talk about customer service. You know all about her habits.'

Mr Grayson smiled ruefully. 'If we didn't, she'd soon teach us. An imperious lady, our Mrs Preston.'

'Then let's see the room before she gets back.'

Grayson hesitated. 'I'll have to tell her you were in her room. And why.'

'Don't worry. I'll tell her myself. And if she causes a fuss I'll flash my badge at her.'

'Oh no,' said Grayson. 'She won't mind that we were in there as long as she knows all about it. If I didn't tell her and she heard about it from another source she'd go ballistic.'

'Ah, I see.'

'She likes to stick her nose into......I mean she shows a lively interest in everything that goes on.'

'They often make excellent witnesses. Come on. Let's go up.'

They climbed the outdoor steps up to the first floor and walked along the wooden pathway which all the rooms opened onto. They stopped at room 15 and Knightly leaned on the safety banister and looked down on the garden, the pool and the death rooms.

'What a great vantage point.' She looked across to her right and could clearly see the first floor outside terrace where people liked to sit and eat. 'Let's go in'

They stepped inside room 15 and Knightly was again amazed at the perfect view the room had of all the death rooms. A small shelter in the garden below obscured part of room 9 but otherwise the view, not only of the relevant rooms but also of the garden and the higher terrace were excellent.

Knightly said. 'If Mrs Preston likes to know what's going on she's chosen the perfect room.' She pointed to a chair pushed neatly against the wall near the window. 'Perhaps she would sit on that chair and look out of the window.'

Grayson smiled and shook his head. 'She used to put it on the pathway outside her front door and watch what was going on. Until it grew too cold. *Then* she would watch out of the window.'

'I think I'm going to like Mrs Preston. But I have to get to Lymington. I'll see you around 5.30'

Inspector Anderson's enquiries into the owner of the abandoned car, Winston Gale, were going great guns. True the registered address of the car didn't turn out to be Mr Gale's address and never had been, but Sergeant Daly had come up with something interesting. He had run a routine check and has discovered that a Winston Gale had a number of convictions for both petty crime and crimes of violence.

A further check of the fingerprints of the remaining right hand showed that the Winston Gale who had a record was the same Winston Gale who was hanged from the tree.

Sergeant Daly had mixed feelings. Another research success pleased him, but it raised his reputation as an ace researcher even higher when, in reality, it was his reputation as a detective he wanted rising. He briefly toyed with not telling Inspector Anderson about it but dismissed the notion as a pleasant fantasy.

He had run fingerprint checks on the three murder victims but John Small, the young woman Lina and the elderly woman were model citizens. Or they had never been caught. One or the other.

They were still no nearer finding an address or anything concrete on Winston Gale and it looked like staying that way. Fingerprints taken from the car matched those of Winston Gale but beyond that they knew nothing.

Sergeant Knightly parked in the usual, convenient car park at the back of the Angel Courtyard in Lymington and walked through to where she immediately saw the familiar diagonal steps going up the white wall with the white handrail as protection against falling.

She glanced at the sign which still advertised "John Small, Solicitor", knocked on the door and entered.

Sammy was sitting at her usual desk reading a magazine. She glanced briefly at Knightly. 'You're early. Very early.'

'Since I've got to drive you all the way to the mortuary and back again I thought we'd get a move on with it.'

'It's a long way to Dorchester.'

'No. We're not going to Dorchester. It's been moved to Boscombe. Just down the road.'

'That's a blessing' said Sammy. 'Time for a cuppa?'

'Afraid not. After the mortuary, I am going to buy you lunch.'

Sammy sat goggle eyed. 'First time I've had lunch from the fuzz.'

'Then come and enjoy it. Is the office all cleaned up yet?'

'Yes. Hampshire coppers went through it and then said I could tidy up. So I did.'

Knightly shrugged. 'Ah well. Come on. Let's go.'

'You're not in a police car, are you? I don't want to be seen getting into a cop car. I've got a reputation to keep'

Knightly wondered what kind of reputation, but she said nothing.

When Sammy saw the red sports car her eyes goggled again. ‘This really yours?’

‘All mine. Get in and let’s go.’

The drive was short and when Knightly pulled off the main road into a grass and tree landscaped area Sammy said, ‘This is nice. It’s good to think that Mr Small is resting amongst the trees.’

One hundred yards later she had changed her tune. ‘Is this it?’ she said pointing to a group of shabby concrete building half hidden by the trees. ‘Is this the morgue? It looks like a group of old bomb shelters left over from the war. It’s disgraceful that people have to come here to find their dead loved ones. Diabolical.’

She continued to air her views all the way to the place where John Small was kept, but then she went silent. She gave Knightly a sideways glance and in return Knightly gave her an encouraging nod. The attendant guided Sammy to the corpse which was covered in a sheet. ‘Ready?’ he asked.

She nodded grimly and the sheet was removed. She gave a sharp intake of breath and had to steady herself. She looked long and hard at the corpse until the attendant said, ‘Is it him? Mr John Small?’

She nodded bravely and then she and Knightly swiftly left the building. But not before Knightly had performed a quick task the mortician would not have approved of.

They climbed into the car and Knightly reset the SatNav.

‘I hope you’re gonna take me home.’

‘After our meal.’ And she swung the car round and drove far too fast through the grounds to the main road.

Inspector Anderson had had something of a brainwave himself. He was sitting at the bar of the Poachers Inn watching Jamie the barman doing his work and enjoying a pint. He knew he was pretty much sitting where John Small had sat on that fateful night and he was imagining the arrival of the invited five. Firstly Lina. Feisty and cold. There under sufferance. Then the older woman, skin weather-beaten making her look older than her years. She also was berating Mr Small. He recalled that both of them had been told by Mr John that there ‘would be something in it for them’.

Then the arrival of the first man who asked for Mr John but didn’t speak with him. The nervous brandy drinking visitor. And finally, the quiet, clipped, calm military type. Silently and stealthily looking round all the time and drinking water.

He called Jamie over and asked for another pint. When Jamie gave him his pint Anderson said. 'You're Jamie, aren't you? You were here the night the murders happened.' Anderson saw Jamie stiffen and back away a little. 'I'm police.' He showed his badge.

'Can't you lot leave me alone.'

'I only want a minute of your time. Do you remember what the two men looked like who came here and asked for Mr John but didn't speak to him?'

Jamie shrugged. 'Sort of.'

'I've got a photograph here I'd like you to look at.' He took a photo from his pocket and placed it on the bar. Jamie took one look at it and vomited. It went down big with the customers who weren't used to this kind of unusual behaviour. But perhaps they had never seen a photograph of a man who had been hanging by his neck for two days.

Jamie returned to his work at the bar which had been cleaned up in the meantime. He looked green and gave Anderson a sulky look.

'Well. Was it one of them?'

'Let me see it again.'

Anderson sat a little further away from him and then turned over the picture. Jamie winced and then nodded. 'That's him. The nervous one who had all the brandy.' Then Jamie turned a little greener and Anderson left abruptly with a spring in his step.

Inspector Loveluck had sent a carefully worded email to Ted Bassington on the Costa del Sol, outlining why he wanted to speak to him. He was surprised to get an almost instant reply suggesting that they could speak by phone now or, better still, by Skype. Bassington had left the relevant details and requested Loveluck's Skype name and a convenient time to talk.

Five minutes later Loveluck was looking on his screen at a bronzed, healthy looking man of retirement age.

'Inspector Loveluck, I presume. Ted Bassington. Delighted to meet you.'

'Call me Jack.'

'Hi Jack.'

Loveluck could see that the man was sitting outside in the shade of the sun but the sunshine and blue sky were clear in the background as was exotic foliage.

‘I understand you want to know about John Small. What has he been up to now?’

‘He’s been murdered.’

‘Has he now? I’m surprised he hadn’t been murdered years ago.’

Loveluck was adjusting to this medium of Skype which he had used before but not often. ‘What can you tell me about him?’

‘At the moment not too much. I’m going out soon, but I’ll give you a swift fill in.’

‘I’d be grateful’

‘OK. He joined the firm when his father Alfred Small died leaving him considerably less than he had been expecting. There was joking around the office that his son had done him in. His father was always up for the main chance and John was certainly a chip off the old block. Or blockhead might be nearer the mark.’

‘How did you manage to stop them from cheating clients and the like?’

Ted sat back in his seat and sighed. ‘With great difficulty and limited success. Alfred was a good solicitor but dodgy. We really couldn’t keep tabs on him all the time without rows. And he *was* a partner, not some office junior, so he had plenty of rights. Could you hang on a sec whilst I pour myself another vino mucho collapso.’

Loveluck waited patiently and wished that Sherborne police station had something interesting to drink.

‘Sorry Jack. Back now. Where were we?’

‘John Small had just joined the firm after his father died.’

‘That’s right. I already said that when it came to sharp practice it was like father, like son but not when it came to ability. The father was a good solicitor, the son wasn’t. He was poor. And it didn’t help that his heart wasn’t in doing a good job, but only looking for juicy pickings.’

‘That must have made things difficult.’

‘Well, it did and it didn’t. We kept him off anything that required real ability and pushed him off onto routine and one off stuff. He was only a junior partner so we had a lot more control over what work he did.’

‘So things settled down after a bit?’ asked Loveluck.

‘Not at all. He grew resentful and there were terrible rows but we other partners had the clout and we more or less held him in check.’

Loveluck was beginning to think that nothing much was going to come of this.

'Until,' continued Ted Bassington, 'the man from the New Forest turned up.'

Suddenly Loveluck was all ears and enthusiasm.

'Man from the New Forest?'

'Yes. It was a strange business. One day this chap turned up at the office. No appointment or anything, just turned up and said he wanted a lawyer. We asked what the nature of the legal business was but he refused to talk about it. He said he wanted to deal with one man and one man only. Which one of us was it to be?'

'How do you mean? Which one man did he want?'

'It didn't matter which man. He just wanted the matter not to go beyond one person from the firm. In other words he didn't want all the partners knowing about it. Just one person.'

'Is that a common request?' asked Loveluck.

Bassington hesitated. 'Well. There is a great deal of secrecy involved with some parts of legal work. Wills are one good example. But usually clients rely upon the integrity of the law firm to preserve any details and keep the matter discrete, as we like to say. Secret as they like to say.'

'But not this chap.'

'No, certainly not this chap. He suddenly grew angry and said that if we couldn't give him the secrecy he required and to keep the details to one person then he would find someone who would. And with that he stormed out.'

'Never to be seen again?'

Bassington shrugged. 'Not by me'

'And that was the end of that?'

'It was as far as I was concerned. But John Small came into my office about half an hour later. Very cocky. Very full of himself. He said he had been listening at the door and couldn't believe how unprofessional we had been in letting a client get away. However, he'd stopped the client and had spoken to him and they had reached an agreement.'

'I asked him what kind of agreement. He said he wasn't at liberty to say as the client wanted complete secrecy with just one person. And he was to be that person. He gave us a sly look and said that he had hit the jackpot. It was a phrase he often used and we didn't pay much attention to it.'

'So how did it pan out?'

'Look Jack, I really have to go and join my friends at the Doghouse. That's a bar just near here.'

'Just tell me how it panned out, Ted.'

'Well, it led to plenty or rows. He was smug and said he was going to the New Forest to do the legal work for the client. Burley, I think he said, in the New Forest. Of course we demanded the case details were written up in the usual way. He refused. We demanded he leave the partnership or we would take steps to have him removed.'

'And?'

'And it went on like this for a while with periods of calm and periods of rows but no real progress. Then one day he came in and said he was willing to be bought out of his partnership. He'd hit the jackpot and didn't need us anymore. So he asked us for a severance payment. We refused and he said that he would stay with the company and make our lives a misery until we bought him out of his partnership.'

'Which you agreed to?'

Bassington sighed wearily. 'Yes. We had no choice in the end. He was beginning to sabotage the firm. It was easiest to pay him off.'

'Which you did?'

'Yes. And what a relief it was to be rid of him.'

'And when did all this take place, Ted?'

'Twenty five years ago.'

Loveluck whistled. 'That's a long time. Do you think it could have anything to do with his murder?'

Bassington shrugged. 'How do I know? Maybe, maybe not. But he came to live here on the Costa del Sol for several years. And there are plenty enemies he made when he was here who would be only too happy to see him murdered. Hard men too. Criminals. The answer might lie here rather than in Sherborne or the New Forest.'

'Just one last thing Ted. Do you remember the name of the client from the New Forest?'

'No. It was a strange name, I remember that. I'll give it some thought. If you want to come and ask around here about John Small you are welcome to stay with me. He only left here to go back to the UK about eighteen months ago.'

'So you have a house there?'

'Yes.' Ted laughed. 'I bought it from John Small actually. He was rushing back to the UK to deal with his Jackpot.'

Chapter 12

Gordleton Mill is a charming conversion on the outskirts of Lymington and on the edges of the New Forest, beautifully situated in the country between the sea and the Forest. It had been a water mill but had been converted and extended more than once. That it still held its old world charm and modern standards are a credit to its owners over the years.

There was an inside restaurant, an outside restaurant and gardens when the weather permitted and a charming front bar to sit and join friends for a drink or dine.

All this Knightly took in as Sammy led her to the front bar.

'Always my favourite bar,' she explained.

They found a table and Knightly carefully noticed how some of the customers followed Sammy with their eyes. It could have been a disapproval borne of past history or it could have been reaction to this shapely woman with masculine features. Either way they soon returned to their own conversations and forgot all about her and Samantha.

'What a lovely place,' said Knightly. 'Really, really charming. Do you come here often?'

'Not really. I've been here a few times. Bit posh and pricey for me. I prefer things a bit more cheap and cheerful. My pocket does anyway.'

They both laughed and Knightly said. 'I'm not sure I dare look at the menu.' Though in fact the menu was reasonable and, if other peoples meals were anything to go by, very good food. 'Did you go out much with Mr Small' asked Knightly.

A cloud passed over Sammy's features and Knightly could see that she was putting two and two together and coming up with four.

'He was my boss. I was his secretary and housekeeper. Why would I go out with him much?'

'Just a question.'

'Well, I didn't.'

'Pity. I'm sure you would have enjoyed coming here. I know I would.'

Sammy offered no more in the way of conversation on this topic and Knightly gave it up.

The meals were ordered and more drinks also. Knightly was on soft drinks in honour of her drive back to Sherborne but Sammy showed a liking for Prosecco which she was happy to drink as long as Knightly bought them. So Knightly kept buying them.

The food was excellent, the surroundings wonderful and Sammy tight as a clam.

Knightly sighed. How much could Sammy drink before she started talking? And would Knightly's money run out first. Thank heaven for plastic.

Sammy launched herself into a large pudding and an even larger Prosecco and finally began to talk. Knightly tried some gentle questions on John Small and Sammy began to get a little sentimental.

'He was a good man. A lovely man. Sometimes he would take me out when he was in a good mood.'

'Did he bring you here,' asked Knightly hoping that she had forgotten she had asked the same question before.

'Sometimes. If he was working.'

'Do you mean that he met clients here?'

Sammy looked stunned, then burst out laughing. 'Did I say he brought me here if he was working? I meant if he was celebrating. Silly me. Silly, silly me.'

Knightly smiled at her but she knew now that Sammy was not silly. Not silly at all. Not silly by a long, long chalk.

Loveluck was sitting in Sherborne Police Station writing a report when Anderson bustled in. He went straight to Loveluck and said. 'Have you seen this? What is the world coming to?'

Loveluck glanced up at him. Anderson was waving a leaflet in his hand. 'Have you seen it? Have you seen what is happening here next week?'

'If you stop flapping that leaflet around I might get chance to read it.'

‘Have one of your own,’ said Anderson dropping a couple more copies onto Loveluck’s desk. ‘It seems the town’s full of them.’

Loveluck picked the leaflet up and studied it briefly. He looked up at Anderson. ‘Annual psychic fair and witchcraft exhibition?’

‘In Sherborne of all places,’ said Anderson. ‘As if we hadn’t got enough with moccasin wearing Indians, or whoever they are, in the woods and people getting their left hands chopped off. Now the place is to be swarming with witches and psychics.’

Sergeant Daly heard the noise and came into the room and leaned against the wall.

Loveluck smiled. ‘Where’s it all taking place?’

‘It does say somewhere on the leaflet. Digby Hall, I think, for the psychics and witches. Did I really just say that? And stalls all round the streets selling all manner of things. Crystals, voodoo dolls, sun catchers, spell kits.’ He turned to Loveluck in despair. ‘Spell kits, I ask you. Every nutter in Sherborne will be casting spells. I can imagine it now when we stop a car on suspicion. ‘Excuse me, sir. Is that a jemmy I see on the back seat?’ ‘No, officer. It’s my spell kit.’’

Loveluck laughed heartily.

‘You won’t be laughing when they turn you into a frog.’

‘I’ll buy you a wand,’ said Loveluck. ‘That should keep you safe.’

Loveluck read the leaflet more carefully. ‘It starts on Friday,’ he said. ‘Goes right through to next weekend. It must be quite a big fair.

‘Starting on Friday is ridiculous. It’s the weekend. The traffic and parking will be a nightmare.

‘Broomsticks don’t take up much room,’ laughed Daly and received a humourless look from Anderson.

Sergeant Pepper, also attracted by the laughing, popped her head into the room. ‘What’s the joke?’

Anderson handed her a leaflet. Pepper read it with relish. ‘Fantastic. Tarot card readings, palm readings. Wow. A crystal ball. And you can find out who you were in a past life. Wait ‘til Sadie hears about this. What do you think of it, sir?’ she asked Anderson.

Anderson turned away but they could all catch the single word which might have been, ‘Warlocks’.

Sergeant Pepper walked in through the open door of Sherborne Abbey. A door that was normally kept closed. She looked round for the vicar, saw no sign of him and set off for the vestry area.

As she walked past the open steps up to the organ loft she felt a tang of admiration for the steel nerved murderer of the organist who had trod those steps in full view of a packed abbey, done the murder and walked down them and away.

She popped her head in the vestry door and called out 'Hello. Vicar? Toby?' Getting no reply she walked on to the verger's office and called out. 'Tom? You there?' The door was flung open and there stood a bear of a man. He looked down at Pepper and smiled.

'Janice. I ain't seen you in months.'

'It's Janine.'

'I was sorry to hear all about what happened to you. If I'd of got my hands on that Tillotson I'd have done for him. I'm not a violent man, Janice, but I am a big 'un.'

'Thanks Tom. And it's Janine. But that was a while a go now. I'm better.'

'Well,' grumbled Tom unconvinced, 'you take care of yourself 'til your proper better. Do you hear?'

'I do, Tom. And I thank you. It does my heart good to see you again. Have you any idea where the vicar is?'

'I don't know. He could be anywhere. There's nothing on in here this afternoon. Did you want him for anything special? Can I help, Janice?'

'No thanks, Tom. Have you heard about the Psychic fair and Witches exhibition?'

Tom laughed his explosive laugh. 'I've heard about little else for days. As if there aren't enough witches in Sherborne already. But I think it'll brighten things up for a bit. They were here a few years back. Lively bunch. Good fun. One or two of 'em takes themselves a bit on the serious side, and one or two are downright scary, but on the whole a good bunch.' He was about to launch into a story of the last fair when Pepper stopped him.

'Tom. Don't look now but who is that man. Over there by the altar steps.'

Tom looked at the man and shook his head. 'The tall slim chap with a face like a wet weekend. Tight lips and mean mouth.'

'That's the one.'

'That's the new curate. Strange sort of chap. Keeps himself to himself, but always seems to be listening in to everyone else's business.'

'He looks a bit spooky. What's his name?'

'Simon Peter.'

'Really?'

'That's what he says and everyone calls him curate or Simon Peter. I keeps out of his way and call him nothing. I'd best be going, Janice. I always think he's doing a time and motion study on me. Writing down how much I talk to the public and the like.'

'OK Tom. See you later.'

'Bye Janice.'

She watched the big man go back to his room and said quietly. 'It's Janine.'

Ted Bassington walked into the bar of his favourite drinking haunt, The Doghouse, and sat himself at the bar.

'Hello Ted. Usual?'

'Yes please, Susie.'

He watched her pour a gin and tonic, Spanish style. No optics, no measures just plenty of ice and gin poured in a good sized glass until it was nearly full and then add a dash of tonic and leave the rest of the tonic to Ted to add when he wanted.

'You know Susie, the first time I saw a gin and tonic poured Spanish style was in a bar in Madrid. My eyes nearly popped out of my head. And when I got the bill I thought I had died and gone to heaven. I knew then that this was the place for me.'

'How come you ended up on the Costa del Sol? And in El Pilar in particular?'

Ted gazed into the past. 'I don't know really. I loved Madrid. Still do. But you know, the time comes for a change. At least it did for my wife. She went back to the UK with a chap she met in an ex-pat church. Nothing's sacred. So I thought I'd give the coast a try. And I'm glad I did. I wouldn't have met the gorgeous Choosy Susie if I'd stayed in Madrid.'

Susie smiled. 'You old charmer.'

'Oh. And speaking of dying and going to heaven. You'll never guess who's just died.'

'If I'll never guess you'd better tell me.'

'John Small. Remember him?'

'Smarmy little creep. How could I ever forget him? What did he die of?'

'He was murdered.'

Susie thought it over for a short while. 'Now how come that doesn't surprise me?'

'Nor me,' said Ted.

'I'm only surprised it took someone so long to bump him off. I felt like doing it myself more than once. How do you know, anyway?'

'I had a copper from England ring me. Well, Skype me actually. Trying to find out a bit about him. When did he leave here to go back to the UK? Do you remember?'

'Two, maybe three years ago. You should know. You bought his apartment off him. How long have you been living there?'

'About that long. I'll look it up. I think the copper is going to contact me again.'

'How long was he here for? Quite a time, wasn't it?'

'Golly yes,' said Ted staring into his gin and tonic for inspiration. 'Must have been getting on for twenty years. Have long have you been here Susie?'

'In Spain? Over thirty years. And when John Small left here he did that in a bit of a hurry. Solicitor to the crooks can be pretty lucrative but pretty dangerous too. He took several of his clients for quite a lot of money.'

'He had nerve, though,' said Ted with a hint of admiration. 'I wouldn't have tangled with his so-called clients. Nasty bunch. I wonder which one caught up with him?'

Susie laughed. 'Whichever one it was, he did a lot of people a favour. Perhaps we should have a raffle for who it was. I might do that. Get a list of the names of the most likely people and have a raffle.'

'If the cops ever catch him,' said Ted handing over his glass for a re-fill. And one for yourself, Susie.'

'Thank you, kind sir. I'll have a two euro top-up,' she said waving her half finished wine at him.

'Susie, darling. How are you this fine evening?' said a voice from the doorway.

'Fine thank you, Roger. What's it to be?'

'I'll have a white wine please and something for my old mucker here, Ted. How the devil are you?'

'Fine,' said Ted. 'Just about to get myself another G n T.'

'I'll get Ted's drink.'

'We've got some news.'

'Good, I hope' said Roger.

‘Remember John Small?’

‘How could I ever forget him? He still owes me 200 Euros, the bastard. What’s the news? Nothing good, I hope.’

‘He’s dead.’

‘That is good news.’

‘And he was murdered.’

‘Even better. I’ll drink to that. What are you having, Susie?’

‘Just a small two euro top-up for me, thank you Roger,’ she said indicating her half full glass.

‘Do we know who did it? And how? And was it slow and painful?’

‘Don’t be horrid.’

‘We’re having a raffle,’ said Ted. ‘Having a list of who dunnit. Who’s your choice, Roger?’

‘My choice for who murdered John Small? Not me, unfortunately. But I’ll go for Stan-the-man.’

‘Oh. Good choice. Let me get a pen and paper. Roger goes for Stan-the-man. Small took him for a tidy penny or two. That *is* a good choice.’ She wrote Roger’s choice under a heading entitled “Who murdered Cock Robin”.

‘And how about you, Ted?’

‘I’m not sure. I should mention that he was killed in the UK. In Sherborne if that helps.’

It didn’t, and Ted was still pondering his choice as the warm Spanish evening sun began to go down and Ted began to go down with it.

Sergeant Pepper and Sergeant Daly were cooped up in Daly’s office and had been for half an hour. They had been arguing back and forth and plotting a simple operation which they had finally agreed on.

‘Are you sure you can get the information.’

‘Yes, said Daly. ‘I’ve told you I can.’

‘By tomorrow at twelve?’

‘They’ve already agreed once. There will be no problems, except perhaps with the amount of data you want.’

‘But you’re sure you can do it?’

‘Yes, yes, yes. Now get out of here or I won’t have time to do it.’

‘I’m going. I’m going. I’ve got to get to the meeting. I’m late’

Chapter 13

The meeting had, in fact, already begun.

Loveluck, Anderson and Knightly were discussing a new initiative. It was Anderson who had proposed it.

'We need to know,' he said, 'who all these people are. The three who were murdered and the hanging man.

'We know who two of them are,' said Knightly. Winston Gale and John Small.

'Sure, we know their names but we know precious little more about them. It's as though neither of them ever really existed. What do we really know about John Small? Naff all. And Winston Gale? Even less.'

'So what do you propose,' said Loveluck.

'I think we should launch a big effort of getting them identified. Get pictures and what names we do have in the press. And on television. We have a good police mug shot of Winston Gale. That should help. And a name for the girl. Lina'

Loveluck seemed doubtful. 'Apart from Gale, the only pictures we have of the others are after they had been murdered. Not pretty for the public to see.'

'That's not quite true, sir' said Knightly. They all looked at her expectantly. 'There was that small picture that the girl Lina had in a locket round her neck. That could be worth a look.'

Anderson brightened. 'I'd forgotten about that. See if the lab boys can blow it up and get a decent image. Somebody might recognise him.'

'And he has the added attraction of being photographed alive,' added Loveluck sardonically.

‘And another thing’ said Knightly brightly. ‘I have the photos I got from Small’s office. They looked interesting from the start. Two were beach photos of a group and the third was of a group cycling if I remember rightly. I’ll get the boys to enlarge those too.

‘Things move along,’ mused Anderson. ‘And about time too.’

‘Changing the subject,’ said Loveluck looking at the others to see it they had finished and getting affirmative nods, ‘I know we’ve had the medical reports from both the Poachers Inn murders and the hanging in the wood. I have the Poachers report and Inspector Anderson has the woods hanging report but we should all have copies of both reports. Is Pepper in work today?’

‘Yes,’ said Anderson. ‘She and Daly have been cooking something up between them all morning. She should be here with the copies now.’

And cometh the hour, cometh the woman. Sergeant Pepper bustled into the room with an armful of reports. ‘Sorry I’m late. So much admin to catch up on. Perhaps you should cut back my admin hours a bit,’ she said looking hopefully at Loveluck.

‘If your admin duties are so onerous that you can’t get them all done, I’m sure we can manage without the minutes for a while.’

‘No, no’ said Pepper quickly alert to the danger. ‘I’ll put in a bit of extra time if I have to. Anything to help.’ She took out her pen and notepad. ‘Right. Actions.’

‘Inspector Anderson to organise publicising the victims with photographs from wherever we can get them. Sadie to get blow ups of the photos she has to help Inspector Anderson. Is that a correct summary?’

‘Not bad,’ admitted Anderson.

‘You can rely on me, boss.’

‘Don’t overdo it Pepper.’

‘No, sir’

‘Right,’ said Loveluck with authority. ‘The medical reports. Dr Ryan states quite clearly that all three of the victims at the Poachers Inn were drugged before they were murdered. No doubt about it. The drug was slow burning but powerful.’

‘Slow burning?’ asked Knightly.

‘Its effects were not immediate. They slowly began to work over a period of time but the effects were powerful. He concludes that the drugs were probably administered with drinks taken before or after the meal.’

‘That cuts it down to Mr Small and the two women at the meal. The older woman and the younger one called Lina.’

‘Why would they want to poison themselves? asked Anderson.

‘So, someone else administered the poison whilst they were deep in conversation?’

‘If they were ever deep in conversation,’ said Loveluck. ‘Jamie seems to think they were arguing more than discussing anything.’

‘The two men who asked for them but didn’t join them look favourite to me,’ said Pepper. ‘Just saying,’ she said in reply to their enquiring looks.

‘It could have happened whilst that dining club were making all the noise and commotion.’ Said Knightly.

‘What dining club?’ asked Loveluck. ‘I haven’t heard anything about a dining club.’

‘It was just something Mr Grayson from the Poachers said. There was a dining club came in whilst the Mr John party were there and sat right next to them. Became a bit of a nuisance.’

‘That could be it,’ said Loveluck. ‘The dining club were just a front to distract everyone whilst the drugs were administered.’

There was a silence which Loveluck didn’t understand.

‘A perfect distraction. A noisy club getting settled and...’

‘And taking photographs and generally making a fuss?’ asked Knightly. ‘Ring any bells?’

Loveluck was genuinely puzzled.

‘I’ve checked out this dining club with Mr Grayson. The booking was made by someone called George.’

Pepper and Anderson both twigged it before Loveluck did.

‘The dining club had a name and a leader called George.’

Now it sank in. The look of sad recognition and faint despair. He looked slowly from face to face as if hoping that they would laugh and it would all be a joke. But there were no smiling faces.

‘It’s them again, isn’t it? The Last of the Sodding Summer Wine Sodding Dining Club.’

‘Looks like it.’

‘So they were there at both murders,’ said Loveluck with astonishment. At the hanging. Even found the body. And there when the drugs were administered.’ He was exasperated. ‘How do they do it? How can that set of eccentric.....’ words seem to fail him. ‘How do they do it?’

‘Getting back to the medical report,’ said Anderson.

‘Yes. Drugs administered and the deaths were caused by the garrotting. They were strangled. The severing of the left hands was done later, for what purpose we don’t know as they left the hands along with the candles between the fingers in the shower of room 11.’

There were no surprises there and attention switched to Anderson. ‘The hanged man was, well, hanged. Death caused by strangulation. Straightforward. His left hand was also severed but not left at the scene of the crime. What was special about his left hand I don’t know. But it was taken away by the murderer, or murderers, for whatever reason.’ No surprises there either.

‘Copies of the forensic reports should be available to everyone later today. Is that right, Sergeant?’ Loveluck asked Pepper.

‘Yes, sir. The reports are lengthy and will take some time. Also the forensic report for the hanging is still not complete as regards the vehicles. But otherwise they have updated us on everything so far.’

‘So,’ said Loveluck as he began to put away his papers, ‘that’s your bedtime reading for tonight. Is everyone available for a meeting tomorrow at ten in the morning?’ Nods all round. ‘Good. That’s it for now.’

The meeting broke up and Pepper and Knightly made straight for the car park. ‘Have you got everything we need?’ asked Knightly.

‘I certainly have. Let’s go lunching.’

Inspector Loveluck chose to go to the Digby Tap for lunch. And he chose to go alone. At least alone as far as the police were concerned. He went into the bar to find Olwen Evans already waiting for him. She hailed him and waved him across to a table she had saved for them by the window.

‘Hello Inspector. To what do I owe the pleasure of this summons?’

‘Just the pleasure of your company.’

‘That’ll be the day,’ she said with a smile. ‘What are you eating?’

He thought briefly. ‘Just a toasted sandwich. Cheese and Onion.’

‘I’ll join you in that,’ she said and made for the bar.

She returned with drinks and they settled down. ‘Is this really just a social drink, or is there something the Dorset Police need to know from a lowly reporter.’

‘A bit of both.’

‘I might have guessed. What do you want to know?’

Loveluck sat back in his seat and regarded Olwen slowly. 'Two things,' he said. 'Firstly, can you ask your reporter friend who used to work on the Lymington Times what, if anything, he knows about a woman called Samantha Alcock? Sammy Alcock as she prefers to be known.'

Olwen seemed uncomfortable. 'I can't keep on going back to Mark for information. For a start, he doesn't work on the paper anymore and hasn't for two years. And also he has a new job to do.'

Loveluck nodded. 'I'm aware of that, Olwen.'

'Then why ask?'

'Because we need to move this case forward. I think there is more to this woman than she's saying. I think it may be very important.'

Olwen shrugged. 'I can ask him. But don't hold your breath. Mark was a bit short with me last time I asked for information. And when I think of the extremes the Sherborne police go to keep information from me, I can tell you, Jack, there has to be a bit of give and take.'

'I know what you're saying.'

'Well, I hope you do.'

They sat in silence for a spell until their toasted sandwiches arrived. 'What was the second thing you were going to say to me?'

'Would you like to come to the Costa del Sol with me for a few days?'

She looked at him in amazement. 'Are you serious?'

'Deadly serious.'

She smiled. 'I'll ring Mark tomorrow.'

Knightly and Pepper arrived at the Gordleton Mill in good time for lunch, and they had no intention of dining on toasted sandwiches. Pepper was grinning from ear to ear. Not only was she back doing detective work but she was doing it in a very splendid restaurant indeed.

'Do you think it's warm enough to eat outside,' she said.

Knightly shook her head. 'I don't think so. Anyway, I want to be where I can question the staff, and that's inside. Come along, my administrative assistant. Let's get to work.'

Knightly guided Pepper into the front bar where she had been before with Sammy. A good mixture of a bar atmosphere, people drinking and people eating. Easier to mix.

They managed to find a couple of empty bar stools and ordered drinks. Soft drinks for them both. Knightly because she was driving and Pepper because of her medication.

Knightly got into conversation with the barmaid. The woman was chatty and seemed a good bet. 'You have a good, lively bar,' said Knightly. 'Is it always like this?'

'Mostly,' she replied. 'It's a good crowd. Will you be eating?'

'Yes, of course. I have a couple of friends who particularly recommended the Gordleton Mill to us.'

'Did they? That's good.'

'You might know them. Have you worked here long?'

'Three, coming up four years. What are your friends called?'

'He is called John Small. A solicitor.'

The woman flashed a very brief but wary eye at Knightly. 'Can't say I know the name.'

'And the woman is called Samantha Alcock. Normally known as Sammy.'

'Sorry,' said the barmaid shortly. 'Never heard of either of them.'

'I was in here yesterday with Sammy. Sat right there,' Knightly said pointing to a corner table of the small bar.

I wasn't working yesterday. Sorry, I can't help you.'

'Oh yes you were,' said Knightly. 'You served us.'

'Look. I'm busy. Do you want to order a meal or not, because other people do.'

'I'd like to see your boss,' said Knightly formally. 'Now.'

'She's busy. We're all busy. I suggest you leave before I call someone to have you removed.'

Knightly stood four square. 'Call someone.'

'I'm not joking,' said the barmaid sternly. 'I'll have you removed.'

'Call someone. I'm going nowhere.'

The barmaid looked about her in confusion, turned back behind the bar and disappeared to a private area before returning shortly with a man not dressed for cooking.'

'Which are the troublemakers?' he asked loudly and theatrically.

'These two.'

'I understand you are upsetting the bar staff,' he said reasonably but firmly. 'They are busy and we don't let our staff be harassed by anyone. I suggest you either take a table in the restaurant where our waiting staff can take your orders, or if that doesn't suit you, leave.'

He waited for a few seconds. 'Which is it to be, ladies?'

'Neither,' said Knightly politely. 'I want to speak to the manager.'

'You are really being very difficult. If you continue to be difficult I will be forced to call the police. I don't want to, but I cannot let this disruption continue. So which is it to be? Restaurant, leave or I call the police?'

Knightly displayed her identity badge. 'We are the police. Your barmaid gave us false information and we are investigating a quadruple murder. Now *that* is important. And serious. I don't want to cause a fuss but I do want to see the manager.'

'The owner/manager is here but busy. I am the restaurant manager. Perhaps I can help you.'

'It depends. I'm seeking information about two people who I believe were regulars here for a while. I think that the front of house staff might be of more use than people in the kitchens. Are you mainly in the kitchens?'

'I'm the restaurant manager but I am not a chef or cook. I manage the smooth running of the restaurant. I am the senior member of staff under the owner/manager. So it depends what kind of information you want. And,' he added reasonably, 'it's lunchtime and we are very busy. Could I suggest you have lunch and we can talk when things are a little quieter?'

Happy to reduce the tension, Knightly agreed.

'I'll show you the way to the restaurant.' As they walked he asked, 'What are the names of the people you are interested in?'

'John Small and Sammy Alcock.'

He stopped. 'Have a good lunch. I'll get the owner to come and join us afterwards.'

They sat at the table and Knightly smiled at Pepper. 'You were very quiet.'

'You're the detective. I'm the administrator. For now. But my time will come when we talk after lunch. And I'm looking forward to it. Watch the girl go then!'

Knightly laughed. 'This is a menu I intend letting myself go on. Waiter!'

Chapter 14

Detective Inspector Jack Loveluck walked out of the Sherborne police station and along Digby Road towards the Abbey. He turned right along Half Moon Street, crossed over the road and round into Cheap Street. Once in the main street he slowed down and took on an ambling gait.

He walked past the Cross Keys pub, casting a wistful glance inside, and continued up Cheap Street. He had the demeanour of a man with a guilty secret, as indeed he had. Gone were the days when he would pop into the Digby Tap for a pint and a pasty, or into the Half Moon for a full meal.

Detective Inspector Jack Loveluck was on a diet.

A chance glance at himself in a pub mirror as he lounged on a chair had startled him. 'Can I really be that fat git in the mirror?' was the question he posed himself and the answer that came back was an unequivocal "yes."'

In truth, he wasn't fat in the usual sense of the word, but there was no doubt that several pounds had been put on recently and it was beginning to show.

He had decided to put pubs and beer and pasties behind him. Now he ate out only in the Three Wishes cafe, and if he wasn't losing weight the reason could be discerned from the first few words spoken by the waitress.

'Inspector Loveluck. How nice to see you again.' She turned and called out to the kitchen. 'Inspector Loveluck special, please. With tea.'

He turned to walk to the back garden as usual when he was hailed by a voice he knew well. 'Jack. Jack. Wait for me. I'll share a pot of tea with you.'

He turned to see the vicar of Sherborne, the Rev Toby Austin, waving excitedly at him, his eager eyes sparkling behind his glasses.'

'Hello Vicar,' said the waitress with just the right measure of respect. 'What can I get you? Just a pot of tea?'

'Is the inspector eating?'

'Heavens, yes. Having the Inspector Loveluck special.'

'Can you do me one as well? I'm a bit peckish'

Toby Austin bounced after Loveluck into the back garden. 'I don't see so much of you these days, Jack. Busy keeping Sherborne safe, I suppose.'

'Doing my best, Toby. How's life treating you?'

'Well.' Toby moved his chair a little closer to Loveluck's and leaned forward in his conspiratorial manner. 'Actually. I've got a little secret.'

'And what might that be?'

'Well' and here Toby glanced around the empty garden to make sure nobody could hear. 'Can't you guess?'

'No. I have no idea what it could be.'

'Go on. Have a guess. I'm sure a copper could deduce it easily enough.'

Loveluck peered wearily at his feet.

'Have a guess. Go on,' urged Toby.

Loveluck sighed. 'All right. They are going to knock Sherborne Abbey down and build a multi story car park on the site.'

'No,' said the vicar playfully. 'Not a bad idea though. Have you seen the traffic in Sherborne recently? Have another guess.'

'Toby'

'No. Go on Jack. Have another guess. It's really easy.'

Loveluck sighed again. 'They've made you Archbishop of Canterbury.'

'Think, Jack, think.'

But Loveluck was spared the effort of any more guesses by the arrival of the food.

The vicar was aghast. 'Blimey. Is all this for me?' he asked.

'Course it is,' said the waitress. 'The Inspector Loveluck special. Smoked salmon, scrambled eggs, muffins followed by three balls of ice cream. He loves it does the inspector.'

She bustled off and the Rev Toby Austin looked at Loveluck with concern. 'Quite a fancy dish,' he said tactfully.

'Tell me your secret,' Loveluck replied eager to change the topic of conversation.

'All right,' he said, eyes again glinting excitedly though his spectacles. 'I'm engaged to be married.'

'Congratulations, Toby. Do I assume that the lucky lady is the Widow Albright? The well known floozy with an admirable knowledge of dirty songs?'

'Jack! She is a lady of distinction.'

'And of money. So you finally got your feet well and truly under her table. Early retirement beckons?'

'Nothing of the sort. I see her as a fine upstanding woman. In fact I see her as my Queen Supreme.'

'As your what?'

'My Queen Supreme. I idolise her.'

Loveluck put on a stern expression. 'Isn't there something in the bible about having no other idols than God?'

'Oh, stop it Jack. You know what I mean.'

'Actually, Queen Supreme makes her sound like a pudding.'

'A pudding?' said Toby with fire. 'It might be true that she is small with a lowish centre of gravity but that doesn't make her a pudding.'

'I only meant the name, Toby. Queen Supreme.'

'Oh. I see,' said Toby calming down. 'My Queen Supreme she is and my Queen Supreme she stays. Do you always eat all this stuff?' he said pointing at the food. 'It's quite a large meal for elevenses. Or does it do for your lunch as well?

'For lunch as well,' lied Loveluck. 'When are you to be married? Have you set a date yet?'

'We have actually pencilled in September 5th.'

'Not this year.'

'Yes, yes. This year. It's very exciting.'

'And very soon,' said Loveluck. 'Not much more than two weeks.'

'I know. I do hope you'll come along, Jack.'

'I will if there's room. I expect the Abbey will be packed. You are having it in the abbey, I assume.'

'Yes, of course. But we are thinking about having a quiet affair in the Lady Chapel. You know. The small chapel behind the altar. Just a few chosen guests. What do you think?'

'I think that would be hardly possible for a man of your standing in the town. You would disappoint too many people.'

Toby sighed heavily. 'That's what the Widow Albright says.'

Loveluck shrugged. 'I'm with the Queen Supreme on this one. Full abbey with all steam and whistles blowing.'

'I suppose you're right. But you see, Jack, although I am still the Rev Toby Austin that Sherborne has come to know and love. Well, tolerate anyway. In my private life I've grown more towards the Widow Albright's outlook on life. She's more bohemian. An aging hippy, if you like. A touch alternative. And I rather like that kind of way of life. It has no contradiction with my faith or that of the Abbey.' Here Toby hesitated.

'But?' prompted Loveluck.

'Well, the thing is, in my private life my way of dress is a touch bohemian as well and, to be frank, I don't want to get married in full vicar outfit or, indeed, full morning suit or anything else like that.'

Loveluck waited with interest as to what was coming next.

'Do you understand what I'm saying? My dilemma?'

'It depends what you are thinking of wearing for the wedding. If it were a bandana with flip-flops I can see that raising a few eyebrows.'

'Not to mention a few blood pressures,' added the vicar.

'Would this have any impact on your job here as vicar of Sherborne?'

Toby shrugged. 'Officially, no. But unofficially, the nods and winks, chats in quiet rooms. You must have read Trollope.'

'Anthony Trollope was fiction and a long time ago,' said Loveluck reasonably. 'Things in the church can't still be like that.'

'Don't you believe it. I've even been tinkering with the idea of running away to Gretna Green.'

Loveluck laughed. 'Come on, Toby. You are a pillar of respectability here in Sherborne and a loved figure. You've played to the gallery for many, many years here in Sherborne. You can play to the gallery once more for your wedding. Give them what they want and then after that you can set up your yurt on Church Green right outside the abbey and wave two metaphorical fingers at them.'

'And why can't I wave two metaphorical, or real, fingers at them before the wedding. Or during it.'

Loveluck leaned over to be nose to nose with Toby. 'Because, Reverend Toby Austin, after the wedding the Widow Albright will be your wife with all that money to keep you from harm. Do it before the wedding and finding yourself in trouble or ridiculed could make her say at the vital moment. Will I? Will I hell.'

Toby licked moodily on a chocolate ice cream ball.

'She is very fond of my standing in the town. Gives her status. Particularly as Mrs Toby Austin.'

'There you go Toby. Look your splendid and regal best at the wedding and you can come out in your beads and bangles and flip-flops at the reception. They'll be so full of champagne they'll just think it a small eccentricity of yours. Dear old Toby. Always was a bit of a character.'

Toby smiled for the first time. 'Right Inspector. I'll do as you suggest. Now for the rest of the ice cream. That shirt fits you a bit snugly, Jack. Best you lay off the ice cream.' And with that he leaned over and scooped up a ball of Loveluck's ice cream and put it on his own plate. 'Darn good meal this Inspector Loveluck Special.' And he smiled his most dazzling, sparkly smile.

In the Gordleton Mill, Sergeants Knightly and Pepper were sitting back metaphorically loosening their belts.

'They certainly serve up a good meal,' said Pepper. 'Not good for the waistline.'

'I couldn't do this every day,' said Knightly, 'though I'd like to.' She looked at her watch. 'It's getting late. Let's see if we can get the owner and restaurant manager back.'

They flagged down a passing waiter, gave him the message and within three minutes both owner and manager had arrived.

'I hope you both enjoyed your meals.'

'Truly excellent,' said Knightly. And wonderful value.

'Delighted to hear it,' said the manager as he and the owner sat down.

'Can I just clear up a couple of points, 'said the owner. 'I'm sorry we got off to a bit of a bad start. We always cooperate with the police as and when the need arises, but I must insist that if you come here again on police business you contact me beforehand and don't just turn up and start questioning my very busy bar staff. As you've been told by my manager, we don't allow anyone to harass our staff and that includes the police.'

Knightly nodded her head firmly. 'I accept everything you have just said and assure you that in future we'll proceed as you suggest. I will apologise to the bar lady before I leave.'

'No need. I'll pass on your apology.'

'Fair enough.' Knightly studied the owner briefly. She was a well organised woman who ruled the roost in her own restaurant. Not one to be messed with.

The owner continued. 'As I said, I'll help the police in any way I can , as will my staff, but the names you mention are not familiar. What were they again?'

'John Small and Samantha Alcock. Sammy, as she likes to be known.'

I'm not saying they haven't been here, but they're not regulars. We try to get to know the regulars.'

I was in here with her yesterday,' said Knightly. 'We were served by the same bar lady as is working today. She denied having seen her.'

'My staff deal with a great number of people every day. They can't be expected to remember them all. Now you say your friends have been here a few times. Not enough for us to get to recognise them. Passing trade doesn't get remembered in the same way as regulars.'

Sergeant Pepper, who had been silent throughout the exchanges between owner and Knightly, now brought out a briefcase. 'How many visits would make them regulars? In a month, say.'

The owner glanced at the restaurant manager who shrugged. 'Maybe every other day. Say fifteen times a month.'

'That would be very regular,' said Pepper. 'Probably in more than most of the part time staff.'

'Yes. It would be very regular.'

'And you think you would remember them?'

The manager shuffled his feet and glanced at the owner. 'Yes. Probably.'

'And,' continued Pepper, 'if they came here every other day for two months? That thirty times in two months?'

'Yes. We would expect to remember them. It depends on what they spent.'

Pepper took several sheets of paper from her briefcase. 'Take a look at these.'

The owner leaned across the table. 'What are they?'

Pepper smiled. 'These are all the debit and credit card transactions Mr Small made in June and July of this year. They are all dated and show the amounts spent. I have highlighted in yellow the transactions made at your restaurant.' She turned to the manager.

‘Would you care to count how many bills Mr Small paid to the Gordleton Mill in June, sir?

He turned to the owner who nodded and said. ‘Count them, Jerry.’

He did so and said. ‘Nineteen’

‘Nineteen, Jerry,’ said Pepper. You must have got to know them very well. And the amounts all indicate that they had meals or a lot of drink. I think that you would have remembered them either way.’

Perhaps you would like to count the payments for July,’ she said to the owner. ‘I’m sorry. I don’t know your name.’

‘Angie,’ she said almost snatching at the papers and running her finger down the figures. ‘Twenty one.’

‘Count them again, Angie.’

She did so. ‘Twenty two.’

‘So,’ said Pepper tidying up the papers, ‘if my maths is correct, and it is because I did it on a calculator at the police station this morning, they visited here forty one times out of sixty one days. A lot more than the thirty one Jerry said would be enough to be remembered. And all their payments suggest they both had meals or a lot of drink. Or both. What do you think, Angie?’

‘What you say sounds likely, but what does it matter? What have they done?’

Knightly took over. ‘We are investigating a quadruple murder. And John Small was one of the four victims. Now, I suggest you shake up your memories and get talking. We know that John Small was a solicitor and we know that Sammy Alcock was his secretary and housekeeper. We’re not so interested in her, but we want to know all about him. He was the boss, the one in charge and the one, in the end, who was murdered.’

Angie nodded. ‘What do you want to know?’

‘What did they talk about? Who did they meet? Were they talking to anyone special? Why they were here is what we basically want to know. Some of those bills suggest he was paying for meals and drink for four people. Maybe more. We need to know who they were.’

There was a silence as Angie mulled this over. She looked troubled. ‘This isn’t easy. There are very influential people get into this restaurant. Some of whom I wouldn’t want to get on the wrong side of.’

Knightly and Pepper waited.

Seeming to come to a decision, she said. 'There was one man they met regularly back in June. A young man in his twenties. A strange man.'

'Does this strange young man have a name?' asked Knightly as calmly as she could.

'Yes he does.'

'And?'

Angie hesitated before saying. 'Jakob'

Knightly and Pepper were in a state of excitement as they walked across the car park. 'Didn't you say that you saw 'Jakob' smeared across a wall or something at John Small's cottage?' asked Pepper.

'Yes I did. But Jakob takes on a whole new significance now. It's only a name we have, which on its own means nothing. But if we put it with the other names like Lina and Winston we now have three names that seem to be connected. And three names are a lot more recognisable than one.'

'Why is that?' asked Pepper.

'Well. If I say the name John to you, what does it mean?'

'Nothing.'

'But,' continued Knightly, 'If I say the names John, Paul, George and Ringo to you, what does it mean now?'

'Still nothing.'

'Philistine! And you have the nerve to be called Sergeant Pepper.'

'Course it means something to me,' laughed Pepper. 'You can't go round with a name like Sergeant Pepper and not get to know just about everything about the Beatles.'

They had climbed into Knightly's sports car when Jerry came running out to catch them.

'Glad I caught you. There was one thing that I think needs clearing up. You were wrong when you said that John Small was the boss and that he made all the decisions. It was her. Sammy. She was the boss. No doubt about it. In complete control.'

'I wasn't expecting that,' said Knightly. 'Can you tell us anymore about Jakob? Description? Anything at all?'

Jerry thought about it. 'About average height. Not tall, not small. Short hair. Spoke in a very clipped way. Had a bit of a military bearing. I didn't like him much. He looked like he could be trouble.'

'Thanks Jerry. You've been very helpful.'

‘Just one more thing,’ said Jerry. ‘I think that Jakob might have been living rough. He had an old motor bike and I saw him a couple of times in the forest. The New Forest, I mean. I couldn’t swear he was living rough but I saw what looked like a tent behind some bushes as I passed early one morning. He was just sitting on the grass.’

‘Do you remember where this was?’

‘Somewhere out Burley way. I don’t remember exactly where. I’ll keep an eye out on the way home later. See if I can remember the spot where I saw him. Drive safely.’

They waved him goodbye and drove away.

‘Well,’ said Pepper. ‘Suddenly Jakob gets a lot more interesting. Short hair, clipped speech, military bearing. It looks like our old friend who turned up at the meeting in the Poachers Inn but didn’t chat to Mr John. And yet they seem to have been old pals.’

‘Curiouser and curiouser.’ Said Knightly. ‘Cling on tight. I’ll show you how fast this baby can go.’ And with a twitch of the throttle they disappeared into the distance.

Chapter 15

Loveluck, Anderson, Knightly, Daly and the minute taker, Pepper gathered for a catch up in Anderson's office. The main news was that all the forensic reports were in and a mass of information available.

Fortunately, the forensics teams had written out splendid summaries and the main points shone through without having to wade through the detail.

The medical forensic report for the three hotel murders had already been gone through and there was nothing to add, and the medical report for the hanged man was predictable. Death by strangulation.

The only interesting point was that the weapon which had severed the hands of the three people found in the Poachers bedrooms was different from the weapon which had severed the hand of the hanged man. It didn't alter their view that the murders were connected but it raised some doubts not only as to whether the murders were connected, but to what extent. It clouded the waters.

More exciting was the forensic report from the hanging scene regarding the vehicle, the group of people in the woods and its role in piecing together the story.

'You all have a copy of the summary,' said Inspector Anderson, 'and I'll run through it. Firstly the vehicle. As we know there were two vehicles. The car parked near the woods and belonging to the hanged man, Winston Gale. We've discussed this before and that car is also getting the full treatment from forensics. Results to come later.

'The other vehicle is the truck we believed was there. And now we know there was a truck there. It was a Toyota pick-up truck.

White. We found a piece of the truck body, rusted, on the ground. It was broken off from the wheel arch. The company have been brilliant and inform us that it was a white model and it is 27 years old. They have given us the most likely model and though they can't help us much with the registration number, our own police department can do that and try and trace it. In truth, it's a bit of a long shot. Our best bet for locating it is our eyes. Look out for a very old white Toyota pick-up truck. We know it's still in use.'

Here he paused and the other four chatted amongst themselves. 'Do you want me to try and trace it on the police computers?' asked Daly.

'Before we come to any decision on that,' interrupted Anderson, 'I just want to point out that there will be a lot of research to be done and a need for sergeants too. I suggest Sergeants Pepper and Daly work out between them who will research on the forensic leads we have and who will work on the other things we need to know about. By which I mean the ritual side of things. The severed hands and what not.'

'I'll do the police stuff, if you like' said Daly. 'I think Pepper would be better than me on the ritual side of things.'

Pepper nodded in agreement. 'Suits me.'

'Suits me too,' said Loveluck. 'Any more on the forensics?'

'Indeed there is. This is the story the forensics have pieced together. Eight people, they are pretty sure there were eight of them, were on the site that night. They suspect waiting. Some barefoot, some wearing slipper type footwear they are treating as moccasins on account of the fact that stitching traces were found in the mud. Moccasins have loose stitching it seems.'

'They do,' said Knightly with conviction.

'They say the truck was parked by some bushes. You will see exactly where on the map provided. This was some little distance from the hanging rope. One interesting fact is that some footprints were found all around the hanging rope. Very small footprints. Child like.'

'They think there were children there?' asked Loveluck sharply.

'Seems so.'

'Who the hell would hang someone in front of a child?' asked Daly with distaste.

'Child *like*,' said Anderson. 'It may have been a very small person. 'Going on, someone with shoes arrived on the scene. This we know fine well was Winston Gale. He was still wearing them when we found him hanging.'

'So he was a late comer to the party,' said Knightly.

'At some point, continued Anderson the truck was moved to the bottom of the hanging rope. We assume that Winston Gale was taken to the pick-up truck and forcibly hanged.

'Pretty gruesome,' said Daly again with distaste.

'The truck was driven away but with much deeper indents into the ground than before suggesting that perhaps the eight members were on and in the truck, giving it greater weight. It then pulled away in the direction of Dorchester. Or, if you prefer, in the direction of the Poachers Inn.'

Anderson leaned back, satisfied with his contribution.

There was a silence as the others thought this evidence over. It was Anderson himself who broke it. 'One thing that puzzles me is that Jamie, the bartender at the Poachers, has identified Winston Gale as one of the men who asked for Mr John, but didn't speak to him. Winston Gale is the link between both murders but we have virtually no information on him.'

Loveluck nodded to Knightly.

'Sergeant Pepper and I went to the New Forest yesterday. We learned that Mr John Small and Samantha, call me Sammy, Alcock were indeed regular visitors. But the most interesting information we learned was that it was Sammy who was in charge of things. Sammy who was the boss, not Mr John Small at all.'

'Are you sure?' asked Loveluck. 'How did you find that out?'

'By luck really,' said Knightly. 'We were just leaving when Jerry, the restaurant manager, came running out and told us.'

'Just came running out and told you?' asked Loveluck.

'Yes. Volunteered the information.'

'Mmm,' said Loveluck doubtfully. 'Go on.'

'Well, he also told us that they had one regular visitor who was called Jakob.'

'More volunteered information?' asked Loveluck.

'Yes,' said Knightly firmly.

'Actually, no,' said Pepper. 'Volunteered but by Angie. The owner.'

'So it was,' admitted Knightly. 'Jerry also told us that he thought that Jakob was living in the woods. Living rough in a tent. Near Burley.'

‘And,’ added Pepper, ‘his description of Jakob was very much like the description given us by Jamie, the barman.’

They let their report hang in the air.

‘Then why,’ asked Loveluck thoughtfully, ‘would Jakob not go and talk to Mr John in the Poachers if they were friends?’

‘Just what we thought,’ said Pepper.

‘And why did Mr John not recognise him?’

Pepper shrugged. ‘Search me, gov. Just reporting back.’

‘I don’t like this case.’ Said Loveluck slowly. ‘I don’t trust it. I’m beginning to hate it.’

This comment caused the others to exchange wary glances.

Loveluck stood up and paced as best he could in the small office. ‘The crime scene at the hanging is just littered with clues. Endless clues. Too many clues, just left there for us to find.’

The others remained silent.

‘And then the meetings in the Poachers Inn are conducted right in front of the bar for the likes of Jamie the barman to hear everything. All the key players have to report to the bar staff and ask where Mr John is. Then argue loud enough for Jamie to hear.’

Loveluck paced with thunder on his face. ‘Even Winston and Jakob had to ask the bar staff which is Mr John, but now we hear that Jakob and Mr John had been having lunch together for weeks.’ He stopped and peered towards the window. ‘Someone is working us like bloody puppets.’ Loveluck pointed at the evidence lying on the table. ‘I’ve a good mind to scoop up the whole damned lot and sling it in the bin. Because that’s all it’s worth.’ And fitting action to his words be brushed all the reports onto the floor.

He roughly grabbed Peppers note pad and ripped out a blank sheet which he threw onto the table. ‘That’s all the evidence we have. Blank.’ He looked at his four colleagues one by one and then quietly said. ‘We start again. From scratch.’ And he left the room.

Word soon spread that Loveluck had ordered that all evidence be discarded and that the investigation should begin anew. The summons from Detective Chief Inspector John Waddington for Loveluck to present himself at Dorchester police station immediately came as no surprise, and within the hour Loveluck was called into Waddington’s room where CC Mackenzie was also present.

Loveluck entered the room to a deep silence. Waddington looked concerned and CC Mackenzie was pure furious.

‘Take a seat,’ said Chief Inspector Waddington. ‘Tell us what it’s all about.’

‘Before you do,' said the CC, ‘pray tell us how long it is since the murders happened.’

‘Just a week sir.’

‘A week?’

‘A week. Yes, sir’

‘A lot of evidence can be collected in a week. At least it can if the investigation team is well and properly led. Wouldn’t you agree?’

‘It depends, sir.’

‘On what?’

‘On the quality of the evidence.’

The CC walked round the room. ‘I believe that a great deal of this evidence has been collected by the Scene of Crimes Officers and analysed by the police forensic teams. Is that correct?’

‘Perfectly correct sir.’

‘Am I to understand then, Inspector Loveluck, that you think that the work of these forensic teams is not to be relied on? Is that the case?’

‘Certainly not, sir. No one has a higher respect for the forensic teams than me.’

‘Really? And yet you throw all their evidence onto the floor with the words “because that’s all it’s worth.” Those were your words, weren’t they inspector?’

‘Yes, sir.’

‘It seems an odd way to me to show your high respect for their work,’ said Mackenzie returning to his side of the desk.

Detective Chief Inspector John Waddington now spoke to Loveluck in his soft, measured way. ‘Tell us. What exactly did you mean when you threw the forensic evidence on the floor and said “because that’s all it’s worth”?’

Loveluck looked up at Waddington and said. ‘I said it because it was true.’

‘True in what way?’

‘True in this sense. The forensic teams not only told us of the evidence they had analysed. Tyre marks, metal shreds from the truck, foorprints and so on. They also told us the story of how they think it all happened. As I listened to Inspector Anderson telling this story yesterday I had the feeling, which I’ve had all along, that this is the story we were meant to believe.’

‘You think the evidence was contrived?’ asked Waddington.

‘Certainly I think it was arranged. You know at police training school and on other courses, I was always told that evidence had to meet certain standards. Not the analytical kind that the forensics do. If they say the tyres came from a Formula 1 car I would believe them.

‘What I’m concerned about is that lack of reliablilty, validity and verification of this evidence. It all needs to be checked through another source. If one source tells you something, it might be true. If two sources tell you the same thing there is a greater probability that it’s true.’

Waddington nodded. ‘You doubt the evidence for those reasons?’

‘I do. And another example. Sergeants Knightly and Pepper went to the New Forest to follow some leads. They reported that when they were in the car park about to leave, the restaurant manager, Jerry came running out and volunteered some valuable information.’

‘What information?’ asked CC Mackenzie.

‘That Sammy Alcock was the real boss and not John Small. And that they dined regularly with someone called Jakob. Both interesting and valuable pieces of information.’

‘They most certainly are,’ said Mackenzie.

‘If true,’ added John Waddington catching Mackenzie’s eye. ‘If true.’

‘Exactly, ‘said Loveluck. ‘Just before I came here I asked Sergeant Knightly how the interview with owner and manager had been. She said ‘difficult. Like extracting teeth.’ But then the manager runs out and tells them all these things. He also told them that he thought that he had seen Jakob camping in the New Forest, near Burley. Again, great evidence if it’s true.’

‘And a worthless distraction if it isn’t true,’ said Waddington.

‘Even so,’ said the CC, ‘You can’t just ignore what could be important evidence.’

‘No. Sir. And we can’t just believe it either. There is some very contrasting evidence. We need to sort out what is true and what is just smokescreen. Is Sammy Alcock really the one in charge and John Small just a figurehead? We need to know.’

‘So what do you propose,’ asked Mackenzie.

Loveluck leaned forward feeling the tide turning a little in his favour. ‘What I propose is this. All the evidence we have received is put through the sternest test to see if it is reliable, valid and has been verified. Who told us? Can they be further and deeper questioned? Is their story backed up by anyone else? Can forensics give us an alternative story of just what they think happened at the scenes of crimes? We need theories to explain the facts and the inconsistencies.'

Mackenzie scoffed. 'That's just basic police work. It should have been done already.'

'Yes it should,' agreed Loveluck. 'But with evidence raining down on us like manna from Heaven it all seemed so easy.'

'Too easy, you mean.'

'Exactly, sir.'

Mackenzie and Waddington exchanged glances and Mackenzie gave the nod.

'All right,' said Waddington. 'I agree.'

All three of them sat back in their chairs. 'Right. Do you have the manpower?'

Loveluck nodded. 'I think so. It'll spread us thin because we still have two crimes to investigate. I don't suppose we could ask the Hampshire police to take over some aspects of the New Forest side of the investigation?'

Mackenzie spluttered. 'I would prefer not. I will see if we can transfer someone from Dorchester or Bournemouth on a temporary basis to help out.'

'Thank you sir.'

'Just one more question, Inspector.' Loveluck turned to Waddington who had spoken. 'Did I understand you to say that Sergeant Pepper and Sergeant Knightly were investigating at a New Forest Hotel?'

'The Gordleton Mill. Yes, sir.'

'Why?'

'It was Pepper's afternoon off sir. She is free to do what she likes. She had lunch with Sergeant Sadie Knightly.'

CC Mackenzie walked over to Loveluck to shake his hand. 'Have a care, Loveluck. No one is indispensible.'

'Yes, sir. I'll remember that. Good day, gentlemen.'

Loveluck raced back to Sherborne and called another meeting.

Anderson, Knightly, Daly and Pepper gathered to hear the outcome of the summons they knew that Loveluck had received. Bad news travels fast.

‘Right,’ he said in a brisk and businesslike fashion. ‘Here’s what we’re going to do. We’re going to cover all the evidence again. All the evidence. Double check.’

‘And how are we going to do that?’ asked Anderson.

‘You,’ he said pointing at Anderson, ‘are going to be me.’

Anderson looked at him blankly. ‘You are going to go over all the things that I did. Interview Jamie, the bar man, bearing in mind we now know that Jakob is probably the military type man and may have known Mr John of old.’

‘What do they mean by Jakob having a military bearing?’ asked Knightly. ‘It makes me think of a retired Colonel with a handlebar moustache of the old school with a ramrod straight back telling endless boring stories.’

‘That’s not how I see him,’ said Sergeant Daly. ‘I see him as a quietly spoken, reserved man who misses nothing and notices everything. He carries a quiet menace. That’s what witnesses say. ‘More a third para killing machine. Or SAS. Keeps very low key.’

‘That’s more my image too,’ said Anderson.

‘I will be Sergeant Knightly and will revisit the Gordleton Mill to see the owner and the manager,’ said Loveluck. ‘I’ll also pick up on Sammy Alcock.’

Sergeant Knightly I want to be Sergeant Knightly and I want Inspector Anderson to go with Knightly to the Poachers Inn. Not only can you repeat my interview with Jamie but you can go round again to see that we missed nothing. Sergeant Knightly can conduct her interview with Mrs Preston in room 15 and make sure we have overlooked nothing and no one at that scene of the crime.’

‘I will meet the head of SOCO at the hanging woods to go through all that again. This way all the evidence will have been looked at through different eyes. And more critical eyes.’

Sergeants Daly and Pepper waited hopefully. ‘Pepper I want to go and interview those nutters at the last of the Summer Wine rambling club, dining club and any other damned club they have set up. Mainly about their meal at the next table to the Mr John.’

‘Excuse me, boss.’ said Pepper. ‘Can we decide whether John Small is going to be called Mr Small, Mr John or John Small, because I’m getting confused?’

‘Hear, hear,’ echoed Anderson.

‘John Small,’ said Loveluck.

‘And me?’ asked Daly.

‘You’ll still be known as Sergeant Daly,’ said Loveluck which brought a laugh from the others and lightened the atmosphere greatly.

‘I want you to go with Pepper to the Crown to talk to the ramblers club. And then I want you to start to design the campaign to try and identify the three bodies in the Poachers and the hanging man. I’m aware that we know who the hanging man is, but I want all the names of the dead people linked. John Small, Lina, Jakob, Winston Gale. There’s a good chance someone will recognise those names if they are indeed linked.’

‘What about the older woman?’ asked Anderson

‘I think she’s the least important of the lot,’ said Loveluck, and in speaking that sentence he very nearly threw away his chances of ever solving the case.

Chapter 16

Pepper met with the Vicar of Sherborne in the Abbey as arranged. She entered and spotted him sitting quietly in a pew. She walked slowly through the quiet church and sat beside him.

'Hello, Janine. Lovely to see you again. I haven't got anything for you, I'm afraid. About the rituals and such. Use of candles with dead bodies is so common and used in so many ways that I can't find anything sinister about sticking candles between the fingers of a dead person.'

'I wouldn't have thought it very common chopping a dead person's hand off to do it,' she said. 'I bet you don't see much of that in Sherborne Abbey at funerals.'

She stopped because a more urgent light had come into Toby's eyes. 'You never said anything about the hand being severed,' he said. 'That makes a lot of difference. All the difference in the world. Which hand?'

'The left one.'

'Mmm. The hand sinister,' he mused to himself. 'And where were the bodies found?'

'The bodies were found in hotel rooms. Each in a different room.'

Toby shook his head sadly. 'Lying down?'

'Yes. On the floor. Is that no good?'

'No. Not really.'

'The hands were found in a different room with the candles between the fingers, set at the points of a triangle with a note in the middle.'

'What did the note say?' he asked eagerly.

Pepper consulted her notes and handed him a piece of paper. He took it and read it out aloud.

'Let those who rest more deeply sleep
Let those awake their vigils keep
Oh, hand of glory, shed thy light
Direct us to our spoil tonight.'

'What does it mean?' asked Pepper.

'Just what it says,' said the vicar. 'The hand of glory is supposed to give a form of protection to people going about bad business. If you are going to burgle someone or murder someone the rhyme asks that those who rest more deeply sleep. Or don't wake up and catch us!! Let those awake their vigils keep. The baddies stay awake. Oh hand of glory spread thy light. The candles. Direct us to our spoil tonight. Show us the way to what we want to steal or to who they want to murder.'

'Is this just old wives' tales or were there such things as hands of glory.'

'Oh yes. There certainly were. It is an old and well established legend. In fact there is a Hand of Glory in the Whitby Museum you can go and see. There is also a rhyme there which is a bit different but says much the same thing. Toby chanted it;

Now open, lock!
To the Dead Man's knock!
Fly, bolt, and bar, and band!

Nor move, nor swerve,
Joint, muscle, or nerve,
At the spell of the Dead Man's hand!

Sleep, all who sleep! -- Wake, all who wake!
But be as the dead for the Dead Man's sake!'

Pepper regarded him oddly. 'You knew that by heart. Why?'

'I told you before. I have some experience in these things.'

She continued to regard him warily. 'You are beginning to scare me.'

Toby smiled. 'It isn't me scaring you. It is the power of the hand of glory as passed down through the centuries.'

‘Do you really think those hands have power?’ she asked

‘No,’ he said brightly. ‘Not the ones you are talking about. To really have power the hand has to be the left hand but it has to be severed from a convicted murderer as he, or she, swings from the gibbet. And yours were found on the floor of hotel bedrooms.’

He had spoken these last words cheerily to reassure her, but he could see that he had failed. ‘What’s wrong, Janine? You look as pale as a ghost.’

‘You don’t know about the hanging man in the woods, do you?’

‘I don’t know what you are talking about.’

‘On the same night as the murders at the Poachers Inn, a man was hanged from a tree by a long rope. His left hand was severed and taken away.’

Toby watched her for several long seconds before saying. ‘You were right to come to me.’

Loveluck had taken a different approach to Knightly and Pepper when he got to the Gordleton Mill. He showed his ID and asked to speak to Jerry, the restaurant manager.

Jerry wasn’t too pleased to see him but kept his composure well.

‘I’m pushed for time, but how can I help you inspector?’

‘When my officers were here yesterday, you waited until they had gone out to the car park before running out and offering them some very useful information. If true. Why did you do that?’

‘I’d just thought of it,’ he said. ‘It just came back to my memory.’

‘I don’t think so,’ said Loveluck kindly. ‘When you were talking inside, I don’t think you listened to the officers saying how John Small was the boss and Sammy Alcock just the secretary but didn’t remember that this wasn’t true until later. So why did you do it? Was it true what you told them in the car park?’

‘Completely true. Absolutely true.’

‘Then why not mention it inside? Do I assume that the presence of the owner might have had something to do with it?’

Jerry looked down at the floor. ‘It’s complicated, Inspector. Look. I get off work when the lunchtime rush dies down in an hour or so. Can I meet you in a pub somewhere?’

Loveluck smiled. ‘I only know one in the whole of Hampshire apart from this one.’

‘What’s the other one?’

‘The Angel on Lymington high street.’

‘Right,’ said Jerry. ‘See you there in an hour or a bit more. Turn left out of the car park, keep going until you see signs for Lymington. It isn’t far.’

Loveluck drove away. He would have time to see the strange Samantha, call me Sammy, Alcock if she was still clocking in to keep drawing her salary.

Sergeants Pepper and Daly entered the bar of the Crown Inn to find two people that Pepper recognised sitting at the bar. George and Lily Bryant. Pepper made the introductions.

‘This is George who is president of the Last of the Summer Wine Rambling Club. This is Sergeant Daly. Who is president of the Last of the Summer Wine Dining Club?’

‘George is,’ answered Lily Bryant. ‘He’s president of all the clubs.’

‘And this,’ said Pepper with a flourish, ‘is the famous Lily Bryant whom I once had the pleasure of arresting for murder.’

‘Of which I was totally innocent,’ added Lily.

‘Of which she was never charged,’ said Pepper pointedly.

Daly smiled. ‘I remember seeing both George and Lily at the station the night that half the pub was arrested.’

‘Happy days,’ said George. ‘How are you, anyway? It was a bad business. Shocking. I don’t know how you survived it.’

‘Well,’ said Pepper with a smile. ‘We’re not here to discuss that now.’

‘Of course not,’ said George in his avuncular fashion. ‘I’ll still never understand what made Olwen Evans say it was you who had the diary when we all knew that Loveluck had it. But like you say. We’re not here to discuss that now. Is it the Poachers Inn murder where our diners club was there sitting next to the murdered three, or is it the woods where we found the hanging man that you want to talk about?’

George smiled broadly and waited for a response, but Pepper was struck dumb and Daly was waiting in the wings for something to happen.

And then it did happen. Pepper fainted.

Pepper was taken to a couch to lie down and brandy was brought. Daly hovered about her being of no use whatsoever.

‘Is she going to be all right?’ asked George nervously.

‘I expect so,’ answered Daly. ‘She’s still undergoing therapy and on some kind of drug regime. Perhaps she has been overdoing things.’

'Don't let her have that brandy if she's taking medication,' said Lily taking control. 'Fetch some cold water.'

'Just let her lie there for a while. I'll ask the questions.' They stayed by Peppers couch whilst Daly began.

'As I understand it, you had the table next to the one where John Small and his two guests were having dinner.'

Lily answered. 'I wouldn't know John Small from a loaf of bread but there was a man and two women at the next table who kept complaining about the noise and the pictures and everything.'

'Pictures?'

'Yes. Photographs. We take pictures wherever we go. Always nice to have a record.'

'Who takes these pictures?'

'Usually two or three of us have cameras. Justin collects all the pics together and turns it into a lovely collection for us. Justin is one of the group.'

'And he discards the bad ones, I assume.'

'Of course.'

'Has he put together the collection yet?'

'No. He's been working away all week in Wales. He'll do it when he gets back.'

Daly let out a huge sigh of relief. 'Contact him. Now if you can. Do you have a phone number for him?'

'Yes. Of course.' The phone number was searched for and found.

'You keep an eye on Pepper will you? I'll call Justin.'

As Daly walked away to make the call, Pepper began to show signs of recovery. Slowly she sat up and apologised for fainting and was mother henned by Lily and fussed over by George.

Daly returned. 'We'll probably come and talk to you again but I think it best to cut this interview short. Just two quick things. Firstly, did you see anyone interfere with their drinks?'

Two heads shook in unison..

'Or anyone acting at all strangely?'

Two heads shook again in unison. 'We'll think about it and ask the others,' said George. 'The photographs might shed some light on things.'

Pepper got to her feet. 'Sorry about that. I'm feeling better now.'

Daly and Pepper walked to the door and out into the street.

George and Lily watch the door close and then turned to each other. George raised his eyebrows in an arch manner. ‘Why didn’t you tell them?’

Lily returned the look. ‘Why didn’t you?’

And with that they turned and ordered another drink.

Chapter 17

Mrs Hermione Preston was a troubled woman. A very troubled woman. From the moment she had heard about the murders in the Poachers Inn, and especially that they had taken place in the rooms alongside the swimming pool, she had sat back and thought about what, if anything, she had seen the night before. And the more she thought about it and the more detail she heard from the hotel staff the more she thought she should tell the police.

But then she had gone to visit her daughter for a day in Dorchester and then had met an old friend for a day in Weymouth and before she knew what had happened, several days had gone since the murders and she hadn't mentioned a word to the police.

Then it somehow seemed too late. If she called the police with her days old information she could end up in trouble herself. She knew about it from the television programmes. Withholding information, they called it. She could get into serious trouble.

And so she had decided to say nothing, even though she knew it was wrong of her. It also made her angry with herself. All the years she had people-watched from her home, hotel rooms, cafes. Anywhere and everywhere. And now when at last she had a good story to tell she had to keep her mouth shut or risk going to prison.

She had called her daughter who had ridiculed the idea of her being sent to prison and told her to contact the police at once, but her daughter didn't watch as many detective stories as she did. Her daughter didn't know about withholding information.

And now this morning that nice manager Mr Grayson had told her that the police had been asking about her and that they needed to speak to her and that they would return. They had actually been in her room, doubtless looking for clues.

Quickly she had packed and determined to leave the hotel at once. But how did she pay the bill without telling Mr Grayson she was leaving? She couldn't just leave without paying the bill. That would put her in even more trouble with the police.

Eventually she decided that she would leave quietly and ring Mr Grayson the next day apologising for forgetting to pay her bill and paying over the phone. She looked out of the window and all was quiet in the garden. It was a dull, cloudy day.

She opened the door, took her case and turned to walk along the first floor pathway when she was suddenly confronted by a man.

'Mrs Preston? I hope you aren't thinking of leaving the hotel just now.'

She stumbled and seemed confused but the man grabbed her. 'Do you have the key to your room?'

'I don't have a room. I mean, I'm leaving the hotel.'

'But you just came out of that room with your case. Unless you've just stolen someone else's case,' he added with a grin. 'You are Mrs Preston. Room 15.

'Well, yes. But you see I'm leaving. I can't stop and talk now. I must hurry.'

'I'm the police, Mrs Preston. Inspector Anderson,' he said showing her his ID card. 'It's very important I speak to you.'

'No, no. Not possible. I'm very sorry but I must dash. Must dash.'

'But Mrs Preston. You are a valuable witness. A very valuable witness. You may be a key witness.'

'Value? Valuable ....witness, you say?'

'Yes. It would be a great help to the police if you would talk to us.'

'Oh, I see. Great help?'

'Enormous help, Mrs Preston.'

'Oh I see. Yes, I see. Well, in that case of course I must stay and help the police. A valuable witness, you say Inspector?'

'Most valuable,' answered Anderson.

She opened the door of Room 15 and was about to enter when she said,' I'm a bit flustered with the shock of bumping into you. Do you think you could have a brandy sent up to me? A large brandy? The shock, you know.'

He contacted Knightly by phone. 'Could you have a large brandy sent up to Room 15? Better make it three. We have a right one here.'

Loveluck parked his car and entered the Angel Courtyard in Lymington. Almost immediately he saw the white wall and the diagonal outside stairs leading up to the door. With a determined step he took the stairs and knocked and entered the office of John Small, Solicitor.

The door opened to his touch and there in the secretary's office sat Sammy Alcock, feet on the table and a glass of something red by her side.

'Boss not in, I take it.'

Sammy didn't move but waved an arm. 'Take a seat. Fancy a glass of Rioja?'

'I Always enjoy a glass of Spanish rioja,' he said taking a hardback chair and studying anew this vision that was Samantha, call me Sammy, Alcock.'

She poured a glass of wine for him and he sat back in his uncomfortable chair and said. 'Still being paid for working so hard?'

She shrugged. 'Dunno. I'll find out at the end of the month. Payday.'

'And if you don't get paid, what will you do?'

She waved her glass unsteadily. 'Sign on I expect.'

They sat in silence for a while, he quietly appraising her and she quietly appraising him.

'I want to bring forensics in here. Go over the place.'

'You'd be wasting your time. I've cleaned everything. Shining like a new pin.'

'Destroying the evidence? That's a serious offence.'

'Doing my job, Inspector. He liked everything sparkling like new.'

Loveluck swirled his wine around in his glass. It was a displacement activity as he studied his adversary.

'I hear that you wore the trousers in your relationship with John Small. Made the decisions. Bossed him about.'

Sammy smirked. 'Who's been telling you that?'

'It seems to be the opinion at the Gordleton Mill'

She smirked again. 'That crowd of gossips. Let me tell you this, Mr Inspector of police. John Small was a very clever solicitor.

Looked up to in his profession. But outside of his profession he was just what his name suggests. Small. Small in height, small in everything. He couldn't make a decision so I made them for him. Socially, you understand. In the office he was boss. Socially, I was boss.' She sat back and took another sip of wine. Swig of wine. 'It's not unusual for a wife to boss a successful husband.'

'He was your husband?' asked Loveluck sharply.

'No,' she said mockingly. 'He would have been my lover had he not been so useless. And he was useless in everything except his profession. The law.'

They fell into a silence.

'I'm a pretty tall woman. Agree?'

Loveluck nodded.

'And he was small. Five foot five at most. Of course I took control. Not because of his height but because his mentality was that of a small man. Do you get where I'm coming from?'

But Loveluck's mind was far away. It was back in the Poachers Inn a week earlier seeing a middle aged man lying on his back on a hotel room floor, a piece of wire round his neck and his left hand chopped off leaving only a bleeding stub. Loveluck was a man with a call to make.

'More wine Inspector?'

'No. I have to go.' And with little ceremony he left the office, ran down the stairs and went into the bar of the Angel.

Inspector Anderson and Sergeant Knightly were on the bed together. A fact which Anderson would dine out on for years to come.

They were perched uncomfortably clutching glasses of brandy whilst Mrs Preston sat comfortably on her chair, brandy on the bedside table. 'What is it you want to know?'

Knightly tried to reach for her notebook but her position made it impossible and she manoeuvred herself off the bed. 'We really want to know what, if anything, you saw on the night of the murder. Your position here is excellent for seeing anything that happened in the rooms opposite where the murders took place. In fact the whole garden and terrace.'

'I'm not the kind of woman to pry into other's affairs, you know. But. I do like to sit here and watch the comings and goings. I'm a people watcher. Just watching people pass by is fascinating for me. Wondering where they are going. Anywhere exciting. Do they look happy or nervous or stressed?' She laughed. 'Sometimes I make up little stories about them. Give them a new life in my imagination.'

Anderson smiled sweetly at her and hoped she wasn't going to start making up stories about them now.

'Well,' said Mrs Preston adjusting her position and clearly getting ready to tell her tale, 'one or two little things went on that evening.'

'And?' said Anderson as she paused.

'Just let me get the order straight, Inspector. I don't want to make any mistakes.'

Anderson rapped his fingers impatiently on his knee.

'I think the first thing I noticed was a gentleman letting himself into Room 7. The one at the end.'

'That's the one where Mr John Small was murdered.'

'Yes I know,' replied Mrs Preston eagerly. 'I remember all the policemen arriving that day. I saw you, my dear.' Knightly nodded in acknowledgment.

'And I have seen you here since. But where was I? Oh yes. The man in Room 7. Well, he went into his room for about half an hour and then he came out and went off towards the bar. Over there.' She pointed towards the outdoor seating area on the first level. 'That's the quickest way into the bar from those rooms by the pool. And I understand he was sitting at a table just inside the door from the seating area where he met his friends.'

Anderson and Knightly both independently were following John Small on his walk to the bar.

'The next thing to happen was the arrival of the older lady. She was in Room 10 if the gossip is correct.'

'It is,' said Knightly.

'It usually is,' said Mrs Preston with a knowing smile. 'She arrived on the back of a motor cycle.'

'She did what?' asked Anderson.

'Arrived on the back of a motorbike, Inspector. A very exciting way to make an entrance. Very impressive.'

'A strange way for a lady of seventy or thereabouts to travel,' suggested Anderson.

'I see you are ageist, Inspector. Is that legal? And you a policeman too.' She tutted playfully having made her point. 'Perhaps you think that I am too old to give reliable evidence. You may take your leave if you do.'

‘Not at all,’ he answered. ‘I was just saying it is an unusual way for a lady of advanced years to travel.’

‘But this was a game old lady, Inspector. She was telling off the young man all the way from the car park to the bar.’

‘Telling who off?’ asked knightly.

‘The young man who brought her here on his motor cycle.’

‘What was she saying?’

Mrs Preston sighed. ‘Now there I can’t help you. She had a very strong accent of some sort and I couldn’t catch the words. But the tone was unmistakable. She was giving him a jolly good ticking off about something.’

Knightly and Anderson exchanged glances and paused for breath.

‘Perhaps time for another brandy,’ suggested the prize witness and her order was phoned down to the bar.

All three walked out onto the pathway outside the room and looked down onto the rooms opposite, the pool and the beer garden. Again Anderson and Knightly forming mental pictures of the events of the evening of the murders as described by Hermione Preston.

‘Didn’t you recognise the accent at all?’ asked Anderson with some frustration.

‘She shook her head sadly. Sorry, Inspector. You may tell from my own accent,’ which was cut glass, ‘that dialects are not my forte.’

Anderson shrugged.

‘But one thing I will say,’ she went on, ‘I may not recognise dialects but I certainly recognise the Queen’s English when I hear it, and I didn’t hear it that night.’

‘A foreign language, you think?’

‘Either that or a very strong dialect indeed. But the rhythm was English, if you know what I mean.’

‘Are you suggesting an English person speaking a foreign language?’

‘I’m not sure what I’m suggesting. I am just trying to explain something which is very difficult to explain. You would probably be better off ignoring what I just said.’

Knightly pursed her lips, glanced at Anderson and said. ‘What happened next?’

‘Let me think. Yes, the young man came back and let himself into Room 7.’

‘That’s John Small’s room. Do you mean that John Small came back?’

'No, Inspector. I said the young man came back because the young man did come back and he let himself into Room 7. You really do think I'm senile.'

'Not at all. I'm just checking the facts,' said Anderson pouring oil over the troubled waters. 'So you mean that he had a key and he let himself in. Is that correct?'

'I don't know if he had a key or if the door was left unlocked. He walked up to the door and let himself in.'

'Did you notice if John Small locked the door when he went to the bar,' asked Knightly.

'No sergeant. I was sitting here having a cocktail and idly watching people come and go.'

'And you have no idea who the young man was? Or what kind of motor bike he was riding?'

'As to the bike, I can tell you nothing. As for the young man. He was the quiet young man from Room 12. He had stayed here for a night. No, I tell a lie. Two nights.'

Knightly was running her fingers down a document she had taken from her bag. 'Did you say Room 12?'

'Yes. Room 12.'

Knightly looked at Anderson. 'According to the list of guests who were staying here around the time of the murders, there was no one in Room 12.'

She handed the guest list to Anderson who checked it. 'I'll get Grayson up here. Are you sure it was Room 12?'

'Absolutely positive,' she said firmly. 'And tell Grayson to bring me a brandy.'

Anderson motioned to Knightly to move away from Mrs Preston. 'If what she is saying is correct,' said Anderson, 'we have a stranger staying here before and during the night of the murder. This changes everything.'

'Not only a stranger,' said Knightly, 'but a motor cycle riding stranger who is quiet and clearly knew the older woman. The very feisty older woman. And we both know who rides a motor cycle.'

Mr Grayson, the manager, arrived smiling. 'How can I help you?'

Knightly showed him the guest list. 'According to this there have been no guests in Room 12 since well before the murders'

'That's correct. Room 12 is one of the rooms awaiting some maintenance work on it. It has been closed for a couple of weeks. There are another couple of rooms in the same position. We carry out all the work at once on these rooms. The contractor is due in a few days.'

'Mrs Preston says that someone had been staying in Room 12 for two days at the time of the murder.'

Grayson smiled again. 'That isn't possible. That room hasn't been let out. You can see on the sheet.'

'And I saw with my eyes a young man using that room.'

Grayson stared at Mrs Preston, sighed deeply and said. 'Come on then. I've got my master key with me. Let's go and have a look. But you're wasting your time.'

But when they arrived at Room 12 Grayson had very different words to say. The sight that greeted them was one of a mess. Empty sandwich wrappers, water bottles, remains of apples and oranges, diet coke tins and other signs of rough living and an unmade bed.

Grayson walked slowly around the room as in a daze. He picked up a sandwich wrapper. Tuna and mayonnaise.

'Leave it,' snapped Anderson. 'We need forensics in here and quickly.

'I don't understand it,' said Grayson. 'The room was locked.'

'You managed to get in,' said Knightly.

'Oh yes. But I've got a master key.'

Anderson looked at him pityingly.

Understanding dawned on Mr Grayson. 'You think he has a master key too?'

'Are there any master keys missing?'

Grayson shrugged. 'I don't really know. We have quite a few,'

'I would suggest you now have one less. Can you trust your cleaning staff?'

'Yes of course,' huffed Grayson.

'Reception staff?'

'Implicitly.'

Knightly shrugged. 'Well. It seems he got one somehow. Perhaps be befriended someone from your staff. That makes it an inside job.'

Grayson stopped huffing. 'I'll get checking straight away on any missing keys. And I'll talk to all the staff.'

'And secure this room. I don't want anyone in here until our SOCO teams arrive. Stand on duty all night if you have to,' growled Anderson.

Grayson scurried off and Knightly said. 'Did you notice the diet?'

Anderson nodded. 'Pretty healthy.'

‘Seems like our friend Jakob has been here.’

They walked down to where Mrs Preston had been waiting patiently for them on the raised terrace. ‘Thank you very much for all your help, Mrs Preston. You have been a very valuable witness indeed.’

‘Ah, but Inspector. My story has hardly begun.’

Knightly and Anderson exchanged glances. ‘Let’s go and sit in the bar, Inspector.’

Inspector Loveluck sat in the beer garden of the Acorn waiting for the arrival of Jerry, the restaurant manager of the Gordleton Mill. He flipped his phone and called a number.

‘Dr Ryan? Loveluck here. Could you tell me exactly how tall the body of the middle aged man we have been calling Mr John Small was. Loveluck waited patiently whilst Ryan consulted his report notes. ‘One metre seventy eight,’ came the reply.

‘What’s that in old money?’

‘Five foot ten.’

‘Thanks Doc,’ said Loveluck as he rang off. He sat chewing this fact over and sipped at his beer. Then he said quietly to himself. ‘If John Small really is five foot five, then who was murdered in Room 7?’

He sipped a little more of his beer. ‘And what’s more to the point. Where the hell is John Small now?’

For all Mrs Preston’s dramatic statement she did, in fact, have little more to tell. The most important fact to come out of their continuing interview was that the young man, who by now they were sure was Jakob, had left on his motor bike at about ten o’clock on the night of the murders. She hadn’t been watching from the balcony at that time of night but had heard the distinct roar of the bike’s engine.

‘It was too cold to be sitting out,’ she had said, ‘and I was tired and in bed but I heard the bike start up.’

‘But you can’t be sure it was the same bike,’ Anderson had said.

‘Oh yes Inspector. I can. When he arrived with the old lady I noticed that the bike was not running smoothly. It was missing now and again. Almost spluttering. It was the same bike. No doubt about it.’

Chapter 18

Loveluck was still thinking over the John Small conundrum when Jerry arrived. He turned down the offer of a drink. 'I can't stay long,' he explained, taking a seat facing Loveluck 'It's a difficult situation at the Gordleton Mill. This topic is, I mean. It caused some problems.'

Loveluck raised his hands defensively. 'Slow down. Take it from the beginning.'

'How much do you know?'

'Assume nothing.'

Jerry looked at his watch. 'I'll try.'

Loveluck nodded in thanks.

'It all started about March time.

'That's six months ago,' said Loveluck in surprise.

'Yes. And we thought it was all over until your two detectives turned up the other day.'

Loveluck raised his hands again. 'I don't know what you're talking about.'

Jerry nodded. 'About six months ago, Mr John Small came into the restaurant with an old friend of Angie. Angie is the Owner of the Gordleton Mill. An elderly man called Mr Nightingale. Quite elderly but in good shape. A little frail perhaps but had all his wits about him. Angie made a great fuss of him as she hadn't seen him for a long time.'

Jerry paused for thought. 'It seems that he was meeting John Small that night over business. Urgent business, he called it. He seemed rather flustered by it all and somewhat concerned.'

'How do you know all this?' asked Loveluck.

'Whenever Mr Nightingale came to the restaurant Angie asked me to take great care of him. Make a fuss of him. He used to come regularly with his wife, but she died a few years ago. He didn't come so often by himself.'

Loveluck nodded his understanding.

'Anyway,' continued Jerry. 'He met with Mr John Small and they had dinner together and a couple of drinks as well. And when they sat back at the end of the meal they began to talk. It was clear that there was some kind of debate or discussion going on. Heated debate over something. I didn't know what. You must understand that I wasn't there all the time. Just popping in regularly to see that they had all they wanted.

'Then the waiter came to me in some alarm saying that their table was becoming noisy and that Mr Nightingale was in some distress. By the time I got there Angie had already been alerted and was there sorting things out. In fact, it wasn't Angie who was doing the sorting out so much as that odd woman Samantha.'

'You mean Samantha 'call me Sammy' Alcock?'

Jerry smiled. 'Yes. She likes to be called Sammy. But she was very good. Mr John Small seemed a bit cowed by her and she smoothed things over very quickly. Buttered up Mr Nightingale and all was well.'

'So what happened then?'

'Nothing. That was it.' Jerry glanced at his watch again. 'Nothing more was heard of them for a few weeks until news came through that Mr Nightingale had died. He fell down the steps of his home whilst under the influence of alcohol. He did drink a bit, it's true.'

'Do you know where he lived?

'Yes. In that rather lovely house opposite Strawberry Field. Sorry. I forgot. You're not local are you? In the New Forest on the Brockenhurst to Lymington Road. At Boldre. Westgate Lodge. One tall chimney. You can't miss it.'

'It hasn't been sold, or anything?' asked Loveluck.

'Oh no. His son lives there. A rather strange young man. Tall, handsome, rich. Bluest eyes you ever saw. The girls love him.'

'He sounds quite the playboy.'

Jerry shrugged. 'Rufus? Not really. He hangs around with a group of people in the forest most of the time. Bit of a hippy or a druid or something.' He laughed. 'They're all the same to me.' He checked his watch again. 'Your detectives can tell you the rest about how John Small and Sammy started coming round again a few months ago. Sorry I haven't been of much help. Got to dash. Bye'

Loveluck watched him hurry off. 'But you have been a great deal of help,' he said softly. 'So. Rufus is his name. And he likes to hang around with a group of hippy types in the forest. Well, well, well.'

'Will you be eating today, sir?' asked a passing waiter, dragging him back to reality.

Loveluck felt the tightness of his belt, grimaced and said. 'Why the hell not. Bring me the menu and another pint of Doom.'

Sergeant Pepper sat in the comfort of her one bed roomed flat in the Maltings, Sherborne. Her medicine was in the drawer and a large gin and tonic in her hand. And murder in her heart. She muttered the same name over and over and over again quietly. Almost in a whisper. 'Olwen Evans. Olwen Evans, Olwen Evans. So I suffered thirty six hours buried alive because of you, did I? I'm shuffling papers in administration because of you, am I? I'm up to my ears in treatment and drugs because of you, am I? You. You told them I had the diary they wanted. Bitch, bitch, bitch.'

She shakily put down her drink and even more shakily poured another one. Then she picked up the anonymous pay as you go phone she had just bought. She typed in Olwen's number with the text message. "I know everything"'

She pressed hard on the 'send' key and said. 'Work that out, you bitch. Put that on your front page. You're going to be your own front page news by the time I've done with you.'

Then she leaned back onto a cushion on the floor, dropped the drink and fell into a deep and dangerous slumber.

The next morning Loveluck, Anderson, Knightly, Daly and Pepper all met in Anderson's office. Sergeant Pepper was looking pale and drawn but she was as excited as the rest at the success of Loveluck's 'start again from scratch' policy. They had all reported back on the results of their repeating the interviews originally done by someone else.

Anderson and Knightly had had them spellbound at their progress following the interview with Mrs Preston and the discovery of Jakob, as they were assuming, in Room 12 for two days prior to the robbery.

Loveluck's discovery that the dead man in Room 7 might not be John Small and that John Small may still be alive was only topped by

Loveluck's further discovery of the name and address of a man who liked to hang about with friends in the forest. Like hippies.

And he had a name. Rufus. Rufus Nightingale of Westgate Lodge, Boldre. In the New Forest.

There was still work to do. Loveluck had still to duplicate Anderson's interview with the SOCO team leader in the woods where they found the hanging man and Daly was still working on the logistics of publicising names to try and identify the young woman killed in the Poachers Inn. Indeed, to identify them all.

But the excitement and progress were palpable.

Tea, biscuits, excitement and good humour were present in spadesful.

Loveluck called them to order.

'We now have to move this investigation forward. It's true we have a lot of confirmed, interesting and conflicting knowledge, but the time of just looking for facts has gone. We must now turn our attention to putting these facts together and forming some theories. And alternative theories. Let's start with the basics. Basic theory?' he asked turning to Anderson.

'Why were the three people summoned to the Poachers Inn and why were they murdered.'

'Exactly,' agreed Loveluck. 'Why were they murdered?'

'And who did it,' suggested Daly.

'Who did it we need to know, of course. But for out theories we need to know why they were killed. There has to be a reason.' Loveluck took up the role of lecturer. 'We all know that we need to know who, what, where, when, how and why. For theories, it is why which is important.'

They all nodded at this re-iteration of basic police methodology.

'Who, what, where, when and how are all pretty well advanced. But we have no idea why they were murdered.'

'And we're not sure who was murdered or who murdered them,' said Knightly. 'The identity of John Small has to be sorted out. People who knew him say he was small in height. The body in Room 7 was above average height. So where is he?'

Loveluck waved his finger at Knightly. 'Didn't you say that you took Samantha 'call me Sammy' to identify the body of John Small.'

'That's right. I did. And so did she. Identify the body, I mean. And she's the one telling us all the time how small he was. Methinks Sammy speaks with forked tongue.'

Loveluck smiled then continued. 'We need to know the role of Jakob in all this. He keeps popping up, both in Dorset and in the New Forest.'

'Where he may be living rough,' added Anderson.

'And now we have the connection with Mr Nightingale and John Small which was not a good relationship. Sergeant Daly,' said Loveluck, 'can you get onto the Hampshire police and see if there was anything suspicious about his death.'

'Yes, sir.'

'You think Mr Nightingale is important?' asked Knightly.

'Yes I do. If only because his son is Rufus Nightingale whom I suspect of being with the moccasin wearing people in the woods where they hanged Winston Gale.'

Loveluck regarded Sergeant Pepper with concern on his face. 'Are you all right, Sergeant? You don't look so good.'

She nodded her head. 'I rather foolishly forgot to take my medicines last night.'

Loveluck wagged a concerned finger at her. 'Don't forget to take them again.'

'Right. We all have work to do. I want us all here by ten o'clock tomorrow morning with theories as to what you think happened. I don't care how off-the-wall or scatter-brained they may seem I want to hear them. As many as you can muster. Long theories, short theories. Sensible theories, daft theories. I want to see evidence of lateral thinking.' He stood up and looked down at them one at a time.

'We've got to get a hold of this case. We've been chasing it for too long. We've got to get some control of it.'

He took a sip of his cold tea. 'I also want to know who you prioritise in terms of importance in this case. Sergeant Daly.'

'Yes, sir?'

'I want to know who the two women were who were murdered at the Poachers. Why did Jakob bring the older woman on his bike? What's the connection there? And the younger woman. We have neglected her so far. Dig.'

'Shovel at the ready sir.'

Loveluck nodded to Anderson and Knightly. 'Can you give me half an hour? Now? Three Wishes garden. It's a lovely morning.'

'There in five minutes, sir.'

Loveluck left them and walked briskly out of the police station. Once gone, the others relaxed. 'The boss seems to be on a roll,' said

Knightly. 'I've never seen him so energised and positive. It's very impressive.'

'Must be all those calories he's been taking in recently,' said Anderson with a grin. 'I'll bet you a pint in the Digby Tap at lunchtime that he has the Loveluck Special in the Three Wishes.'

'You're on,' said Knightly. 'In fact, dear Inspector Anderson, I might just have one myself.

They left with cheerful banter until they were too far away to be heard, leaving Sergeant Pepper and Sergeant Daly sitting silently alone in the room. They looked at each other, both used to being sidelined when the real detective work began. Pepper because she hadn't yet been passed fit to return to detective duties and Daly because he still seemed to spend most of his time on the computer doing so-called research.

Daly smiled. 'Remember the time we interviewed Sherborne's leading business man in the Digby Tap after about six mojitos?'

Pepper smiled. 'We were pretty tipsy.'

'I haven't had a Mojito since then.'

'Me neither,' said Pepper. 'It's a nice drink.'

'What are you doing for lunch?'

'Going with you to the Tap.'

'Not a very good idea,' said Daly. 'Mixing alcohol and prescribed drugs.'

'Bugger the drugs. The Digby Tap at one o'clock it is,' she said standing up. 'Now I must go and write up the minutes of the meeting before I forget them.'

'Why don't you record the meetings? The station has voice recorders and Dictaphones. Save yourself endless note taking.'

'Sounds like a good idea.'

'It is,' said Daly. 'I always use my Dictaphone.'

'Really?' said Pepper sweetly. 'I always use my finger.'

When Anderson and Knightly arrived at the Three Wishes, Loveluck was sitting there with a modest cup of tea and two scones with jam and cream.

'Not having the usual?' asked Anderson.

'I don't have a usual,' replied Loveluck pointedly. 'I asked you over here because I really want to pursue this New Forest connection. Today, for example, Sergeant Knightly and I are going to The New Forest to call on Rufus Nightingale and see what we make of him.

Also to keep a lookout for a very old Toyota pickup truck. And also to see if we can find our old friend Jakob. Jerry said he might be camping out there. Certainly someone is camping out there near Burley.'

Anderson looked concerned. 'How do you hope to find him?'

'The same way we hope to find the white pickup truck.'

'You don't mean just cruising around the place. Do you?'

'Yes. Just cruising around the place.'

'You're mad. The New Forest is a vast area. And if he is camping in the woods you'll never find him. It's a crazy mission.'

'There isn't really that much woodland.' Said Knightly. 'Most of it is like,' she stopped and struggled for a word, 'like wild grassland with animals and bushes and streams.'

Anderson didn't look convinced. 'If my conception of Jakob is correct, he won't be camping where passing motorists can see him. And if has was involved in the murders, and we have no evidence that he was, he certainly won't be camping where passing policemen can see him.'

'And policewomen,' added Knightly.

Anderson nodded in acknowledgment. 'And policewomen.'

'What I really want you to do, Mike,' said Loveluck feeling slightly uncomfortable using Anderson's first name as he did with all his police staff, 'is to push on with the publicising of the names and photographs of the murdered people. And I think we can throw Rufus in there too. We now have a good collection of names to offer the public, though nothing much in the way of photographs.'

'That might change,' said Anderson with a twinkle in his eye.

'Do you know something we don't know?' asked Loveluck.

'I do, actually. My sergeant told me that your friends from the Last of the Summer Wine Dining Club - 'he paused as Loveluck groaned audibly. 'Don't groan. Sergeant Daly thinks they might come and rescue us from our ignorance.'

'That'll be the day,' mumbled Loveluck.

'Because,' said Anderson and then paused teasingly.

'Tell me the worst.'

'Because they were taking photographs at the Poachers at the very next table to John Small and his two lady guests.'

This news galvanised Loveluck. 'Have you got the photographs?'

Anderson shook his head. 'No. Justin from the Diner's club has them. He's working away but should be back in a couple of days.'

Loveluck's eyes were picking out every corner of the garden as if following his scattered thoughts. 'This could be the big breakthrough we need. This IS important.'

'It *could* be,' said Anderson not as convinced of the importance of the snapshots. 'But then again they could just be a lot of pictures of the Last of the Summer Wine Dining Club. Don't get your hopes up too high.'

'No, no. You're right. Even so. Here comes your food.'

He turned to the waitress. 'Another tea for me, please.'

He watched as the waitress put down two Loveluck Specials and left for his tea.

'You two want to watch your waistlines. You have five minutes to finish that, sergeant. If the ice-cream is too much for you I'm always willing to help you out.'

Through mouthfuls of smoked salmon, scrambled egg and muffins, Anderson brought up the subject of the Psychic Fair and Witches Exhibition. 'They've started rolling into town. There's loads of camping and caravanning space put aside for them. And for the public who are also flocking into town to see the show. I had no idea it would be so big.'

'Where are the camp sites going,' asked Loveluck.

'Up on the terraces. Plenty of good, flat fields there. Also in the fields alongside the railway track from Castleton right along to the main Dorchester Road. And,' he added conspiratorially, 'I hear the boy's school have put aside part of the playing fields for public camping.'

'You mean at Carey's Fields?' said Loveluck in surprise.

'So I've heard.'

'That does surprise me.'

'You might find yourself a sexy little witch, Jack.'

'I don't think so,' said Loveluck smiling.

'You might have no choice,' said Knightly. 'Once those witchy women get mixing their potions and casting their spells you might have just no choice at all.'

Loveluck smiled. 'You make it sound quite exciting. Do you recommend white witches or black witches?'

'Do you mean the colour of the magic or the colour of the witch?' asked Knightly.

Loveluck laughed. 'Either. Both. Let's change the subject and let me help you out with your ice cream.'

‘Certainly, Inspector. Vanilla or chocolate? And you can’t have both’

Chapter 19

Loveluck parked his car next to Knightly's. She had got there fifteen minutes earlier. They both walked briskly towards the diagonal steps which led up to the lawyer's office.

'I want to know why she identified the dead body as John Small when she knew quite well it was someone entirely different,' said Loveluck grimly. 'I think our friend Sammy has a lot of explaining to do.'

But this time the door didn't yield to their touch. Or to their knocking. Or to their calling to Sammy by name.

Loveluck and Knightly exchanged glances.

'Bolted?' asked Loveluck. 'Or just popped out for a minute to the shops?'

Knightly shrugged. 'Do you want me to run down to Lentune Cottage and see if she's there?'

Loveluck considered this for a moment. 'I'll come down with you'

Together they walked out of the Angel Courtyard, down the high street and onto the cobbles which led them to the harbour and to Lentune Cottage.

Brisk knocking at the door brought no response and peering in through the windows at front and back showed no sign in anyone there.

A head appeared over the garden fence. 'If you're looking for Sammy, she's gone.'

'We rather gathered that,' said Knightly. 'Do you know where?'

'On her holidays. Now that Mr Small has passed over she's taken an aeroplane and passed over as well. To Spain.' He chuckled at his own joke.

‘When did she go?’

‘This morning. Bright and early. Are you the fuzz? ‘Cos if you are she left you a note.’

‘We are the police, yes.’

‘Inspector Loveluck?’

‘Yes. Can we have the note please,’ he said irritably.

‘It said best of luck with your investigation. Sammy.’

‘How do you know what it said?’

‘Cos I opened it. I’ve got it in the house. You can have it if you want?’ He disappeared into his house and returned a moment later with the note inside a neatly opened envelope.

Loveluck glanced at the note. It said exactly what he had said it did.

‘Do you know where she went?’

‘Yes I do.’

‘Where?’

‘Spain’

Loveluck counted to five and said tersely. ‘What’s your name?’

‘Trevor. Trevor Smith. Pleased to meet you.’

‘Mr Smith.’

‘Call me Trev.’

‘Mr Smith. Do you know where in Spain Sammy Alcock went?’

‘Malaga. At least that’s where she was flying to. That’s all I can tell you. Toodle Pip.’ And with that he was gone.

Knightly threw an urgent glance to Loveluck. He shook his head. ‘Let him go.’

Mr Trevor Smith went inside and sat on the sofa next to Sammy Alcock. ‘All go well?’ she asked.

‘Perfect. He thinks you are now in Malaga.’

‘Thanks Trev. I have to leave. Got a flight to catch.’

Loveluck and Knightly walked along the quay and stopped to stare at the boats. ‘I’ve never lived by the sea,’ said Knightly. ‘Have you?’

Loveluck shook his head. ‘I couldn’t stand the noise of those damned gulls.’ They both watched the sights in the busy harbour then Loveluck turned to Knightly. ‘Now for Mr Rufus Nightingale who likes to hang out with his hippy friends.’

Knightly smiled. ‘I hear there were gypsy dancers on Church Green last night. Very erotic dancing.’

‘That’ll have the vicar tearing his hair out.’

‘I wouldn’t be surprised if Toby joined in. Can you find this house of Rufus Nightingale?’

‘Sergeant Daly gave me the post code. You got your Sat Nav handy?’

‘Of course.’

‘Then lead on, Macduff.’

‘That should be lay on Macduff. Not lead on.’

‘Just get on with it.’

They continued their walk to the car park.

‘When’s your birthday?’

‘Don’t tell me. You’re going to buy me a SatNav.’

‘Yes I am.’

‘To drag me into the twenty first century.’

‘Exactly’

‘And Sergeant Pepper is going to buy me a smart phone for the same reason.’ Loveluck stopped. ‘Why do I need technology when I have two perfectly capable sergeants?’

Knightly shook her head in despair and they walked on.

The drive to Westgate Lodge was short and they didn’t see much of the New Forest en route. The SatNav guided them there unerringly along the Lymington to Brockenhurst Road and they pulled into a small country lane which ran beside the house which was on the main road.

Loveluck and Knightly parked as best they could and walked back to the house. They strolled round looking it over. Knightly smiled in appreciation. ‘Not a bad little pile.’

Loveluck nodded in agreement. ‘I’m not surprised Rufus wants to hang around with his friends in the woods. He probably owns half of them.’ They entered by a small gate and knocked on the metal knocker in the shape of a lion.

‘They should hear that without much problem,’ said Knightly strolling on the edge of the garden. ‘It’s very attractive. The house is a little smaller than it seemed at first. Terrific property, though.’

Loveluck knocked again.

‘I hope we aren’t going to have to search the woods for him and his pals,’ said Knightly with a sigh. ‘Not having much luck today.’

‘Search the woods for whom and his pals?’ came a voice from a wooded part of the garden.

They both turned round to see a figure emerging from the shadows. 'Hi. I'm Rufus Nightingale. And who might you be?'

Loveluck gazed in interest at the young man standing before him. Tall, slim, wavy fair hair and astonishing blue eyes. A male counterpart to Sergeant Knightly almost. Apart from the colour of the eyes.

'Well? Who are you?'

'Sorry,' said Loveluck. 'I am Detective Inspector Loveluck of the Dorset police and this is Detective Sergeant Knightly.'

They both proffered their identity badges and he took Knightly's badge from her and studied it, then Knightly and then the badge again. 'Very curious.' He gave it back to her and smiled. 'The picture doesn't do you justice.'

He stood back and regarded them both. 'So what can I do for the Dorset police?' He guided them to a garden table and waved them both into seats. 'I prefer to be outdoors when possible. If you get cold we can go inside, of course.'

It was a pleasant late August day and they were content to be outside. Loveluck began the interview. 'I understand your father died recently. I'm sorry to learn that.'

'Yes. A few months ago. It came as a bit of a shock really. It was an accident, you see. He fell down the stairs.'

'Did he trip, or have a seizure or something?' asked Loveluck ingenuously.

'Not really sure. He'd been drinking quite a lot. He never used to drink much until my mother died a few years ago. I think he was lonely. Anyway, I assume he tripped or lost his balance or something like that. The autopsy showed a very high level of alcohol in his blood.'

'It must have been a great shock. Was he under any kind of pressure at the time? That can lead a man to drink.'

Rufus regarded Loveluck carefully. 'What kind of pressure, Inspector?'

Loveluck shrugged. 'Business pressures? Money problems?'

Rufus sat back in his chair. 'Would you like some tea and biscuits and sandwiches? Or cake? I get the impression this is going to be a long interview.'

'I don't want to put you to any trouble,' began Loveluck but Rufus was already on his phone.

'Weston? Tea, sandwiches, biscuits and cake for three people on the lawn. Thank you Weston.' He turned to Knightly. 'It'll only be a few minutes.'

Then he turned back to Loveluck. 'Let me give you some idea of the set-up here, Inspector. What you see here,' and he swept his arm out to encompass the house and grounds, 'is really the family home. I was born here. I've always lived here. But my father also has an apartment in St James' in London. A very valuable property. But the income for the family comes from tenant farmers. The family owns land. There are four farms all rented out to tenants. My father wanted me to study Land Management at an agricultural college and become manager of the estate, which includes the four farms.'

'And did you?' asked Knightly fascinated by this young man and his background.

He smiled. 'Farming wasn't for me. I went to Oxford to study modern languages.'

'And do you work for a living?' asked Loveluck.

'No. After Oxford I travelled around Europe to use some of these languages I'd studied so hard to learn. And to study the cultures.'

'Do you have a favourite country to visit?'

'Oh yes, Inspector. Spain. My father kept an apartment there also. And I've kept it on. But I've inherited everything and must keep an eye on the estate until the new estate manager has got a grip of things and then I'll travel again.

'I take it you are an only child,' said Knightly.

'Me? Only child? No. I have a sister Angela.'

'Didn't she inherit anything?'

'No. It's family tradition that the whole estate is passed onto the eldest son.'

'So your sister got nothing.'

'Correct. It is, however, also a family tradition that the eldest son, having inherited, takes care of the remaining family.'

'So you provide for your sister. Angela, was it?'

'Yes I do. Or at least I would if I had the faintest idea where she was.'

The food and drinks were brought out by Weston at this point and a very fine spread it was too.

'I have taken the liberty of bringing some dry sherry out for your guests, sir.'

'Thank you Weston.'

Weston retired and they set about the food.

'Can you explain about your sister?' asked Loveluck.

'Certainly,' said Rufus and he spoke very carefully between mouthfuls, not with a mouthful.

'My sister and my father didn't get on. Not for as long as I can remember. It wasn't too bad when mother was alive but after she died the rows became terrible.'

'Do you mind if I ask how old you are?'

'Not at all. I'm twenty five.'

'And your sister?;

'Twenty four.'

'Quite close together. Were you close?'

Rufus considered this. 'Yes and no. We were quite close when we were young. Kids I mean.' A broad and very winning smile spread across his face. 'When she was about six or seven she became fascinated with dancing. She would dress up and dance all the time.' Memory brought a softer smile to his face. 'We used to call her Angelina Ballerina. She was called that for years.' He got lost in thought and said again softly. 'Angelina Ballerina. But then she got too big and dancing went out of the window.'

'So what happened to her?'

Rufus shrugged. 'She changed. She got in with a strange crowd from Southampton. I think drugs might have been involved. She started coming in late, wearing outrageous clothes. You know the kind of thing. Father objected, they rowed, things went from bad to worse and at the first opportunity she left home.'

'And you don't know where?'

'For a while we did. She went to Brockenhurst College to study secretarial work. She wasn't academically inclined like me, but very quick. Very sharp. A bright girl. Once qualified she said she felt liberated. She could earn a living anywhere.'

'And?'

'Excuse me a moment.' He took another sandwich and poured three dry sherries.

'She worked in Lymington for a while. Then she had a job in Rye. She liked it down there. The last I heard she was working in Bournemouth, but I haven't heard from her for probably three years.'

'No phone contact? Email?'

He shook his head. 'She changed her phone number ages ago. Her email address doesn't bring any response.'

‘Poor old Angelina Ballerina,’ said Knightly.

‘Not so old. Twenty four.’

They all paused to pick at the remains of the meal and Rufus poured them all another dry sherry. ‘Dry sherry isn’t really my drink,’ he said apologetically, ‘but Weston has been pouring it for forty years and I don’t think I can stop him now.’ Once again the smile took any offence away from his words.

‘But,’ he continued, ‘you haven’t come all this way from Dorset to pry into my family. So what is it you do want?’

Loveluck thought this through and was deciding on his next line of questioning when Knightly suddenly said. ‘Do you own an old Toyota pick-up truck?’

He looked slightly startled. ‘No’

‘Are you sure?’

‘Of course I’m sure. I don’t own a pickup truck at all. Not an old one or a new one. Not a Toyota or any other make.’

‘Do you know anyone who does?’

‘No. Nobody I know of.’

‘How about Moccasins?’

‘How about them?’

‘Do you own any?’

He sat back slightly bemused. What Knightly could see with her eyes was a handsome young man in a casual shirt and shorts wearing trainers. Like any one of a million other young men. She began to feel slightly silly and she could sense rather than see Loveluck’s disapproval.

‘No I don’t own any moccasins. I wish I did. Proper ones I mean. Hand stitched. Do you know where I can get some?’

Knightly was about to speak when Loveluck pitched in first.

‘Thank you very much, Mr Nightingale. For both your time and your frankness. Can I ask you one thing?’

Rufus smiled, though a little wearily. ‘Go on.’

‘I understand you like to spend time with your friends in the woods.’

‘Yes I do,’ was the curt reply. ‘Weston will show you to the gate.’

Rufus went into the house and Weston came out and duly showed them to the gate and no further. As he returned to the house Rufus said ‘The Moccasins?’

‘Dumped in a recycling bin on a Southampton council estate with the other garments, sir.’

'Thank you Weston.'

'Thank you sir.'

As Loveluck and Knightly reached their cars Knightly said. 'What now?'

'Now we cruise the New Forest looking for Jakob and his camp site and also the pickup truck. White, Toyota and very old.'

Knightly studied his face for clues. 'Are you serious, sir?'

'Yes, of course I'm serious.'

'Have you any idea how big the New Forest is?'

'No, I haven't, sergeant, but I'm about to learn. One of the main objectives is to get me, and you, a bit better acquainted with the area. Right now it's all a bit of a mystery. I want to find Burley as that has been mentioned a couple of times. Jerry, the Gordleton Mill restaurant manager, thought it was near Burley where he saw Jakob.'

'Or what he thought might be Jakob.'

'Yes. But I really want to get a better idea of the whole area and the towns and so on.'

'As you say, boss.'

'So.' Loveluck glanced at his watch. 'In exactly thirty minutes from now I will meet you in the local pub in Burley. Meanwhile, happy cruising.'

Knightly watched him get into his car, turn it awkwardly in the narrow lane and pull onto the main road.

Knightly got into her own car and made the same manoeuvre, but she had to pull up quickly when she saw Rufus standing in the road.

'Nice wheels,' he said walking up to her and giving her the benefit of his smile. 'They must pay you well in the police force.'

'They pay me to do my job, which I will continue doing now if you would just move out of the way.'

'Of course. It's just that I know I was a bit abrupt about getting rid of you both. I'd got bored with answering questions. Particularly questions that didn't seem to be going anywhere. Just prying into my family.'

'Don't worry about it.'

'But I do, sergeant. Manners are everything.'

'I forgive you.'

'If there are any other questions you would like to ask.....'

Knightly thought it over. Why not? She had thirty minutes which might be better spent questioning Rufus than cruising about the New

Forest. 'All right.' She got out of her car and joined Rufus back at the same table minus the food and drink. Weston was nothing if not efficient.

'So how can I help you Sadie?'

'You know my name.'

'It is on your police badge which you showed me earlier.'

'Tell me. Do you know anyone by the name of John Small?'

Rufus' face clouded over. 'Yes I'm rather afraid I do. Though I certainly wish I didn't. What do you want to know about him?'

'Just about everything. What did he look like? Do you have any pictures of him?'

'Pictures? No. As to what he looked like, I can't help too much there either. I only ever saw him once when he came here to see my father.'

'Do you know what he came to see your father about?'

No I don't, but whatever it was it left my father more upset than I have ever seen him. I think it helped lead to his death.'

'What do you mean by that?' asked Knightly sharply.

Rufus smiled. 'Nothing sinister. Just that I think my father's drinking increased from that moment on. He was worried all the time. It seemed to age him and drive him to drink at the same time.'

'And you have no idea what the problem was?'

'No. Not a clue. I know it was all tied up with John Small, but in what way I have no idea. Sorry I can't be of more help.'

'Thanks. You have been of help. But I have to go and meet my boss. But just one last thing. How tall was John Small?'

'In feet and inches I couldn't say. But he was small. Small for a man. Maybe five foot six. Or less.'

'Oh. And just one more thing.'

'You can have as many last things as you like, sergeant.'

'Do you know Samantha Alcock? Usually known as Sammy.'

'Big butch woman? Yes. She used to get in the Angel Hotel in Lymington sometimes.'

'Oh, do you get in there?

'Sometimes. If I'm in Lymington. Why? Do you?'

She laughed. Not very often. I live in Cerne Abbas and work in Sherborne.'

'Now there's an interesting thing. I'll be spending a few days in Sherborne next week. There's a Psychic fair and Witches Exhibition going on there. I'm very interested in that kind of thing. Perhaps we could meet up?'

She smiled and passed him her card. 'Call me if you have any information which might be of interest to me.'

He tucked the card into his wallet. 'I certainly will.'

She pulled away and began her touring of the New Forest, but within two minutes of leaving Rufus she pulled in and fed 'Burley' into her Sat Nav. No getting lost for her.'

Jakob sat by his tent amongst the bushes near the road leading into Burley. In his hand he held a very used piece of paper. He read it as he had read it many, many times before. It was a copy. The original he had preserved in pristine condition tucked safely amongst his belongings in his rucksack.

He glanced up as a very special red open- topped sports car passed by with a very attractive woman in it, hair blowing in the breeze.

Once again he studied the piece of paper. It was A4 size and covered in tightly typed text but even so he knew it by heart. A piece of paper which could change his world if the balance tipped in his favour. And could destroy his world if the balance tipped the other way. Could destroy him.

He screwed the paper up and petulantly stuffed it deep within his rucksack. He had come so close to tipping the balance in his favour. Close but not close enough. Now the balance was swinging about erratically and nobody knew where it would end up.

He needed a new plan. A clever plan. He dug in his pocket and took out an energy bar.

As he chewed slowly on it he noticed the red open-topped sports car pass by in the opposite direction. It was going much more slowly and the girl's hair was not flowing. The speed limits were low in the New Forest to protect the animals but she was driving much more slowly. And she looked carefully in his direction as she passed.

Swiftly and in a much practiced manner he prepared his camp for moving. He camped in such a way that he could strike camp and be gone in five minutes.

And in five minutes he was gone. In six minutes the red sports car passed by again and the driver thought she must have taken a wrong turn. The camper appeared to have gone.

From five hundred yards down the road, Jakob watched the red sports car pass and pass again. His motor bike was well hidden and he was lying flat on his stomach watching through binoculars.

He would recognise the car again. He had the registration number. He would recognise the girl again. In fact, he had seen her before. He had seen her at the Gordleton Mill asking awkward questions.

She was police and she was dangerous. And much more than that, she was now in real danger herself.

Loveluck was waiting outside a pub in Burley centre and he flagged Knightly down as she drove by. ‘See anything?’ he asked.

She told him of her sighting of a tent and a man sitting by it. Of her return to see him still there. Her third run to find him gone. Loveluck came to the same conclusion she had.

‘You blew it.’

‘I rather think I did, sir. He must have noticed me going passed the second time. But there was no vehicle in sight.’

Loveluck shrugged. ‘He rides a motor bike. He can lay it down. Let’s get back.’

They drove separately back to Sherborne. She would tell him about Rufus and John Small later.

Chapter 20

Sherborne was in a state of excitement. The psychics, witches, warlocks, gypsies, clairvoyants and all manner of people with the 'gift', 'second sight', 'the touch' and many other skills and talents were there.

Along the main streets of Sherborne from Cheap Street itself, along and past the Parade with bemused drinkers sitting outside the Cross Keys pub, along Half Moon Street and spilling onto Church Green itself right outside the abbey, which would soon have the verger and Rev Toby Austin himself out remonstrating, down Digby Road all the way to the railway station and spilling over into the park of Pageant Gardens.

Stalls were being set up, Ouija boards being laid out, tarot cards, crystal balls and impossible to guess paraphernalia were being laid out, some starting to be covered with tent like structures for privacy.

But even more eye catching were some of the costumes being worn by women and men alike. The hair, makeup and dress were stunning in the colour, decoration and effect.

Finger nails long enough to rival the fingers for length, dramatic face make up and confidence, confidence, confidence everywhere.

It took the breath away and brought smiles to the face in equal measure. Love it or hate it – you certainly couldn't ignore it.

To Sergeant Pepper it was simple. She loved it. Sitting on the low wall at the gate to the driveway to the abbey she watched it with child-like wide open eyes. Her eyes missed nothing and marvelled at everything. This was a life beyond anything she could imagine. So far removed from the humdrum toil of her own life. And the lives of everyone she knew.

And she marvelled at the confidence of everyone involved. Was it theatre or was it real? Pepper neither knew nor cared. She knew that she loved it and wanted more of it.

And the music.

Not the raucous noise of the roly poly circus music or the deafening noise of fairground music, but a still and haunting spiritual music. Music that seemed to draw you into belief that there was indeed another world. A spiritual world with experiences far beyond our known world.

Pepper let her gaze roam over the busy bustle of the stalls. Already customers were lining up to have their fortunes read in one way or another. Some were being turned away as the clairvoyant in question was not yet ready for them. Not yet at one with the spirits.

The Ouija board was attracting early customers outside the little tent. Pepper shook her head in bewilderment. She was trying to decide where she would go first. A difficult choice but there was no doubt that she was going to be a very good and loyal customer to the Show.

She crossed the street and walked down Digby Road towards the police station, but as she passed the Digby Memorial Church Hall she saw a commotion going on and joined the mass of people outside who were trying to gain entry.

And there was the Vicar of Sherborne himself, The Reverend Toby Austin standing in the doorway waving his arms windmill style and calling for quiet.

'Will you please be quiet and be still,' he called out. 'I will not have this behaviour in my hall.'

Pepper smiled fondly. The Rev Toby Austin always liked to call church property 'My Hall' or 'My Shop'. It was a pretty conceit and one which endeared him to her. Though not everyone thought of it in those terms.

He was clearly struggling to get order so Sergeant Pepper forced her way to his side by the judicious use of her police badge and her elbows. 'Police. Let me through.'

Toby wiped his brow. 'Janine. Am I pleased to see you. There was almost a stampede earlier. I was getting quite concerned for the safety of the psychics and witches.'

Pepper smiled again at the easy acceptance of the stallholders as 'psychics and witches.'

‘Is this some kind of demonstration against the psychics and witches?’ she asked.

‘Quite the opposite. They want to get in to have their fortunes read and to contact their dead friends and families. I had no idea it would be so popular.’

‘I’m surprised you allowed them to use your hall,’ she said pandering to his small conceit.

‘Oh no. It’s very good for the abbey. Good publicity. And they are paying through the nose for the use of the hall. These things are important in this wicked world, Janine.’

She laughed. ‘I know that the abbey knows how to charge. I remember coming to a choir performance here. That cost a pretty penny.’

‘But worth that pretty penny. And you had the performance not only of a top notch choir but you had it in the beautiful abbey.’

‘I agree. I have no complaints Toby. Worth every penny. Which reminds me. I hear you’re getting married soon.’

‘Yes I am. Very soon.’

‘Then congratulations both to yourself and the very splendid Widow Albright. You are getting married in the abbey, I assume.’

‘Yes,’ he replied without much enthusiasm.

‘How much are they charging you to be married in Sherborne Abbey?’

His face clouded over. ‘Don’t ask.’

‘Or are you getting it for free. A perk of the job,’ she teased.

‘Certainly not. You know, when I marry someone in the abbey, in my capacity of vicar you understand, I don’t receive a single penny. Not a penny.’

‘Where does all the money go?’

He sighed deeply. ‘When you have an hour or so to spare I’ll tell you. Right. I’d better sort this out.’

He turned back to the waiting crowd which by now had settled down but showed no signs of dispersing. ‘Can I have your attention please?’

The crowd quietened down.

‘I will not be opening my hall tonight. The witches and psychics are arranging their displays and stalls and they will be opening at ten o’clock tomorrow morning.’

A disgruntled rumble came from the crowd but they took the news on board and slowly dispersed.

The vicar made another deep sigh and turned to Pepper. ‘A vicar’s work is never done.’

Pepper and the Vicar walked slowly back to the abbey end of Digby Road. ‘Can we have another talk one day soon?’ she asked.

‘About.....’ He nodded his head to encourage her to speak.’

‘About those things we discussed before. You know.’

He thought for a while. ‘That thing we talked about before. The Hand of Glory. That’s a pretty dangerous area. We’re talking about someone being murdered, their left hand being severed, pickled and then used in a criminal or murderous way.’

‘I know.’

‘When you first came to me, Janine, I thought you were interested in witchcraft and pentangles and suchlike. What you are into here is something different altogether. Something altogether more serious. And altogether more dangerous.’

She stared at her shoes and thought this over for a while. ‘Are you getting scared?’

He looked at her keenly. ‘Yes I am. Scared for you.’

She continued to look at her shoes, eventually saying. ‘Don’t desert me, Toby. You don’t know how much this means to me.’

‘I’m not deserting you, Janine. I’m advising you.’

She smiled a false bright smile at him and he smiled one back. ‘Talk soon.’

He turned to go when she caught him by the arm. ‘That man standing by the corner. Almost out of sight.’

‘Where?’

‘Just a couple of yards away.’ She moved to look but he had gone.

‘Did you recognise him?’

‘Yes I did. It was Simon Peter.’

‘My new curate?’

‘Yes. Now there is a man that really scares me. Is he as weird as he looks? He acts like a spy.’

‘Out of the mouths of babes’ muttered Toby quietly as he crossed the road to the abbey and made his way to the vicarage.

In Sherborne police station, Sergeant Daly was piecing together the final details of his collage of the main unknown players in this tragic drama. It wasn’t impressive. What had he got?

He ran his eye over the collage.

‘Elderly lady. No photo. No name. Middle aged man who might or might not be John Small. No photo. Young woman. Twenty five ish. No photo, name might be Lina.

Another middle aged man. Winston Gale. Police mugshot. Youngish man. Twenty five to thirty ish. Jakob. No photo. Rufus. All details known. Might be involved with the moccasin brigade or might have nothing to do with it.’

He wasn’t proud of his efforts. True, he had three more mug shots taken after death. They weren’t pretty. They might be all right to run through the police computer but he doubted if The Western Gazette would run them. He mused that it might be best to stick with ages and what names they had.

He further mused on whether he should include Samantha, call me Sammy, Alcock. That was probably a decision for Inspector Anderson. He also mused on calling Olwen Evans, ace crime reporter of the Western Gazette for some advice on how to present the information.

But most of all he was wishing upon a wishing star that the photographs of the Last of the Summer Wine Dining Club would turn up trumps and they would have perfect photographs of everyone at the meeting in the Poachers Inn.

Thoughts of the Last of the Summer Wine Dining Club also brought his mind back to the point at which Sergeant Pepper had fainted. The faint was very sudden and the feeling kept coming back to him that it was something that someone had said that had brought it about. But think as he would, he couldn’t recall what was being talked about when she had fainted.

He rubbed his eyes and yawned. He wanted to be out of the station and doing detective work. He glanced at his watch. He might just pop down to the Crown Inn and see if any of the Diners Club were there. And even better if Justin was back from working away. And with the photographs.

He slipped on his jacket and strolled out of the station and watched with interest and amusement all the comings and goings and the stalls and the clothing and everything Sergeant Pepper had seen earlier. All the way from the abbey to the top of Cheap Street he took in the displays and people of the Psychic fare and Witches exhibition, and then with reluctance he slipped down Back Lane and across to the Crown.

Inspector Jack Loveluck pressed the button and his computer began to call Ted Bassington. In a matter of seconds Ted answered breezily. 'Hello Inspector. What can I do for you this time?'

'Hello Ted. Just a couple of things carrying on from our conversation the other day.'

'Fire away, old chap. It's damned hot here on the Costa del Sol so you'll excuse me if I have glass of something cold.'

'Yes of course. I only wish I was there enjoying the weather.'

'Nothing to stop you coming. You'd get a damned warm welcome at the Doghouse Inn. I'm off there myself in a minute. I have to see a chap about a ....something or other.'

'OK. Let's move on Ted. First question. How tall was John Small?'

'How tall was he?' repeated Ted a little taken aback. 'Well. I don't know. I don't think I ever measured him.'

'I mean was he tall or small.'

'Mmm. Sort of in-between.'

Loveluck sighed. 'What I'm trying to get at is, if I asked you to describe him so I would recognise him, would you say he was much smaller than most men or much bigger. Or what?'

Ted laughed loudly. 'If I wanted to describe him so that you would recognise him I wouldn't mention his height at all. Just look at his face.'

'His face? What was wrong with his face?'

'Well. There was nothing actually wrong with it. Just sort of memorable.'

'Memorable?'

'Yes. Oh for pity's sake. Let's call a spade a spade. He was damned ugly. Sort of bulbous face, if you know what I mean. Not deformed or anything, but he wouldn't win any beauty contests.'

Loveluck let this sink in for a while. Nobody had mentioned this before.

'You still there, old chap? Only I have to go to the Doghouse to see a man about a dog, if you know what I mean.'

'Sorry Ted. I was miles away.

'Well. You are miles away,' joked Ted with a satisfied laugh. 'You should come over here. Loads of people knew John Small better than me.'

'I think I'll have to do that. I don't suppose anything has been seen of him over there recently, has there?'

'I should hope not. He's dead. At least I think that's what you told me last time we had a chat on Skype.' Ted drained his glass. 'Is that all? Only I, er, have to see this chap.'

'Just a couple of quick points, Ted. Does the name Nightingale mean anything to you. Mr Nightingale.'

Ted mused silently for a few seconds. 'I don't think so. Not Nightingale. Why? Should it?'

Loveluck pondered on how to begin. 'Do you remember you told me last time we talked about a man from the New Forest. A client who turned up one day at your office. He said he wanted to deal with one person and one person only. He didn't mind who but he only wanted one person to know his business.'

'Yes,' said Ted Bassington vaguely. 'I do remember something of the sort.'

'Please think, Ted. You turned him away but John Small went after him and he, John Small that is, became the one person who knew of his business.'

'Yes. I do seem to remember that.'

'John Small said he had hit the jackpot.'

'John Small said that all the time. But I do remember the incident. It caused a hell of a lot of problems.'

'Do you remember his name?'

'Mmm. Not sure.'

'Could it have been Nightingale? Mr Nightingale of the New Forest?'

'No,' said Ted Bassington quite firmly. 'It was definitely not Nightingale.'

Loveluck breathed out deeply with disappointment. How badly he wanted it to be Nightingale. That would give the investigation some focus.

'OK Ted. Thanks anyway.'

'I know it wasn't Nightingale because it was definitely the name of a place. A town probably. And, as far as I know, there is no place called Nightingale.'

‘And no place that I know of either. But thanks, Ted. If you do remember the name of the place you will let me know, won’t you?’

‘Of course I will. Is that it?’

‘No. Just one more thing, Ted. Do you know of a woman called Samantha Alcock? She likes to be known as Sammy. A friend of John Small.’

‘Well, do you know I might just remember something about that. Can’t bring it to mind. My memory is better in the morning.’

‘Before you start drinking,’ thought Loveluck but said nothing.

‘I’ll give it some thought. And I’ll try and think of that man’s name. The New Forest chap. I know it’s the name of a place.’

‘Don’t worry about it Ted. You’ve been a great help.’

‘I’m so glad. Got to go, old man. Got to meet a chap in the.....’

‘No! Don’t go.’ Said Loveluck urgently.

‘Oh. Well, if you really don’t want me to. But I have to meet this....’

‘I want you to think, Ted. Think hard.’

‘Well. I’ll try.’

‘The name of the town. Think hard.’

‘I’m trying.’

Could it have been Berkeley?’

‘Berkeley?’ muttered Ted. ‘Damn you, Inspector. It *was* Berkeley. How on earth did you know that? You must be a genius or a magician or something.’

Loveluck smiled broadly. ‘Just a detective, Ted. Just a detective. And when did this happen? You told me before it was about twenty five years ago.’

‘That’s right. When Bassington, Small and Peacock became just Bassington and Peacock. And then just Bassington.’

‘What happened to Peacock?’

‘Another messy business. I’ll tell you another time. I’ve got this chap to meet in the Doghouse Inn’

‘Ted. You’re a fine man.’ And leaving Ted to mull over these words he signed off Skype.

Chapter 21

Sergeant Knightly arrived at the police station the following morning with a spring in her step and headed straight for her pigeon hole. Today was the day the boys from the police photographic laboratory had promised her the photographs back from the three small framed pictures she had found on the table at John Small's house plus the very small picture she had found in the locket of the younger murdered woman they were calling Lina.

And there they were. 'About flipping time, as well' she grumbled as she headed for the kitchen and an early morning coffee.

'You're cutting it fine,' said Pepper who was piling drinks and biscuits onto a tray, 'I thought you weren't coming.'

'Why? What's going on?'

Pepper started at her, arms akimbo. 'Have you really forgotten?'

Knightly shrugged. 'I was going to do some paper work.'

'No you aren't. You're going into the meeting in Inspector Anderson's room to give him your theories. Remember?'

'Oh Flip. I'd completely forgotten.

'Have you got any theories?'

Knightly shook her head thoughtfully. 'Not one. Perhaps I can deflect his attention by telling him about the photographs.'

'And the best of luck with that,' said Pepper edging past her with the trays. 'Can you bring my note pads and Dictaphone?'

'Oh. Fancy. A Dictaphone. That should save you some effort.'

Together they entered Anderson's office and Pepper handed round the cups and laid out the biscuits. 'Where's the boss?' she asked.

Nobody seemed to know. 'And where's Sergeant Daly?'

‘Standing at the station door,’ answered Knightly. ‘Waiting for some photographs.’

‘If they’re the Last of the Summer Wine Dining Club photographs, they’ll outshine the ones you’ve got,’ said Pepper quietly to Knightly.

‘Oh earth. Open up and swallow me,’ said Knightly with feeling.

They were disturbed by the entry of Loveluck and Sergeant Daly. ‘Morning everyone,’ said Loveluck brightly. ‘Glad to see we are all here. I’m afraid we’ll have to cut this meeting short. I have to go to Dorchester for a meeting. So if we can get off to a quick start.’

The relief on everyone’s face was palpable. Theories aren’t that easy to come by.

‘Firstly a snippet or two of news. I was talking to Ted Bassington, boss of Bassington, Small and Peacock solicitors of Sherborne. Or should I say ex boss. He is retired and living in Spain as you probably remember. Well. Firstly he tells me that when it comes to describing Mr John Small, it doesn’t matter how tall he is. The fact is, he is plain ugly. Bulbous, was how he described him. And don’t ask me what he meant by that. We all know what bulbous means. Don’t we Sergeant Daly?’

‘Eh? Me?’

‘Yes. You.’

‘Well. Bulbous means like a bulb, I suppose.’

‘So a person with a bulbous face would have a face that was?’

Daly looked about him in panic. ‘Er. Lumpy?’

‘Very good sergeant. Yes. Lumpy, bulging. Has anyone described John Small like that?’

Loveluck saw five heads shaking.

Loveluck joined in the head shaking. ‘Why not? If it was so obvious.’

‘How many John Smalls are there out there,’ asked Anderson. ‘Tall ones, small ones, bulbous ones. And is he living or dead?’

‘There is another snippet of information for you. Mr Nightingale, father of Rufus, is indeed the man from the New Forest who went to Bassington, Small and Peacock twenty five years ago and demanded one and only one solicitor to speak to.’

‘And he got John Small,’ said Knightly.

‘Well, strictly speaking he was turned away, but John Small went after him and got the job. His jackpot he called it.’

‘That’s a great link,’ said Anderson. ‘Can we be sure it’s him?’

'Ninety five percent. I want warrants to search John Small's office, John Small's home and Rufus Nightingale's home. His father's home as was. They are being drawn up now. We need to cooperate with the Hampshire police.'

'That's quite a lot,' said Anderson.

'I have the photos back from the lab,' said Knightly. 'Just arrived'.

'The ones we found in John Small's place?'

'Correct.'

'Good. Quite a fruitful morning.'

There was a knock at the door and the station officer popped his head into the room. 'Delivery for Sergeant Daly. One pen drive.'

He passed it through and Daly took it. 'From the diner's club,' he explained.

'Keep your fingers crossed on that one.' Said Loveluck. 'Right. Just time for a quick theory or two. Any volunteers?'

Volunteers were slow in coming forward.

'Mike?' said Loveluck.

'Yes,' said Anderson. 'I'll give you the bones of a theory I'm working on. 'Firstly, I don't think that any of us have come close to meeting John Small, living or dead. We know there was a John Small working for Bassington, Small and Peacock twenty five years ago. My money is on the body we found in the Poachers Inn not being John Small. And not just because he didn't have a bulbous face.

'My money is on the small chap who was at that Gordleton Mill for several weeks not being John Small either. We must find out if he had a bulbous face. My theory is that John Small is somewhere safe, quietly pulling the strings with these fake John Smalls going round the place. I'd like to know what happened to the small chap who was with Sammy at that restaurant. Dead John Small number two in my view.

'And the person who knows a lot and is forever misleading us is Samantha, call me Sammy, Alcock. She's protecting him. Shielding him. Pointing us in the wrong direction. I'd like to bring her in for prolonged questioning.'

'Slight problem there,' said Loveluck. 'She's gone on holiday.'

'To Spain?' asked Anderson.

Loveluck nodded.

'Are you still planning to go over there?'

Loveluck nodded again. 'For perhaps three days.'

'Good,' said Anderson. 'I think he might be there.' He turned to Knightly. 'Do you speak any Spanish?'

She shrugged. 'Uno poco.'

'Get off as soon as you can, is my advice,' said Anderson.

He turned to Daly. 'What's your theory?'

'Me again?' moaned Daly.

'Yes. You're the star of the moment. Give us your theory.'

Daly got wearily to his feet. 'My theory rests on mathematics.'

'Mathematics,' laughed Anderson. 'Then perhaps you better use the white board, Sergeant Daly. Or should I say Professor Daly.'

Daly smiled, walked to the white board, picked up a marker pen and wrote in very large characters the number 25. Then he sat down again.

'Is that it?' asked Loveluck.

'That's it. The number 25 is at the root of this case. When did Mr Nightingale appear at the offices of Bassington, Small and Peacock? 25 years ago. When did the murders take place? 25 years later. How old is the son, Rufus? 25. How old is the daughter, Angela? 24. How old is Jakob? 25 or thereabouts. When did Mr Nightingale die? 25 years after he met Mr John Small. When did Mr Nightingale die, part two? Just before John Small. If John Small is dead.'

There was a quiet for a spell. Loveluck said thoughtfully. 'The theory is a good one. There are a couple of inconsistencies. The daughter Angela is only 24.'

'I'll bet you a Loveluck special at the Three Wishes that she's 25,' replied Daly. 'And so is Jakob.'

'I don't see how she can be,' said Loveluck. 'Unless she and Rufus are twins.' Daly began to reply but Loveluck stopped him. He paced the small room several times then turned abruptly to Knightly. 'Do you remember what the Nightingale family used to call Angela when she was young and keen on dancing?'

Knightly smiled. 'Yes sir. Angelina Ballerina.'

Loveluck nodded. 'They stretched out the name Angela to Angelina.' He paced the floor two more times and then stopped. 'Suppose, just suppose, in later life, Angela took her childhood name of Angelina and shortened it.' Loveluck regarded them all in turn waiting for an answer. It came from Anderson.

'From Angelina to Lina?'

'Exactly. The dead woman Lina we found in the Poachers could be Angela Nightingale.'

Loveluck turned to Pepper. 'Check the birth certificates of Rufus and Angela Nightingale. We have a photo of what could be her dead. We need to go back and get a photo of Rufus.'

'All done, sir,' said Knightly. 'When you left yesterday he came out to apologise for being rude in hustling us out quickly. I took a photo of him.'

'With his permission?'

'No, sir.'

'And what was your motive in taking this surreptitious photo.'

'I thought it might come in handy,' she said blushing from head to foot. No one believed her.

'Get comparing them. I want your first thoughts. Then ship both photos to the lab for proper analysis.' He turned to Daly. 'Excellent theory. If your diner's club photos come up trumps, this will have been an important day for you.'

Daly and Knightly formed an impromptu team. Daly to dig out the photograph of the young woman Lina from files and Knightly to download the photo of Rufus from her phone. She hoped the hastily snapped photos of Rufus would be good enough to make a decent comparison.

Daly also uploaded the photographs from the pen drive given him by Justin to his laptop. He had barely begun to scan them when Knightly said. 'OK Ready?'

'Sure.'

The comparison was difficult. The photograph of the dead girl had eyes closed and looked deathly. The picture of Rufus had captured his face but he was looking the other way and it was almost a silhouette. She enlarged it on her screen and it looked better, but still not possible to make a sensible comparison.

'Do you think the police photographic lab will be able to tell us if these people are twins?'

Daly shrugged. 'Doesn't look like it from here. Still, they do work near miracles down there. We'll have to wait and see.'

Loveluck's meeting with CC Mackenzie and Detective Chief Inspector John Waddington had gone well. Very well. Congratulation all round were offered for Loveluck's tactics of revisiting the witnesses again using different officers and the amount of new or better quality information it had unearthed.

The update on the visit to Rufus Nightingale and the possible sighting of Jakob were also welcomed. The meeting was going better than he could have ever dreamed until Loveluck moved onto the two theories he had heard that morning.

As he recounted them he could see the CC appearing more and more solemn and even Chief Inspector Waddington allowed his eyebrows to rise once or twice. Bravely he battled on with his account until he came to an end.

The CC and Waddington stared long and hard at him. It was the Chief Inspector who spoke first.

'How seriously are you taking these theories?'

Loveluck splayed his hands open. 'First theories. Get the team to start thinking about WHY it happened instead of just who, what, where, and when. Change the mind set.'

The CC said. 'You know you are changing the facts to fit the theory? One of the first things you learn not to do in police training.'

'The so-called facts might be wrong,' said Loveluck.

'Sergeant Daly's theory was that 25 was the key number to it all. Don't get me wrong, I like the idea that 25 turns up several times in one way or another, but Rufus said his younger sister was twenty four. A fact which you conveniently altered to twenty five and now Sergeant Pepper is chasing up birth certificates to see if Rufus and Angela Nightingale are twins.' The CC shook his head. 'Quite unacceptable. And what if they are twins? What difference does it make?'

It was a question that Loveluck had no answer for. But the CC hadn't finished yet.

'And chasing around the New Forest after these periphery members of the investigation is allowing you to lose focus on the chief suspect. In my opinion the chief suspect. And by that I mean John Small. Three descriptions from people who knew him. All as different as chalk and cheese. Small man, tall man, bulbous faced man. He's damned slippery is this John Small. Get after him, Jack. He's the one we want.'

There was a silence which Waddington broke, asking quietly. 'I hear you're going to Spain. Is that after Samantha Alcock or John Small? Or both.'

Loveluck collected his thoughts and took his time doing it as the two senior offices waited. 'In the same way that Sergeant Daly's 25 theory has all roads leading to the number 25, so the Spanish theory, which is my theory, has all roads leading to El Pilar.' Loveluck noticed the blank faces and added.

'El Pilar is a small area between Marbella and Estepona on the Costa del Sol. John Small used to live there. I'm beginning to think he might still live there. Also Samantha Alcock has gone to Spain, though as yet we don't know where. And thirdly Ted Bassington also lives there. And he lives in a house that used to be owned by John Small.'

More blank faces brought the footnotes from Loveluck. 'Ted Bassington was the Bassington part of Bassington, Small and Peacock. The solicitors in Sherborne twenty five years ago where we first came across John Small.'

'Twenty five again,' muttered the CC thoughtfully. 'When are you thinking of going?'

'On Friday, sir. With Sergeant Knightly.'

The CC grinned a knowing grin at Loveluck. 'Weekend in Spain with Sadie Knightly? Nice work if you can get it.'

'Yes sir, thank you sir' said Loveluck with scarcely concealed disdain. 'Probably for two or three days.'

'Do you have any contacts there? Somewhere to start?'

'I have Ted Bassington. Also the Doghouse Inn. A sort of ex-pat bar as far as I can tell in El Pilar. John Small used to go in there a lot it seems.'

The meeting petered out and Chief Inspector Waddington walked Loveluck to the door. 'I have to agree with the CC, Jack. Keep John Small as your focus. Find him and we find all the answers.'

'If he's alive,' said Loveluck.

'Oh, I think he's alive. Someone is pulling all the strings and it has to be him.' They shook hands and parted, both men knowing they had a lot to think about and a long way to go to solve this case.

As Loveluck climbed into his car, his phone rang. It was Olwen Evans. 'Hi Jack. I was beginning to think you were dead. Can we talk?'

Talking to Olwen Evans was not top of Loveluck's agenda. Sooner or later, and probably sooner, he would have to tell her that his promised trip to Spain with her was off. Even worse, he'd have to tell her that he was going with Sergeant Sadie Knightly.

'Are you there?' she persisted.

'Yes, Olwen. I'm busy. What is it you want?'

Olwen balked at this rebuke. 'I have been getting threatening messages. On my phone. Can we talk about it?'

This just reminded him what a pain mobile phones could be. 'I suppose so. I'm in Dorchester at the moment.'

'Can you come into Yeovil?'

'Where in Yeovil?'

'Er. On second thoughts, let's meet at your place in Cerne Abbas. The Royal Oak. About twenty minutes. OK?'

Loveluck agreed and rang off.

He sat in his car but didn't start the engine. He felt weary. They seemed to continue to unearth evidence at a good rate, but they still didn't seem to be making progress. He felt tired and in need of a rest. Lethargically, he started the engine and pulled out of the Dorchester Police Station car park taking a country route back north towards Cerne Abbas.

He pulled in at a rural church, parked his car and walked over to a grave. He read the inscription he knew so well. Angela Loveluck. Beloved wife of Jack Loveluck and devoted mother to Richard Loveluck.

As always he wanted to say something but could never find the words to say to her. Much like the last couple of years of their marriage when they hardly spoke at all. Until the day she connected a hose to the exhaust pipe, ran it through the car window and turned on the engine. And put an end to their communication for good.

His eyes fell on the words Richard Loveluck. His son, now seventeen and not seen by Loveluck since the day his mother died. And that was six years ago. Ricky. Ricky who blamed his dad for the suicide. Come to that, everyone blamed his dad for the suicide. And everybody was right.

He turned to go, then stopped and said. 'I hope you're at peace now, Angie. Because I'm buggered if I am.' And on these first words he had spoken to her for six years, he returned to his car.

Back in Sherborne the town was heaving with people. The fair had got itself fully under way and the public had turned out in their thousands. From Sherborne, Yeovil, Dorchester, Weymouth, Shaftesbury, Sturminster Newton and all points of the compass.

The music was a little louder and many a clairvoyant's palm was being crossed with high value notes. The atmosphere was electric, the mood friendly, the expectations sky high and the delivery of those expectations first class.

Everything imaginable was on sale, from magic pyramids to witches potions and the business was brisk. Everywhere fortunes were being told, palms were being read, tarot cards were being read, astrological charts being consulted and charted.

Move along a few yards and there were Moon readings taking place, Reiki healing, Dream interpretation. Psychic reports were available on romance and relationships. Psychic secrets, Seduction secrets.

Next stall is selling Spirit Rocks and the dreaded Spell Kits which were going to transform the modus operandi of all the Sherborne villains. Stalls stretching out of sight and happy and eager customers stretching with them. The wildly popular Animal Healing tent was awash with potential customers clutching their pets.

Chapter 22

In the Royal Oak the atmosphere was a little more tense. Loveluck and Olwen Evans sat facing each other and saying very little. They sipped at their drinks and picked at the toasted cheese and onion sandwiches and shared bowl of chips with little enthusiasm.

'What's all this about you getting strange messages on your phone?' asked Loveluck.

'I'm not really sure. They are text messages. Short ones. Very unnerving.'

'Have you got the number?'

Olwen shook her head. 'They withheld it.'

'I didn't know you could do that on mobile phones.'

'Course you can. Something to do with Data protection I suppose. Do you think you clever policemen can trace it for me? Identify where the call is being made from?'

'It depends on how serious it is. What do they say?'

Olwen flicked her phone on and called up her inbox. 'First one says, I know everything. The second one says You're going to end up on the front page of your own newspaper. The third one says You messed with the wrong person when you messed with me, bitch.'

Loveluck appeared unimpressed. 'Probably someone you wrote an article about. They'll get over it. Have you been to see the Psychic fair and witches exhibition in Sherborne yet?'

'Sod the witches. What about these threats?'

'Wait until you get some more and we'll look at it again. Anyway, I'm not sure if we can trace texts. I'll ask someone at the station.'

'Well, thank you Policeman Plod. That's set my mind at rest.'

Loveluck sighed deeply within and wished this day would end.

'Fancy another drink?'

Loveluck nodded. 'Get a bottle of something. Rioja.'

She went to the bar and came back with Prosecco. Loveluck took one look at the sparkling wine, called the waitress and ordered a very large Gin and Tonic.

If only I can get through the evening without Spain being mentioned I'll be a happy man, thought Loveluck.

And lucky he was. A female friend of Olwen's came bouncing over, air kisses were given, hands were shaken and the two women went on a five year catch up leaving Loveluck to sip gently at a gin and tonic or three and relax.

His mind wandered from the case to his dead wife, to his long lost son, to John Small.

And when he finally made his apologies for leaving early he was scarcely noticed as the girls talked and talked and he slipped away to his house just a few yards away, went inside and drifted off to sleep on his sofa.

The pictures from the Diner's Club were in the main disappointing. They were hastily taken snaps of members of the club. Daly poured over them as they flashed onto his screen and began to file them into different folders. Three folders. Folder number one was titled 'Club Members'. Folder number two was titled 'Club members including others'. By others he meant non club members. The trouble was he didn't know all the club members so he kept that folder to go over with Loveluck who knew them all well.

Folder three he titled 'General shots of pub'. These were usually poor photographs of nobody in particular. But he knew better than to delete any of them. Any picture could contain a small gem of information. Or not.

Feeling that he had done all that he could at the computer he decided to take himself off to do some real detective work. Months of doing computer research had blunted his enthusiasm for the job and he had decided to do the best job he could with the Last of the Summer Wine Diner's Club photographs.

He was going to go back to the Poachers Inn and draw up a plan of exactly who was sitting where on that fateful night. This he could do with the help of Jamie the barman and the general layout of the room.

If Jamie said that Jakob was leaning against a certain pillar and he could identify a photograph of someone leaning against that very pillar, then he had a photo of Jakob.

Theoretically, that is. In reality it was a bit of a long shot but he was going to worry at this particular bone until he had shaken all of the stories out of it that it had to tell.

The first problem was going to be negotiating the clogged up roads surrounding the police station. As he left the office and walked to the door he bumped into Sergeant Pepper.

'Where are you going?' she asked.

'Going to do some detective work at the Poachers. Do you want to come?'

She shrugged. 'I've finished work for the day. Nearly. Why not?'

And together the two truants headed for the door.

Inspector Anderson was pouring over the collage Sergeant Daly had put together. The face photographs of the dead were a non-starter as far as the press were concerned. He would check it out with Olwen Evans at the Gazette but he was pretty sure what she would say.

Which left a police photograph of Winston Gale, the hanging man and he was the least of their worries.

Daly had added a copy of Knightly's photo of Rufus but again, Anderson wasn't so certain about including a perfectly innocent man in the publicity to identify the people who might lead them to the suspects.

They *knew* who he was, they knew where he lived. He had been interviewed and had been perfectly candid with Loveluck and Knightly.

At least that was the impression he gave. Anderson was still convinced that he was very likely involved with the moccasin brigade at the scene of the hanging man. More than that, Anderson believed that he and the others in his sect were certainly responsible for the hanging. And the severing of the left hand, whatever all that was about.

Which left them with no photographs and no useful names. He didn't consider Winston Gale and Rufus particularly useful names. Only Lisa and John Small. And they didn't even know if Lisa was her name. And as for John Small, the mysterious disappearing man. Or men, as there appeared to be at least three of him.

Anderson was beginning to get a secret admiration for John Small. The man certainly knew how to pull the strings and have the police at a loss.

He strolled to the window and gave it a lot of thought as he gazed out at the hordes of people in Digby Road enjoying the Psychic fair.

Suddenly he came to a conclusion. Unless Sergeant Daly came up with some good photographs from the Diner's Club he was going to go with names alone.

He rehearsed the names in his mind. 'Do these names mean anything to you? Jakob, Rufus, Lisa, Winston, John Small?

Looked at from this angle they seemed impressive. Looked at from another angle they looked weak. He shook his head and turned away from the window. He would leave it for a while and come back to it. Clear his head. Think about something else.

And then he came to another decision. He would go outside and seek the help of a psychic. Which is exactly what he did. Impressed with his own boldness he strolled the street for a while looking for a stall that appealed to him.

Then he went into the Digby memorial church hall and was impressed with the layout in there. He surveyed the stalls and tents and looked at the names. That's the one for me; he thought and entered the tent.

The name above the tent read 'NEMESIS'

Sergeants Daly and Pepper were having a frustrating time at the Poachers Inn. The place was busy and they were having trouble keeping Jamie the barman's attention for any length of time.

They had identified the three yards or so of bar which Jamie normally patrolled and they had identified the table used by the John Small party and also the table used by the Diner's club. Or tables, for they had pushed two tables together to accommodate their numbers.

Much of this they had known before, but now that they were looking at it with a new purpose it took on a whole new meaning.

They pummelled Jamie with questions.

'Who was taking the photographs.?'

'A woman'

'Which woman?'

'Just a woman. Like my mum.'

'Would you recognise her again?'

'Probably'

'Did she take all the photographs?'

'I dunno. She had some taken of herself too,' he added after a pause.

And so the questioning went on until Jamie started taking a very long time serving drinks.

'He's avoiding us,' said Pepper.

'I'm not surprised. We have been giving him the third degree rather,' said Daly with a smile.

The next time they had his attention again Pepper said. 'We have just a few more questions for you. Jamie.'

He sighed deeply but said, 'Go on then.'

'Can you remember where Jakob stood when he was in here? I remember you saying that he stood looking around as if looking for someone.'

'Who's Jakob?'

'Jakob? The one you described as being of a military type. Didn't say much. Drank water.'

'Oh, him. He leaned against the wall. Further back. By the door to the outside terrace.'

'OK Show us where,' he asked walking to where Jamie had pointed to.'

'No. Other wall. By the door to the terrace.'

'The other wall,' said Pepper in surprise. 'He could hardly see the John Small party from there.

'I don't think it was the John Small party he was looking at. Like I said, he seemed to be looking for someone else.'

They went through the same procedure for Winston Gale and all members of the John Small party. Jamie was surprisingly patient but began to lose that patience when asked where the entire Diner's Club party sat.

'There were loads of them. And they were all over the place. Changing seats. Bothering other diners. They were a right nuisance.'

Sergeant Daly ordered sandwiches and drinks and sat with Pepper at the table the Diner's Club had used, studying the photos.

'This should be roughly the place where most of the pictures were taken,' said Daly. 'It should help us identify who was where.'

Pepper squeezed his arm and raised her Mojito to his. 'Cheers. There is a lot riding on these photos.'

He smiled. 'Long time since we drank Mojitos together,' he said joining her in a toast.

Sergeant Daly put the first of the photos onto his laptop screen.

Sergeant Knightly was also looking at photographs, but in her case she had only three of them. They were the three small photos taken from the small table in John Small's office and they couldn't have been more different from Sergeant Daly's photographs.

Daly had a lot of pictures taken from a very modern digital camera which he could enlarge on the screen of his laptop pretty well as much as he wanted. Knightly had three pictures taken many years ago and long before digital cameras were commonplace. In fact, she suspected that the camera used to take them was already very old by the time they were taken.

The photos were post card size. Two were views of a group of men on a beach and the third was of a group of cyclists lined up on their bikes posing for the camera.

She studied the two beach photos. They were clearly taken at the same time and each had five men in. They were not the same five men and Knightly put this down to a switch of photographer so that everyone would be in at least one photo. She soon worked out which man had disappeared from one photo and which new man had appeared in the other photo. Convinced that this had indeed been done to swap photographers she looked more carefully at the pictures themselves.

The police lab had enlarged them as best they could but there was a limit to what could be done with these old pictures. It didn't help that she had no idea what John Small looked like but she would go round the people who had met him, or someone saying they were him, and see if there was any identification possible.

One of the people in the pictures interested her. There was some faint recognition registering in her head. She couldn't pin it down but something deep down definitely registered something.

The photo of the cyclists was of little value as all the cyclists were quite a way back from the camera in order to get everyone in the shot. She scoured the faces from the slightly blurred enlargements for the one that had registered something with her.

And there he was. Straddling his bike. Not very small, not particularly tall and not, as far as she could tell, with a bulbous face. But that same slightly familiar face none the less.

Chapter 23

Inspector Anderson sat down in front of the psychic called Nemesis and regarded her with curiosity. A lady of middle years, proud looking rather than attractive with an impassive stare from threatening eyes that seemed to pass straight through Anderson. And into his soul.

If it wasn't for a totally sceptical attitude to all this psychic stuff he might have been intimidated. As it was he wanted to laugh out loud at her attempts to cow him into believing her.

'What is it you want me to tell you,' she asked.

Anderson shrugged. 'I don't really know.'

She looked him fully in the face. 'It will be twenty pounds for the reading whether we sit here in silence or we talk.'

'At that price I suppose we'd better talk.'

'And the clock is ticking,' she added meaningfully, 'so perhaps it would be best if you told me what you wanted.'

Anderson sat back in his chair. 'It's hard to explain.'

'I suggest you try.'

'Well. It's a work problem really.'

'And what is your work?'

'I'd rather not say,' he said uncomfortably. Deep down he wished he had never got himself into this nonsense.

'Sit quietly,' she said with quiet authority. If you won't tell me what is bothering you I'll have to divine it.'

She sat very quietly, hands hovering over a crystal ball which also made Anderson want to laugh out loud. For many long minutes she sat there, eyes closed, hands hovering just over the crystal ball, almost touching it.

She began to make a slow, deep noise. Deeper than Anderson would have thought possible. He shuffled uneasily in his chair. He felt it starting to get to him.

Now she made different noises. A cross between wailing and singing. 'Pure theatre' Anderson told himself. 'She isn't communing with anything.' But if it was wailing with her it was bravado with him.

Suddenly the wailing took the form of a word.

'Death,' she called out loudly. 'In your profession you are dealing with death.'

Anderson sat still and quiet.

She opened her eyes. 'You are dealing with death. Professionally. This is true is it not?'

Anderson shuffled in his chair again and cleared his throat. 'Yes. I suppose you could say that.'

She raised a single finger to quieten him and closed her eyes once again. More long minutes passed until she said softly. 'You are seeking something. No. You are seeking someone.'

'I am seeking several people,' he said trying to sound jolly.

'No. You seek one man.' Again she went silent. Then she opened her eyes and said. You want to know if someone is alive or dead.' Anderson remained silent. 'This is correct, yes?'

'I suppose so.'

Here a small smile crept across her face. Her eyes showed a higher level of understanding. She nodded slowly. 'You want to know if this man is alive or dead. Would you like to know that?'

Again he shuffled in his chair. 'Yes. Yes I would,' he said in as firm a voice as he could muster.

She smiled again. 'He is alive. The others are dead. As you know.

The witches of Sherborne and the Witches of the New Forest have been at war with each other for as long as anyone can remember and for a long time before that.

What started it nobody knows, but every so often an incident would occur and old rivalries would resurface.

The Psychic fair and Witches exhibition in Sherborne had reopened old wounds with a vengeance.

The Sherborne coven had been expecting the New Forest coven but they were shocked when they turned up in such numbers and with such wares. It quickly became clear that the Sherborne girls were being outshone, outclassed with what they had to offer and the public were flocking to the New Forest witches.

A council of war was called by Astra, the leader of the Sherborne coven and the girls were gathered to discuss how to fight back. The meeting took place in the Digby Tap which was already very busy. With the public returning to their own towns there was some breathing space in the Tap for the first time that day and the girls found a corner by the window.

Outside, the gypsy girls were on Church Green dancing to the sound of the gypsy boys' fiddles to a large and appreciative audience. On some tunes the gypsy boys danced too and the dancing verged on the erotic to an even more appreciative audience.

Inside the Digby Tap the Sherborne Witches were verging on the tipsy and growing belligerent with it. This war council was good and ready for battle.

Olwen Evans glanced at the text which had just pinged on her phone. It read. 'Don't go out alone after dark. I'm coming to get you soon. Very soon'

She leaned back in her office chair at the Western Gazette and turned this message over in her mind. And the other messages she had received from the same person.

There was something in the use of language that was almost comical. Like children trying to sound like the tough guys on television programmes. Could it be kids fooling about? She considered the possibility but discarded it.

On the other hand she couldn't ignore it.

She read all four messages again. Something about the use of language. Someone trying to sound tough. But someone who wasn't that tough?

She tapped her fingers on her desk. 'Come on, ace crime reporter. What kind of person fits that description?' she said to herself.

Then a smile passed her lips. 'Ah ha,' she said again out loud. 'Perhaps I am dealing here with a woman.' Then the smile was just as suddenly wiped from her face. There was only one woman with genuine cause to want to harm her. With very good cause, in fact.

Olwen again tapped the table with her fingers, but more urgent and nervous fingers than before. 'But how could she have found out? How could she have learnt that it was me who had said that Pepper had the vital diary which had led to her kidnap and burial alive? Led to this awful change in her life. The only person who knew was George.'

'Bloody George. He must have told Pepper the whole story.' She was still talking out loud. Now she stood up and paced the room.

What to do now? Pepper on the warpath for her. Pepper still undergoing therapy and subject to violent anger bursts. An unstable woman with a fierce and justified revenge to wreak.'

She reached for her phone to ring Jack Loveluck, but paused. She sat on the edge of her desk and gazed out of the window. This needed thinking through. After all, it might not be Pepper sending her the messages. But if not, then who? It had to be Pepper.

She sat back down in her chair, put her feet on the desk and said softly. 'Now how can I turn this to my advantage.' And she sucked the end of her pencil and began to think deep thoughts.

Meanwhile Pepper was still working with Daly trying to work out just who was sitting where at the time of the John Small meeting in the Poachers, and they were making some progress. Jamie, the barman, was being particularly useful. He had a terrific memory. Either that or he was making it up.

There were some good clear photographs of John Small, the older lady and Lina. They already had good photographs of them dead but to see them alive for the first time was a slightly eerie experience. Particularly knowing that all three were probably only an hour or so from their deaths.

The photos of these three were not posed photos for the camera, but incidentally snapped as the diners club took pictures of each other.

They appeared in several pictures and Pepper noticed that the older woman seemed always to be peering at the younger woman, Lina. And it was a certain look that had meaning but Pepper couldn't quite put her finger on it. She would have to see if Rufus recognised her as his sister. What a breakthrough that would be, though exactly what kind of a breakthrough she couldn't yet work out.

Jack Loveluck and the Vicar were once again sitting in the back garden of the Three Wishes. Loveluck had bowed to the ever tightening of his trouser waist and had settled for a tea and a cheese and onion toasted sandwich. The Rev Toby Austin had tea and cake. A pleasant interlude.

‘I’m glad you have found time to meet me, Jack. There are a couple of things worrying me.’

Loveluck nodded for him to continue.

‘I don’t know if I ever mentioned it to you, but I have had quite some experience of, shall we say the occult or paganism in all its various forms.’

Loveluck was suitably surprised. ‘No. I didn’t know of this. Quite a man of many talents.’

‘So you might say,’ he said doubtfully. ‘Either way, I’ve been talking with Janine Pepper about this aspect of the case. She tells me it is her role to research it.’

‘Well, yes it is. But I meant computer research.’

‘Be that as it may, she came to see me about it and as we talked it became apparent that you are into some very serious elements indeed.’

Loveluck lifted a hand to stop Toby saying any more. ‘Before we go any further, can I just say that my position on all this occult and pagan business is that I don’t believe in it. At least I am not into forces and spells.’

‘Will you hear me out, Jack?’

‘Please go on.’

‘We are dealing here with the Hand of Glory.’

Loveluck shrugged. ‘The Hand of Glory being?’

‘It is a hand which is taken from a convicted and hanged murderer. Sliced off whilst he or she is still hanging. I believe you have had such an occurrence.’

Loveluck nodded. ‘Yes we have. But what can the Hand of Glory do? Does it have some kind of special powers?’

‘Yes. According to old records, if the hand is properly prepared, picked, smoked under certain conditions, then it has powers.’

‘What powers?’

The vicar repeated the conversation he had had with Pepper touching on the power to keep your foes asleep and keep your own people awake. Also to open locked doors. Loveluck listened on, his face showing clear scepticism.

‘So who has this Hand of Glory?’ continued the vicar. And how and where and on whom do they intend to use it? And what for?’

‘That I can’t tell you, except to say that at the scene of the hanging we found evidence of a group of people who may have been wearing moccasins. One of them may have been called Rufus. Rufus Nightingale from the New Forest. Apparently, he likes to hang about in the New Forest with a group of people. Probably the same people as at the scene of the hanging.. Have you heard of him?'

Toby shook his head. 'I'm not one to tell you your job, Inspector,' he said carefully putting in the rank, 'but there seem to be a lot of 'may have beens' in your statement. If you really thought that this Rufus chap had something to do with the hanging, you'd have arrested him by now.'

'True. I personally think it highly likely he is involved, but I don't have a shred of evidence linking him to it. We also found a makeshift circle at the hanging scene, made up of twigs and leaves with the footprints of five people inside it. Would that mean anything to you?'

The Rev Toby Austin, Vicar of Sherborne, looked long and hard at Loveluck. He knew fine well that Loveluck was a sceptic. A self confessed one. And he knew how difficult it was to show people the extent of pagan powers, such as they were. He settled in for a thankless task.

'Let me deal with the Hand of Glory first. Someone has hanged a murderer. That someone has also severed the left hand and is probably even now preparing it. This is not the work of someone toying with a bit of the occult. These are dangerous people who take the occult very seriously indeed. And if they do, so should you.'

They sat in silence. Loveluck in two minds and the Vicar wondering if he himself was out of his depth.

'As for the circle with five footprints in it. If they were all female I would say fairly confidently they were witches.'

'Are you being serious? In this day and age?'

'Just take a look at the streets of Sherborne today.'

Loveluck nodded acknowledgement.

'And one thing more. The Witches of Sherborne and the Witches of the New Forest have been sworn enemies for centuries. If the two covens go to battle with each other you'll see signs of spiritual power that will frighten you.'

'How many witches can we expect?' said Loveluck with concern.

'Both covens have thirteen witches. It's usual to have thirteen.'

Then with one nimble leap from a serious mood to a flippant one he said. 'Got to go Jack. I've got this wedding to arrange. If only I'd known what a kerfuffle arranging a wedding is, I would have been much kinder to the poor souls who come to the Abbey for their wedding. Particularly if it's their first marriage.' He smiled at Loveluck and stood up. 'I do tend to bully them a bit, you know.'

Loveluck smiled too. 'How is the delightful widow Albright?'

'Enchanting, as usual. Now there's a woman who knows how to bully.'

'I'm sure you'll be very happy together. Toby. Can I ask you something?'

'Go ahead.'

'Will you help us with this investigation? The aspects which you seem to be expert in.'

Toby hesitated and sat down again. 'There might be a problem there.'

'Really?'

'Yes. You see, Astra has asked me if I will sort of lead the Sherborne witches and other mystics in any confrontation with the New Forest witches. And I've agreed.'

'Astra?'

'Chief witch in the Sherborne Coven. Works in Sainsbury's during the day.'

'Then can I call on you for advice?' asked Loveluck.

'Of course, Jack. But I want a favour in exchange.'

'Name it.'

'Will you be my best man?'

Jakob sat by his tent in the New Forest. He had already packed his belongings and was preparing to move over to one of the sites in Sherborne put aside for visitors to the Psychics Fair and Witches Exhibition.

He pulled an envelope out of his rucksack. Across the seal was written 'Only to be opened in the event of my death. Ronald Nightingale.'

Well, Ronald Nightingale was dead and he had opened it the moment he had received it from Mr John Small. Inside the envelope were several copies of the letter and he read a copy now. He had made and read many copies. He read one several times a day, looking, searching for a slightest opening which would give him a clue as to whether his world was going to improve rapidly or fall apart. The stakes were high but, as always, the letter told him nothing new.

He put the envelope and contents back into his pack. Trained in the finest fighting corps in the British Army, he was calm under fire but it hid a fierce temper. A temper he had learned to keep under control but this business was trying his patience and his sanity to the limit. He knew his time in the New Forest had been largely wasted having achieved very little. His informant had told him that the Sherborne Witches were going to oppose the New Forest Witches. And that meant opposing Rufus. Jakob would join forces with the Sherborne Witches.

When Sergeants Pepper and Daly returned from the Poachers Inn they were in very high spirits. It had been a long and painstaking job finding the positions of everyone, but they had completed the task as far as it could be completed. It was as if they were actually there on the night of the murders.

Pepper had stood by the bar saying. 'John Small sat right there and the two women on either side of him. Jakob was leaning against the wall over there. Winston Gale sat here. It was like constructing a play. Telling the actors where to stand.

Daly left to do some more work on the photos and Pepper walked to her pigeon hole. She had a message from Administration. How lovely to talk of administration as someone else, not her.

But the message was surprising. Very surprising. It read, 'There are no records of the birth of Angela Nightingale on the date given by her brother Rufus Nightingale for her birthday. Not in the New Forest region or any other region. There are also no records of Angela Nightingale being born on the same day as Rufus Nightingale. Rufus Nightingale's birth certificate is on record and correct and a copy is enclosed. We can find no record of Angela Nightingale's existence.'

Chapter 24

Detective Inspector Jack Loveluck and Detective Sergeant Sadie Knightly sat in silence as the plane headed south to Malaga in Spain. They were both deep in thought and their thoughts had more in common than either of them might have deemed possible.

Knightly could see little point in the trip. The only reasons offered were that John Small used to live in the region. A retired solicitor, Ted Bassington, with little else to do except enjoy the wine and the weather had worked briefly with John Small twenty five years earlier. And finally John Small used to frequent an expat bar called the Doghouse. So she sipped her coffee and read her magazine and decided that she, too, would enjoy the wine and the weather and see what transpired.

For his part, Loveluck had somewhat higher hopes but if anything, lower expectations than Knightly. He now was fairly certain that the murders and the reasons for them were somehow tied up with the visit of Mr Nightingale to the offices of Bassington, Small and Peacock twenty five years earlier and that Rufus, Jakob and the others were involved somewhere along the line. So many people involved somewhere along the line and no clear pointers to exactly how.

For Loveluck, and CC Mackenzie who Loveluck found himself oddly in unison with, the trail had to lead to John Small. Without him the solution couldn't be guaranteed. But was he alive or dead? An elusive individual. But was he an individual or were there many John Smalls? Some paid to act the role of John Small, others paid to die if only they knew it.

Loveluck had a pad and pen with him and had written large across the top of the first page; Trip to Spain. Objectives. So far he had only one. Find John Small.

Knightly glanced at the list and turned away trying to hide a grin. She sat back and tried to decide what her own objectives were. Ten minutes hard thought later and her list was even shorter than Loveluck´s.

They had booked a rental car with satellite navigation and a lot of faith in Knightly's schoolgirl Spanish. They passed smoothly through customs and came out of the Malaga Airport terminal building into glorious, hot sunshine. They both automatically and in tandem turned their faces to feel the full heat of the sun.

'God. It makes you feel good to be alive,' said Knightly feeling the warmth doing her good already. 'Shall we have a drink?'

'I will,' said Loveluck. 'You're driving.'

Knightly felt the injustice of this and sulked slightly as they made their way to the Gambrinus bar. 'I'll have agua con gas,' she said brightly.

'I think you'd better get them,' said Loveluck a little embarrassed at his lack of language skills. 'You need to practice your Spanish. A pint for me.'

He went to sit down and Knightly ordered him a large lager and for herself a bubbly white wine. She felt good. Both the heat of the sun and the buzz of being in Spain were getting to her.

'What's that you're drinking?' he asked.

'Agua con gas.'

'Oh yeah. I thought so.'

Knightly smiled. Fizzy water. Fizzy wine. If Loveluck didn't know the difference she wasn't going to tell him. 'Cheers. And welcome to Spain.'

They collected the rental car with no problems, set the SatNav for El Pilar 28680. 28680 being the postcode. Knightly pulled out of the car park and off they went under the directions of a Spanish lady who offered them instructions in rather rapid Spanish.

Loveluck watched the SatNav screen and gave instructions in English, largely to Knightly's irritation as he had the habit of repeating them with much pointing and a raised voice.

Once they had found the motorway their progress was simple and fast. They by-passed Marbella and came off at San Pedro de Alcantara and were surprised to find themselves being taken off the main road and told they were at El Pilar.

Parking up, they walked in the direction of a bar. The Orange Tree. Walking inside and passing to the bar Loveluck tried in his best English, and with prompts from Knightly in curious Spanish, to ask for the Dog House. 'What's dog?'

'Perro,' replied Knightly.

'And house?'

'Casa.'

'Looking for the Perro Casa. Perro casa.'

The barmaid smiled at him. 'Just round the corner, love. Fifty yards.'

And indeed it was. It had a small terrace outside sheltered from the sun where small groups of people were enjoying a drink and conversation. They passed inside to what looked exactly like an English pub. Apart from the lack of real ale.

Emboldened, Loveluck went to the bar. 'A beer for me and?' he raised his eyes to Knightly waiting for her order.

'Vino de Verano.'

'You don't have to show off your Spanish. They speak English here.'

'It's called vino de verano in any language.'

They were both conscious of being watched by the people inside the bar. 'I think we're a bit over dressed, sir.'

Loveluck nodded. Everyone was in T-shirt and shorts, sun glasses and all either carried or wore hats.

The barmaid brought the drinks. 'Are you in the area on holiday? Or just passing through?'

'Neither really. We're working. In fact, I'm hoping to meet someone in this bar. Ted Bassington. Do you know him?'

She smiled. 'Everyone knows Ted.' She eyed them cautiously. 'I'm Sue. I'm one of the owners of the Doghouse.'

'Hello Sue. I'm Jack Loveluck. This is my....er....this is Sadie.'

'Are you the two police officers Ted was talking about. Come over here to find out about John Small?'

'I see that word travels fast.'

'No secrets here.'

'Detective Inspector Jack Loveluck and Detective Sergeant Sadie Knightly. How long have you been in Spain, Sue?'

'Thirty years or more.'

'So you would have known John Small.'

'Yes. He was a regular here. Lived nearby.'

'What did he look like?'

'Tall? Small?'

Susie gave a shrug. 'About average really.'

'What about his face? Anything special about it?'

'I saw too much of it, if that's what you mean? Otherwise he was sort of normal. Not a very good looking man. I suppose that's why he grew that huge beard.'

'Beard?' Loveluck and Knightly exchanged glances. 'What sort of beard?'

'Just a beard. Big and bushy. It was always wet and had bits in it. He was pretty horrible in lots of ways. I can't say I'm sorry he's dead. Can you excuse me? It's our busy time just now. We can chat later if you like.'

'Thanks, Susie. Can I get you a drink?'

'Just a two euro top-up for me,' she said flashing her ever ready half full drink. 'Red wine.'

Knightly spotted a spare table outside and they sat in the shade of the terrace, relaxing and wondering on the ever-changing John Small.

Hidden amongst the trees and bushes in the New Forest sat Jakob. His tent was erected and he was making a tasty meal of bread, cheese, pickle and tomatoes. It made a cosy scene. He was too far from the road to be seen easily, if at all, but he was suddenly and acutely aware of someone moving. Not an animal. There were plenty of those in the forest but they didn't move stealthily. This person was moving very stealthily indeed.

He sat stock still. Listening. Judging time and distance. Speed and angle of approach. Then the person stopped moving. He sat. And waited. And waited. Then he said. 'I know you're there.'

'Do you know what I have in my hand?' came the soft reply.

He didn't reply for a long time. Then he said. 'Water'

The person moved quietly up behind him, stooped and put soft hands round his throat. 'I could kill you if I wanted to.'

'Do you want to?'

'Why would I want to?' She stooped further and kissed his forehead.

He held her hand and smiled. 'But you don't want to. Do you?'

'No. Not I. But there are others who do.'

'Come, Kayra. Sit down and tell me the news. Good news would be a sweet change.'

She smiled wanly. 'The news grows worse. Rufus knows about your past.'

'I know that,' replied Jakob tetchily. 'That fool John Small told everything in that letter of invitation he sent to us all. He did it intentionally to set Rufus and me at each other's throats.'

'And a fine job he did of it,' said Kayra.

'Let me have the water.' He drank from the plastic bottle and handed it back to her. He looked at her fondly and she returned a concerned look.

'The news,' she said. 'The news is many. The police have been to visit Rufus and had a long interview with him. I don't know what was said but he seems very pleased with himself.'

Jakob threw the plastic bottle onto the ground. 'I feel so impotent. I sit here doing nothing except circle the forest and drive past the house. Rufus' house.'

'Why don't you kill him? That would solve your problems. All of them.'

Jakob watched her thoughtfully. She turned her head and began to sing in her haunting, foreign tongue. 'You have the training,' she said at last. 'In the British Army. Trained to kill. Rufus wouldn't have a chance against you.'

'And if I did that and the secret came out. Our secret. Yours, mine, Rufus'. Where would that leave me? In prison for life. That's where.'

'He'll kill you given half the chance. You know he will.'

He lay back on the grass and she moved nearer to him and stroked his temples. It seemed to calm him a little. 'Remember when we used to go camping? When we were children?'

He smiled. 'You were a wood-elf then and you still are.'

They remained in silence for a while. 'There is more news.'

Jakob groaned.

'Nemesis, the chief witch of the New Forest witches, has joined Rufus' side.'

'To hell with your witches.'

'They are a powerful force. They also have a hand of glory. And that is very powerful.'

Jakob covered his face with his hands and yawned.

'The Sherborne witches want to take on the New Forest witches. There is a very old feud between the two covens. This is their excuse to use whatever powers they can muster to defeat the other coven.

'If we move quickly, Jakob, we can organise the Sherborne coven.'

'Keep your damned witches to yourself. I'm an army man. We deal in bullets. Go back to Rufus before he misses you.'

'And the police deal in prisons,' she replied sharply. 'It needs to look like an accident. We're all going to the big psychic fair tomorrow in Sherborne. Many of the women are already there. Setting up stalls. Working. I'll look for opportunities. For an accident, I mean.'

Jakob took his hands away from his face and smiled. 'I don't know what I'd do without you.'

She smiled back. 'I know.' And she stared lovingly at his face.

Back in the Sherborne police station Sergeant Daly was also staring at Jakob's face. But not quite so lovingly.

'Are you sure?' said Pepper. Absolutely certain?'

'You heard what Jamie said. 'That's him' were his words. We have a photo of Jakob. That's a real breakthrough.'

Pepper appeared unconvinced. 'So. We have a photo of Jakob. And a very poor photograph it is. Would you recognise him if you saw him in the street?'

Daly had to admit that he probably wouldn't recognise him anywhere except in the exact same place in the Poachers as he was in the photograph.

'Where does that take us anyway? That's all we know about him. He stood against that wall a couple of weeks ago. Hardly damning evidence.'

Daly gave her a knowing look.

'Now what are you thinking?'

He slowly walked about the room. 'I have been having quite a few thoughts about our Jakob recently. And even more thoughts about Mrs Preston. Remember her?'

'Yes. The old dear who was staying at the Poachers and watched folk come and go.'

Daly nodded. 'She told us some very interesting things indeed. I think her evidence hasn't been given sufficient weight. Or followed up.' He watched her ponder the point. 'But I have something even more important to tell you.'

'Get on with it then. What is it?'

He smiled and said. 'I've put in for a transfer. I'm hoping to be leaving Sherborne nick for somewhere else.'

It was a cruel twist of fate that brought Sergeant Daly and Sergeant Pepper to sit and look with joy and some pride at the poor photograph of Jakob.

Had it been Inspector Loveluck and Sergeant Knightly who had seen the photograph their reaction would have been very different. But they hadn't seen the picture. Daly and Pepper had considered sending a copy by email to Loveluck, but preferred to keep the big surprise until Loveluck and Knightly had returned home.

A decision that was to cost lives.

Instead they sent the excellent photograph of the older lady and Lisa.

Back at Wootton Bridge in the New Forest, the car park had several cars in it. Kayra was back from her visit to Jakob and was once again in the stream singing in her strange foreign language. A full coven of thirteen New Forest witches stood and talked tactics of how to deal with the Sherborne witches.

The four men of the group sat in silence. They knew the confrontation would be ugly and possibly bloody. They knew also that much was at stake but were ignorant of the details.

Nemesis sat on a log staring lovingly at the Hand of Glory. She felt a shiver of excitement at the power of the relict she held in her hand. The dead man's hand. Taken from a hanging corpse.

She called the others together. The witches, the men, Kayra and Rufus. She spoke impressively.

'We leave for Sherborne very soon. We will need all the combined force of your powers. The coven powers, the powers of our men. The leadership of Rufus. And.' Here she stopped and showed them the Hand of Glory. 'The most powerful of all. The Hand of Glory. They cannot defend against this. Let us begin to bring out the power of the Hand.'

She nodded at one of the men who used two pieces of wood to tap out a rhythm. And they chanted.

Now open, lock!
To the Dead Man's knock!
Fly, bolt, and bar, and band!

Nor move, nor swerve,
Joint, muscle, or nerve,

At the spell of the Dead Man's hand!

Sleep, all who sleep! -- Wake, all who wake!
But be as the dead for the Dead Man's sake!'

In Sainsbury's in Sherborne a cold shiver passed through the body of Astra, Chief witch to the Sherborne coven.

Chapter 25

Loveluck and Knightly checked into their hotel rooms and met at an arranged time in the hotel restaurant for an early dinner.

They chatted of inconsequentials, had a little fun with the Spanish menu which had an English translation of the Spanish dishes. Scrambled eggs became broken eggs and in this harmless way they spent a pleasant and relaxing time.

Over coffee they began to plan out their objectives both for the evening and for the weekend. They felt they could do little more than chat to Sue behind the bar and the locals and elicit what they could about John Small, where he had lived and who he knew best all in the hope of some snippet leading to greater things.

The demeanour showed two people with little faith in their chances of success.

It was at dinner that the photograph of the older lady and Lina arrived on Knightly's phone. 'Look at that,' she said excitedly passing her phone to Loveluck. He peered intently at the shot. 'You don't have to look that carefully to see that they are mother and daughter.'

'They are certainly very similar,' he conceded.

'Are you saying that you don't think they're mother and daughter?'

'No. Family resemblance is striking. I agree, Mother and daughter.'

Loveluck looked good in his choice of clothes for Spain. Casual. Chinos, smart sports shirt and light jacket. Knightly looked stunning in a little white dress and heels.

As they stepped outside the evening was very warm and Loveluck took off his jacket and put it in the back of the car. The sun was still out though having lost some of its burning heat of the day.

It was perfect.

As they drove the short distance to El Pilar and the Doghouse Knightly asked. 'Do you think she'll be here?'

'She? You mean Sammy?'

'Yes. We know she came to Spain. It's my guess she'll have come here. Perhaps John Small is here and she's joined him.'

Loveluck glanced at her. 'You really think he's still alive, don't you?'

She nodded firmly. 'I'm convinced of it. He's a string puller. A man of many faces, or none depending how you look at it. Laying a path for us to chase our tails trying to follow. He's alive all right.'

Loveluck reflected on this. 'You could be right. How do you think Sammy fits into all this?'

'Sammy! She's another manipulative piece of work. Secretary and house keeper? I don't think so!'

They parked as close as they could to the Doghouse and strolled the short distance to the bar. Plenty of people were sitting in the covered outside part of the bar but fewer inside.

They were surprised not to find Sue behind the bar. They asked the new barmaid if Sue would be in later that evening.

'Yes. Susie will be in any time. She'll be behind the bar soon. I'm Rose. Sue and I own the Doghouse together. I assume you are the two people from the UK doing some investigating?'

Loveluck ordered drinks. 'John Small. Do you know him?'

'Never heard of him. I've been in Spain for years and years but not so long at the Doghouse.'

They took their drinks and moved away from the counter. 'Bit of a washout this is turning out to be,' said Loveluck with a sigh.

'Excuse me, good people' said a loudish voice. 'I'm Roger. Excuse me if I sit down. I buggered most of my body up playing rugger until I was nigh on forty, and time has buggered the rest of it. I play golf almost every day now. I play like a tosser because nothing works properly but I still get out there and play. And then I come to the bar. What are you drinking?'

Amid protests he offered a round of drinks.

'I understand you're asking about John Small? Want to know who killed him. Have a look on the board up there,' he said pointing. 'My money's on Stan-the-man. Hard bugger who didn't like Small. Nobody liked Small.'

Knightly went to look at the board. 'Who's Nick the Dick? He sounds promising.'

'Nasty bit of work. You don't want to cross him.'

'Tell me, Roger. What do you know of Samantha Alcock? You must have seen her plenty of times. Likes to be called Sammy.'

'Never heard of her. Do you want to sit on my knee? Er...'

'Sadie.'

'Sexy Sadie. Like in the Beatles song?'

'Dunno. Some might think I'm sexy, I suppose. Tell me about John Small. What did he look like?'

'Ugly bastard. Not you. I mean Small.'

'What way ugly?'

'Just sort of ugly. Used to hide his face behind a big beard. Probably to hide from the clients he had swindled out of money. I'm not sad to hear that he's been murdered.'

'Well now. That's just it. He may still be alive. We might have been mistaken when we thought he'd been killed. Where did he live?'

'I don't know. He had an apartment just up the road, but I know he also had a villa somewhere. Here. Susie might know.' He turned to flag down Sue who had just walked in the bar.

'Sue. Where did John Small live? The flat he had near here?'

'La fuente del paraiso. Ted Bassington lives there now. It's just a hundred yards or so away. I'll show you if you like?'

They left their drinks with Roger and started along the road. Knightly asked. 'Do you know a woman called Samantha Alcock. A friend of John Small.'

She shook her head thoughtfully. 'No. I never saw him with a woman. I mean, not a close friend or girlfriend.'

'I understand he also had a villa somewhere.'

'Yes he did. I don't know where it was. Somewhere in Guadalmina Baja. Sorry. That's a place just a mile or two up the road.'

They came to large gates with 'La fuente del paraiso' on them and Sue tapped a code into an entry device and the gates buzzed open.'

'Seems like you've been here before,' said Knightly with a smile.

'Too often. We have to help Ted Bassington home from time to time when he's had a glass or two too many.'

They walked through beautifully kept gardens, passed a swimming pool and several apartments, and along a path until they arrived at the apartment. Sue knocked on the door several times and was about to let herself in when Ted opened the door to them.

Sue left them as she had to get back to the bar and Ted invited them in.

'Just going to the Doghouse myself to see a chap, you know. Do you want to look round? It's quite spacious for an old chap like me.'

They wandered onto the terrace which was also spacious and held a table, sofa and a collection of pot plants.

'I spend most of my time out here,' said Ted. The evidence was plain to see. Two glasses and three bottles of wine. 'Shall we go to the Doghouse now?'

The evening at the Doghouse livened up by degrees until it became a very jolly evening indeed. Loveluck and Knightly decided on a taxi for later and so settled down to talking with new found friends and drinking the largest gin and tonics they had ever seen.

Knightly was in full flirt and Loveluck in very high spirits cosying up to Susie.

Olwen Evans strode purposefully into Sherborne police station and asked for Inspector Anderson. She was duly directed to his office and found him sitting there with his feet on the table and a half full cup of cold coffee balanced on his forehead.

'Bravo, Inspector,' she said clapping. 'The age of variety isn't dead yet.'

Anderson laughed and, slightly embarrassed, stood up and shook Olwen firmly by the hand. 'It's my grandson's birthday on Sunday and I always do a few party tricks. Card tricks and a bit of magic.'

'I am impressed beyond words, Inspector. All I can do is waggle my ears. Not a mean feat, though. It's not as easy as it looks. Do you want to see me do it.'

Anderson laughed. 'I'll save that pleasure for another time.'

They let the moment linger then moved into business gear. 'I suppose you are here about the publicity we're giving to certain people's names and faces. Trying to fill in a lot of background detail to the case.'

'That's why I'm here my fancy prestidigitator.' She looked squarely and appraisingly at him. 'You know, Inspector. I think you are my hero.'

Anderson blushed.

'Are you sure you don't want to see me waggle my ears?

Anderson smiled. Save it for a rainy day.

She smiled at this avuncular, friendly policeman. ‘Come on then. Let’s see what you have for me.’

Anderson hesitated. ‘I suppose you must have been surprised when you got my invitation to meet me here at the station.’

‘Surprised hardly describes it. I thought you must have had an ambush set to kidnap that amoral woman from the Gazette. Scarlet woman of the press I have heard myself described by you.’

‘And with good reason too, at the time. But I want to put out the hand of friendship and make use of your great hold of the public.’

‘Steady on boy. You’ll have me blushing next. Give me the details.’

Anderson laid before her the mock-up of the names.

“Do these names mean anything to you? Jakob, Lina, John Small, Samantha Alcock (likes to be known as Sammy), Rufus, Winston. If so please contact Sherborne police on....” and the mock-up went into contact details.

‘What do you think?’

She nodded. ‘Not bad. Why have you only given John Small’s and Samantha’s surname? I understand you have more surnames. Winston and Rufus.’

Anderson shook his head in disbelief. ‘Where do you get your information from? Heaven known that Sherborne is full of witches at the moment, but none to match you.’

‘You silver tongued old devil,’ she said with a smile. ‘I’ll gloss it up a bit but it will tell exactly the same message. I heard you had some photos. And before you start it’s very unlikely we’ll print photos of the dead.’

‘I was thinking of trying the names first. Then the photos if nothing comes of the names.’

‘No stiffs,’ Olwen said firmly.

‘No. We have live photos now of quite a few of the main players in this affair.’

‘Good. I’ll knock a piece up for the names. My editor, as always, is happy to help the police. At your service.’ She turned to go then turned back. ‘Is Jack Loveluck around?’

‘No. He isn’t.’

‘Do you know when he’s likely to be in?’

‘Not until next week. He’s gone to Spain as part of the enquiry. He and Sergeant Knightly are following up some leads.’

'Knightly! He's gone for a weekend in Spain with Knightly! Old Miss 'perfect cheekbones' herself. I see.'

She strode out of the station with the headlines already forming in her head. "Senior police officer and young female sergeant on jaunt to Spain at taxpayers' expense". 'So. Take sexy Sadie Knightly instead of me, would you? Without so much as a word, would you? Once again we will see if my pen is mightier than your truncheon Inspector Jack bloody Loveluck.'

As William Congrave would have said, "Heaven has no rage like love to hatred turned, Nor hell a fury like a woman scorned"

Chapter 26

Loveluck was lying in bed the following morning when a sharp tapping came on his bedroom door.

'Sir? Can you wake up sir?' This brought no response from Loveluck, deep in sleep from travelling for hours and a rather more than usual alcohol intake at the Doghouse. 'Sir?' The tapping turned to banging. No reply.

She took out her phone and rang his mobile. It rang and rang and she offered an apologetic smile to the two men waiting with her. 'He's old fashioned in some ways. He often turns his phone off.'

The blank and bleak look she received back from one of the men, clearly the main man, made her shudder.

She banged again. 'Sir,' she yelled. No response.

The main man nodded. 'Your room.'

'Can't we talk here?' she said nervously.

'Your room. Now.' They moved three doors down the corridor and she unlocked her door, then hesitated.

'In you go. Don't worry. You're quite safe with me.'

Strangely, that made her feel quite safe with him. But she was a police officer and she could recognise a dangerous man when she saw one. And she saw one now. He was average height, quite good looking in a suave way, London accent and a clear aura of violence. They stepped inside.

'I'm known as Stan the man,' he said when the door was safely shut behind him. 'You might have heard of me.'

'I've heard the name,' she said.

'I understand that I'm the prime prize suspect in the Doghouse raffle for "Who killed Cock Robin". Only in this case it's "Who killed John Small" Am I correct?'

'Perfectly correct.'

‘I think it’s time I paid a visit to the Doghouse. Sell them a little health insurance. I don’t like people making fun of me.’

‘I don’t think they were doing that.’

‘I understand it was Rugger Bugger Roger put my name forward.’ Knightly shrugged her “I don’t know” reply. ‘I don’t think he’s got any bones left to break that haven’t been broken already. That’s a pity. I like Roger. Used to like him, should I say.’

‘What is it you want?’ said Knightly a lot more boldly than she felt.

‘You and your copper buddy are down here looking for John Small. Correct?’

‘Correct again.’

‘I want him.’

‘So do I.’

He took a step closer to her. ‘I want him more. Got it? Any info comes to light about him, I want to see it. Any hint of where he might be, I want to hear it. You following me little girl.’

‘Perfectly,’ she said firmly then turned to pour coffee. ‘Little man.’

There was a silence and the second man took a step back. He didn’t say ‘Here comes trouble’ but it was written all over his face.

‘Where do you think he is?’

‘I’ve got no idea,’ said Knightly. ‘Have you?’

He walked to the coffee tray and indicated that he wanted coffee. She indicated that he was welcome and so the dumb show rolled on.

‘I don’t know where he is,’ he said. ‘But I haven’t come all the way from the UK to look for him. I heard he was dead and that you were looking for his killer. Which is true? Are you looking for Small, or his killer.’

Knightly considered this and then decided to tell him about it. Who knows. The police had worked with villains for information since the force was first formed.

‘OK. I’ll tell you. We don’t know if he is alive or dead. He’s a slippery customer.’

‘You can say that again,’ said Stan the man helping himself to biscuits.

‘Do you know Samantha Alcock? Calls herself Sammy.’

He nodded his head. ‘Heard the name. That’s all.’

They were disturbed by a sleepy and hung over looking Loveluck who let himself into the room.

‘What time’s breakfast?’ Then he stopped as he saw the two strangers. The he looked at Stan the Man closely. ‘Well I’ll be damned. Stan Barrett. Stan the man. Haven’t seen you in years.’

‘Of all the lousy coppers I had to bump into I get Jack Loveluck. How the hell are you?’

The two men embraced to the astonishment of both Knightly and the silent second visitor.

‘When I saw the name Stan the man on the raffle board I thought of you. But every two bit pickpocket in London calls himself Stan the man. You’re the original.’

The two of them went off into Loveluck’s room for a private conflab leaving Knightly and the silent second man.

‘Interesting man, you’re boss,’ she said.

‘Father. He’s my father.’

And as that seemed to be both the beginning and end of the conversation she sat down to read a magazine and he stood there shuffling his feet and staring at the wall.

In Sherborne the witch’s coven was in emergency session. Firm word had reached them that the New Forest witches were to visit the psychic fair and witches exhibition and whilst there use their powers to settle some dispute. They were vague on the reasons for the dispute or even who the dispute was between, but they knew that they had a chance to clash with the New Forest coven and any reason was good enough for that.

‘Nemesis is already here, though I hear that she travels up daily from the New Forest. She has a stall in the Digby memorial church hall.’

The ladies of the coven exchanged nervous glances. Astra was a fine and powerful leader of the coven, but Nemesis was known far and wide as being one of the finest witches in the country. They were convening in the small church hall in Digby Road, not far from the Digby memorial church hall. It was cold.

‘I hear they have a Hand of Glory,’ said one of the women.

‘And it’s true,’ replied Astra. ‘I felt its power today. I have a plan forming of how we can counter their forces.’

‘Counter the hand of glory?’ asked one in astonishment.

‘Certainly,’ said Astra with great if empty bravado.

They huddled into conversation as to how best to fight the New Forest coven. Ideas for spells came thick and fast and they were down to two main spells of attack when the door opened and the vicar of Sherborne, Rev Toby Austin came in.

'Sorry I'm late ladies. Vicar duties called.'

He was followed into the room by a small, slender girl who hummed softly to herself. 'This is Kayra,' he said. 'She has a story to tell.'

'Too late for stories. We need action.'

The vicar calmed them down. 'I think you should listen to this story.'

This quietened them and they stopped and stared at this waif like girl. Kayra held out her hands and danced in a small circle singing a tune with words which nobody understood.

'What are you doing, Kayra?'

She smiled sweetly and danced on. 'I'm dancing with my brothers and sisters.'

In two seconds Kayra had grown in stature and held the women in awe. 'Come dance with us.' And the coven of thirteen witches, Kayra, the vicar and the brothers and sisters that an outsider couldn't see danced to the sweet singing in that sweet foreign tongue.

The singing stopped. The dancing stopped. 'Go now, children. Go home.' She waved the children goodbye and turned to face the women.

Kayra now spoke quietly, clearly and carefully in a sing-song voice. Everyone strained to listen.

'In the New Forest in Hampshire there is a man named Rufus. Rufus is a bad man. Also in the New Forest there is a man called Jakob. Jakob is a good man.

'Rufus and Nemesis and all the New Forest witches are trying to kill Jakob.'

'Why?' asked one of the women.

'Because Rufus is a bad man.'

'The reason? What's the reason?'

'Jakob needs help to stop Rufus and the witches from killing him. I want you to help. The Sherborne coven. And the vicar as well. The vicar is a knowledgeable and powerful man. I'll join you too.'

Quiet conversations went on round the room. Discontent was everywhere. Only the hatred of the New Forest Coven held them together.

'Why are Rufus and Jakob trying to kill each other?' But in reply all they got was the same lilting tune sung in words they didn't understand.

'Is it true they have a Hand of Glory?'

Kayra bowed and smiled sweetly. 'Yes they have.'

'In the hands of Nemesis that could be too much for us. How do we defend against the hand of Glory?'

'Easy. Very easy,' said Kayra humming.

'How?' came the desperate reply. 'How!'

Kayra danced a short but intricate dance around the small hall and swept up to Astra until they were nose to nose. 'Kill Nemesis,' was the harsh answer.

Inspector Anderson walked into his office to see Sergeant Daly leaning back in Anderson's chair. 'Comfy enough for you, sergeant?'

'Sorry, sir. I was waiting for you and I didn't want to miss you.'

'That's all right. What do you want me for?'

'There are a few things which I don't think have been covered very thoroughly.'

'Anything I've done?' he asked jokingly.

'Yes sir.'

'Oh. I see. You'd better tell me all about it,' he said pulling another chair up to the desk and joining Daly in a lounging position.

'It's about Mrs Preston.'

'I thought that Sergeant Knightly and I did a pretty good job on Mrs Preston. Got a lot of information out of her. Good information.'

'I agree, sir. It was a good job. But not good enough.' Daly was aware that these were strong words to use on his boss but he continued. 'I think there were things that should have been followed up. She saw Jakob arrive with the older lady with a strange accent. I believe she spoke to Jakob.

'I don't think she did. Does it matter?'

'Yes it does,' said Daly adjusting his position to a more dynamic one. 'I would like to know if they had the same accent. I would like to know that very much.'

Anderson pondered these words carefully. 'You think they might be mother and son?'

'I think it very possible. They arrived on the motorbike together. Odd thing to do for a stranger.'

Anderson sniffed. 'Yes. I suppose you're right. Mind you, dragging your elderly mother around on a motor bike isn't exactly a common sight.'

'Could be a financial necessity. They can't afford a car, perhaps'

'You're good at theorising. And I liked your Theory 25. So did the Chief Constable, I understand. You're performing well.'

'Which brings me to another matter I wasn't going to mention until later, but now seems as good a time as any.'

'Go on.'

'I've put in for a transfer. You might know that already.'

'No I haven't heard anything yet. But I will soon. And I can't say I'm surprised.'

'No. I'm sick and tired, sir, of desk-bound research work on the computer. I'm a Detective Sergeant. But I'm not detecting. Not really.'

'I know. I know. And I take responsibility for not getting you out and about sooner. I'm sorry, lad.'

'Me too gramps.'

They both smiled. 'I'll give you the best reference possible, and you'll have earned every word. But I'll miss you.'

They sat in an embarrassed silence for a while.

'Getting back to the case,' said Daly. 'I think it is possible that the older lady who was murdered and Jakob were mother and son. Let's assume that's true for a while. This might be a sort of family gathering. Look. I've got something else to show you.'

He took some photographs out of a folder and laid them on the table. They showed clearly Mr John Small, the older lady and Lina, the younger girl.'

'If Lina is her name,' warned Anderson.

'Let's call her Lina for now.' It showed Lina looking in the direction of the camera, John Small looking down at presumably some papers or his lunch and the older lady looking at Lina. 'What kind of look would you call that?'

Anderson peered carefully at the photograph and a small smile passed over his lips. 'I think I know what you're getting at.'

'Look at this next picture,' said Daly with enthusiasm.

It showed the older lady and Lina both laughing out loud and staring straight into the camera.

Anderson smiled broadly. 'If that isn't mother and daughter I'll eat my hat.'

Daly nodded in satisfaction. ‘Perhaps I’ll make a decent detective one day.’

‘That day’s already arrived.’

‘So it could be,’ said Daly hurrying along, ‘that we have mother, son and daughter here. A family gathering.’

Anderson waved to Daly to slow down. Let’s take a longer look at this. There was dinner booked for five. Only three turned up. John Small, the older lady who we will now call mother, and Lina. Two were missing. Let’s assume that Jakob was one of them. So who was the fifth person? And why didn’t Jakob join them? And what about Winston Gale, the unfortunate hanging man. What was he doing there? Was he a member of the family?’

Daly shook his head firmly. ‘Definitely not. We know a lot about Winston Gale from police records. His background was completely different.’

‘Have you got a photo of Jakob? A decent one.’

‘I’ve got two photos of him. One is no good at all and the other is not too bad, but not good.’

Anderson peered at the photos of Jakob leaning against the door. ‘Try the police lab. And get their view about the mother and daughter connection. If these three were a family group, then I’m sure it means something but I’m not at all sure what.’

Daly left the office and Anderson leaned back in his chair. ‘I’d give a lot to know who the fifth person was who didn’t turn up,’ he said to no one in particular.

Sergeant Pepper and the vicar of Sherborne sat down in a pew in Sherborne Abbey.

‘I hear you are leading the Sherborne forces against the New Forest forces. What will the bishop think?’

‘What will the Widow Albright say is more to the point. The wedding’s nearly on us and I don’t have two minutes to pay her attention. Or to do my job for that matter.’

‘How serious is this supposed feud that’s going on?’ she asked.

‘Deadly serious as far as I can tell. Two men are feuding. In the red corner is someone called Rufus from the New Forest who has teamed up with the New Forest witches.’

‘And in the blue corner?’

‘A strange young man called Jakob who has teamed up with the Sherborne witches. And a strange young girl called Kayra who has teamed up with both sides.’

‘And you?’

‘I’d like to think that I was in the middle trying to keep the peace.’

‘And are you?’

‘No.’

‘So, what’s your position?’

He leaned forward conspiratorially and he was wise to do so for Simon Peter, the new curate was sitting very silently behind a pillar within earshot of his vicar. ‘My position is this. There is no doubt that the New Forest witches are more powerful than the Sherborne witches. And they have the Hand of Glory. This makes Rufus more powerful than Jakob and I hear that Rufus is suspected of the murder of Winston Gale and also of the murder of the three people at the Poachers Inn.’

Pepper shrugged indecisively.

‘Which means he could murder Jakob who, as far as I can tell, is a charming young man.’

‘I’m not sure Rufus is a suspect. There is some very poor circumstantial evidence which might link him to the scene of the hanging. That’s all.’

‘Even so,’ continued the vicar, ‘I think the War of the Witches will be a very one sided affair in favour of the New Forest contingent. If it turns nasty, I will offer the Sherborne witches sanctuary in the abbey. It is the most I can do. The best I can do.’

They sat in silence for a while.

‘What do you really make of all this witches business, Toby? Do you believe any of it?’

He gave her a tired smile. ‘Janine. If I can believe in God I can believe in witches and their powers. If I can believe in heaven and hell then I can believe in other worlds. If I can believe in the resurrection of Christ I can believe in Astral projection. I deal in beliefs. It is my life and my ministry. It isn’t for me to mock or denigrate other people’s beliefs.’

They sat in another pleasant silence. ‘Toby. You are a remarkable man.’

He sat up straight. ‘I just hope I can keep people safe from harm in this struggle.’

‘Do you know what the feud is about?’

He shook his head. 'No. Do you?'

She shook her head. 'No. It all seems to revolve around John Small. And we can't find him.'

'Go and ask one of the psychics where he is.'

'Are you serious?'

'Yes. Go and tell a psychic the story as far as police protocol allows. There are dozens and dozens of them there. Use them. But don't use one called Nemesis. She is leader of the New Forest coven.'

She stood up and turned to walk away but stopped. 'Have you been to one of the psychics?'

'Yes I have.'

'In your entire vicar's garb? Dog collar and all?'

'Of course.'

She sat down again. 'Don't they think it's strange you going to a psychic?'

'Why should they. Psychics go to church. Some of them anyway.'

'Yes but, psychics believe in magic and things. So different from you.'

He smiled and took her by the hand. 'What do you think the raising of Lazarus from the dead was? The feeding of the five thousand?'

'They were miracles,' she said firmly.

Toby laughed. 'And you find it easy to believe in miracles but not in magic? What's the difference?'

'Well. Jesus performed the miracles. He was special. These are just ordinary men and women.'

'Jesus was a carpenter's son. Jesus could be sitting out there in my hall right now waiting for you to go to him for help.'

She sat mesmerised for a spell, then said. 'You are the most remarkable man I have ever met.'

'Go to the psychics. Who knows. Jesus might be waiting for you. And he really *would* be a remarkable man to meet. I must go Janine.'

Janine watched him walk away and then turned to leave. She had got halfway to the door when she was overtaken by Simon Peter, the curate.

'I need a word with you before you go,' he said brusquely.

'I beg your pardon.'

'I need a word with you. You've just been talking with the vicar. I need to know what you were talking about.'

‘Get out of my way.’ She tried to push past him but he grabbed her arm tightly.

‘What were you talking about! Tell me. Tell me. I order you’

Pepper said through gritted teeth. ‘I will give you three seconds to let go of my arm and get out of my way before I do it for you.’

I need to know what you were talking about and you *will* tell me’ he said holding her arm even tighter and stressing the word “will”.

And then the floodgates burst. Everything flashed before her eyes. The evil men who pushed her into a coffin despite her cries and struggles. The evil smiles as they carried her out to the field and put her in the grave. The cruel jokes of ‘We’ll be back next week to get you out.’ The cold, the terror of being buried alive. Of dying. The treatment, the anger therapy. All to no avail now as another man tried to force her into telling him things. Only this time there would be no grave.

The anger and the fury burst out of her like an explosion. She screamed and howled at him, she tore herself free and attacked him with the strength of the wronged and the training of the police. He went to the ground and she hit him and kicked him and screamed at him time and time and time again.

Other people in the abbey shied away and hid from this mad woman. The vicar had already left the church.

How far she would have gone is impossible to tell. Two brave men in the church tried to overpower her and she screamed at them and attacked them too. In a matter of a few minutes, uniformed police arrived on the scene, overpowered her, arrested her, handcuffed her and took her to the coffin of a police cell. There she collapsed in an exhausted and spent heap.

Doctors were called. She was taken away. She was subjugated, sedated, her details tabulated, her files were in piles and she became as helpless as if she had been put into a coffin and buried alive again.

She rested.

Chapter 27

Sergeant Knightly and the son of Stan the man kept their silent vigil. Knightly had showered, dressed and was sitting reading a magazine. The young man was staring at a banal painting on the hotel with the same intensity that he might have stared at the Mona Lisa.

It was with some relief that the door opened and Stan stuck his head in and said to his son. 'C'mon you.' He nodded acknowledgement at Knightly and left. Outside he said to Loveluck. 'Remember what I said Jack. Consider John Small dead. I don't know if he's dead or not but you consider him dead. If you do find him, you'll know why.' The two men shook hands. 'I might pop into the Doghouse tonight. Just to put the wind up Roger. Nice to see you again Jack. Are you diddling your young sergeant?'

'No. Of course not.'

Stan shrugged. 'It takes all sorts. Maybe see you tonight.'

Loveluck watched him walk away. Knightly joined him in the corridor. 'Now there walks a man with a story to tell,' said Loveluck. And half the police districts in the UK would love to hear it.'

'I quite liked him,' said Knightly airily. 'We've missed breakfast.'

'I'll buy you breakfast in a bar somewhere.'

'You're very generous kind sir. With the police budget.'

In fact they drove into Estepona and had a late breakfast on the sea front, sitting outside a bar and watching the Med lazily lap up to within ten yards of their feet.

'Could you live in a place like this?' asked Loveluck.

'Like a shot. Couldn't you?'

Loveluck shrugged. 'Maybe.' He shuffled uneasily in his seat.

'Are you all right, sir?'

‘Yes. I’m fine.’ In truth his belt felt tight and his diet had hit the buffers since they landed in Spain. ‘Did you notice anything odd about Ted Bassington’s flat yesterday?’

‘Yes sir.’

‘What?’

‘Two glasses on the terrace table. He didn’t look like the sort of man to have house guests. He likes to do his drinking in the Doghouse. Didn’t you find that odd?’

‘I don’t know if I did or not,’ said Loveluck. ‘Two glasses and three bottles of wine. It could be that he poured a glass of wine, put the glass down. Forgot where he had put it and got another glass.’

‘Not so, Inspector Loveluck. I may not be a domestic goddess but I can spot how these things work. Follow my deductions carefully.’

Loveluck smiled. ‘Yes, Holmes.’

‘The man has a cleaner who comes in probably every day or every other day.’

‘How do you know that?’

‘The place was spic and span. Do you think that Ted Bassington dons his pinny and goes round the place with his feather duster every day?’

‘She didn’t do a very good job of the terrace. Three wine bottles!’

‘I don’t think she does the terrace. The bottles, the glasses. And did you notice the newspapers? Days old. No. That’s his little domain and she doesn’t go there. That’s my theory anyway.’

Loveluck mulled it over. ‘You might be right. But both glasses could have been his.’

‘My money is on him having someone there for a drink.’

‘It’s hardly against the law. Leave the poor man alone.’

Knightly relaxed. ‘I expect you’re right. What did your friend Stan the man tell you? Anything useful?’

‘Not really. He said to consider John Small dead, whether he was or not. If we did find him we’d know why.’

‘Meaning?’

‘Your guess is as good as mine.’

They sat in an uncomfortable silence. ‘We’re not getting anywhere,’ she said flatly. ‘We need to speak to the Spanish police. See what they have on him. He can’t live here all these years without leaving some kind of footprint, probably in the form of a paper trail.’

‘We can probably get them to find out where this villa is he owns,’ said Loveluck. ‘That would be something at least. We’ll try the Doghouse this lunchtime. Perhaps pick up some tittle tattle. OK. Next stop Marbella police station. Do you have the directions?'

'Yes. Do you want me to drive?'

'Si.'

Knightly smiled. 'Perfecto.'

They drove into Marbella and got caught up in the town centre traffic. Sitting at the traffic lights idly watching the passers by Knightly suddenly opened her door and started to get out. 'Take the wheel. Park up somewhere,' she said urgently.

'You can't get out here.'

But she already had. 'There,' she shouted over the hooting horns. The lights were green, 'Going into that restaurant,'

'Who?' asked Loveluck desperately.

'Sammy. Samantha Alcock.'

Knightly dashed across the busy duel carriageway that ran through the centre of Marbella whilst Loveluck ran the gauntlet of hooting horns and angry shouts to get into the driver's seat just in time for the lights to turn red again and the hooting increased.

Knightly ran into the restaurant which was closed except for the cleaners and waiting staff who were setting up for the lunchtime session. She ran towards the kitchen and stopped when Sammy and a cleaner spun round to see who had just rushed in.

For Knightly it was a moment of complete understanding and for Sammy it was a moment of complete discovery as the two women stared at each other in thunderstruck astonishment. Knightly's face said "I know everything now" and Samantha's face said "I have been discovered". But within seconds that flash of inspiration and knowledge had fled from Knightly's brain and as it did a sly smile crept onto Samantha's face.

Frustration filled Knightly as she pleaded in vain for that half-second of knowledge to return. Like having a word on the tip of your tongue but you just can't bring it to mind. Then it was gone.

What was that spark that flashed in Knightly's brain the second their eyes had met? A spark they both recognised and understood.

'Sergeant Knightly. How lovely to see you. You should have told me you were coming to Marbella. We could have met up for a drink or a nice meal like we had in the Gordleton Mill.'

'I want to talk to you, Samantha.'

'Call me Sammy.'

'Can we go somewhere?'

'Of course we can, dear. Mariposa here is my cleaner. When she's not working for this restaurant, of course. I've just come to ask her to come in a couple of mornings this week to do a bit of cleaning.'

She broke off into rapid Spanish as the arrangement was made.

'Where's your nice inspector what's his name.'

'Loveluck.'

'That's him. Inspector Loveluck.'

'Probably being lynched by a horde of angry motorists by the sound of it.' They both listened to the noise.

'Let's have a small drink and a chat, shall we?' said Sammy. 'Nice little bar just a couple of doors along the road.'

They seated themselves at a table on the street and waited for coffee. Loveluck had called to find out where they were and they waited patiently for him to appear.

'Your Spanish is very good.'

'I have a bit of a gift for languages. Don't know why. I was never much good at anything else at school.'

'I need to ask you a couple of questions. Who was the small man who you went to the Gordleton Mill with for a month or two most nights.'

'Who do you think it was?'

'I have no idea who it was. That's why I'm asking.'

'Course you know. It was Mr Small. John Small'

'Then who was the man you identified that day in Bournemouth. Remember identifying the body?'

'Yes of course I do. It was very distressing. Poor Mr Small.'

'Mr Small in the Gordleton Mill was five foot five inches tall. Mr Small in the morgue was five foot ten inches tall. And if their heights differed by so much one might well assume they were different people with different faces. Why did you say it was John Small?'

'Because it was,' said Sammy sobbing. 'I thought it was. I was very upset at seeing him like that.'

Knightly leaned back in her chair. That was Sammy's story and she was clearly sticking to it.

Loveluck joined them. 'Hello Samantha. Are you all right?'

She dabbed her eyes theatrically and said sadly. 'Yes thank you. I was just thinking of my poor, dead Mr Small. He was very good to me.' Loveluck and Knightly passed amused glances.

'Where do you stay when you are in Marbella?' asked Loveluck.

'Usually in an hotel. A cheap hotel.'

‘Let me rephrase that. Where are you staying on this trip?’

‘Nowhere special.’

‘Sammy!’

‘An old friend of Mr Small is putting me up.’

‘Not called Ted is he by any chance, Sammy?’

‘What if he is? Not against the law is it?’

‘Ted Bassington?’

‘All right. Yes it’s Ted Bassington. What’s your problem? And why do you keep hounding me? Why can’t you leave me alone?’

‘OK. Will you come and talk to us tonight in the Doghouse?’ asked Loveluck.

‘In the where?’

‘In the Doghouse. Ted’s local pub.’

‘Oh that place. I’ve never been in there. Don’t like the look of it.’

‘Why not?’

‘Just don’t. Can I go now?’ She started to stand up and Loveluck gave her the nod. See you tonight.’

Sammy left the table and Loveluck played with his coffee cup. ‘Do you think she’ll turn up tonight?’

Knightly shook her head. ‘I doubt it. We can’t make her. Anyway, what can we get out of her? She claims she knows nothing and perhaps it’s true.’

‘You don’t believe that.’

Knightly smiled. ‘No I don’t. I think the scheming cow knows everything. Including where John Small is. Fancy a beer?’

They ordered two small beers and relaxed a little.

‘Where’s the car?’ asked Knightly.

‘I’m not sure. Have you seen the warren of small winding roads between the main road and the sea? And the crazy drivers? But I’ve got a landmark for it.’

They sat moodily sipping the cold beer and watching the world go by when Loveluck suddenly said. ‘She lied to us.’

‘She’s done nothing but lie to us.’

‘I mean about staying with Ted.’

Knightly sat up sharply. ‘The glasses on the terrace. No lipstick!’

‘Ted would never have a house guest, certainly not Sammy.’

‘She hadn’t heard of the Doghouse, but Ted practically lives there.’

‘We fed her the information about Ted and the Doghouse and she just sat there saying ‘Yes. Yes.’’

Knightly sat tight lipped and squeezed the words out. 'That clever, cunning, conniving, two faced woman.' Then she stood up suddenly. 'Quick. Mariposa. If she is the cleaner she knows where to go and clean. And it isn't Ted Bassington's place.'

They hurried back to the restaurant, Knightly filling Loveluck in on Mariposa being Sammy's cleaner. Mariposa saw them coming and ran off to hide but Knightly was in and after her and soon sussed out her hiding place in the cleaning cupboard.

Senior restaurant staff joined them to protect Mariposa but Knightly produced her police badge. The badge may have meant nothing to them but Knightly saying 'policia' had the desired effect and an English speaking waiter interpreted and the crying cleaner was made to tell them where she cleaned for Sammy.

Once outside they looked again at the address. Calle 6A, Guadalmina Baja.

'Any idea where that is?'

'None,' said Knightly. 'But I know who will know.'

Loveluck smiled. 'Do I see a trip to the Doghouse coming up?'

'The people in there know everything.'

The early results from the publicising of the names were in. The names had been published in all the issues of the Western Gazette, not only in Sherborne but in Yeovil and other areas within the readership of the Gazette.

Olwen Evans had written a short lead story but the rest was the names and why and how to contact the police or the Gazette.

Similar Stories had appeared in the Lymington Times and covered New Milton and other areas around the New Forest.

In Sherborne the local radio station Abbey 104 ran a small piece on it as did BBC Radio Solent who covered a vast area including Southampton and Bournemouth.

The results varied in details and proportions but there was no doubting that Jakob and Lina never had their names coupled with each other which came as a great disappointment to Sergeant Daly and Inspector Anderson who had all but convinced themselves of a family connection. The occasional one off coupling of names occurred but were treated as statistically insignificant.

Winston alone had a few mentions, as did Jakob and Lina, but the essential linking of names was not there. The respondent ringing in or emailing and saying "yes I know Jakob, Rufus and Lina" didn't exist.

Samantha Alcock topped the list with a large number of mentions. John Small received none. The man continued to elude them.

Anderson threw the lists on the table.

'Early days, sir' said Daly encouragingly.

Anderson stared out of the window. Disappointment clearly visible from his stance. 'How can we have no clear, positive linkings at all? Apart from the odd one off,' he said dismissively.

He walked to the door. 'We need to use photos. We have photos of all of them live, don't we?'

Daly nodded. 'Except John Small, of course.'

'How about Samantha?'

'Knightly has some pics of her. Taken without Sammy knowing.'

Anderson came back to the centre of the room. 'Can we use them? I mean taken without permission.'

Daly said meaningfully. 'Well, we *can*'

Anderson smiled. 'So we can. Oversight if anyone asks. Organise it with Olwen.'

'Olwen?' Daly raised his eyebrows. 'We're on first name terms now, are we?'

'Do you want that transfer?' said Anderson with a smile.

'I'll arrange it at once, sir.'

'That's better.'

'With Olwen.'

'I'll pretend I didn't hear that,' said Anderson as he passed into the corridor.

Chapter 28

When the call came through to Olwen Evans from her informant at Sherborne police station that Sergeant Janine Pepper had been arrested for attacking a curate, two members of the public and several policemen it was like all her Christmas' had come at once. She turned immediately to her computer and was about to start typing when she stopped. She swivelled in her chair and put her feet on the table.

'Easy, girl,' she said to herself. 'Nice and slow. Let's get this just right. No going off at half cock. There's mileage in this story.' She nibbled the end of her pencil and thought.

'So, Sergeant Pepper. I'm going to be all over the front pages of my own newspaper, am I? Well. We'll see about that. But first, to get *you*, dear Pepper, all over the front pages.'

Thirty minutes later she was still chewing her pencil with her feet on the table but now she looked more content. She had marshalled her ideas. With a decisive nod she began to type. Just in time for the electronic version of the Western Gazette to greet people coming home from work.

Olwen read her report on the Sergeant Pepper incident in the abbey.

Sherborne detective in violent attacks in Sherborne Abbey.

A young female detective sergeant is being questioned at Sherborne police station following three separate attacks on people in Sherborne Abbey. Police have confirmed that Detective Sergeant Pepper is helping police with their investigations into attacks on the Sherborne curate, Simon Peter Peacock, two as yet unnamed members of the public and four uniformed police officers.

Sergeant Pepper was the victim of a terrible trauma herself earlier this year and has being undergoing anger therapy. The Gazette understands that she has been designated administrative duties until her therapy is complete. What was she doing in the abbey interviewing the Vicar of Sherborne?

Your ace crime reporter wanted to put these questions to her supervising officer, Detective Inspector Loveluck, but has discovered that he is spending a weekend on the Costa del Sol in Spain with another young female police officer.

We taxpayers expect the police to protect the public from violent attacks, not to attack the public themselves. And if officers are working restricted duties, we expect their supervising officers to supervise them. Not to go off to sunny Spain.

The Gazette has just learned that the Sherborne curate Simon Peter Peacock is also helping police with their enquiries.

Olwen read it through with satisfaction. 'Now that´s what I call killing two birds with one stone.' She said softly.

Loveluck, Knightly and Susie arrived at Calle 6, Guadalmina thanks to Susie's directions. It was a fine villa and situated on the edge of the Mediterranean. The two police officers walked up to the door whilst Susie waited by the car. A neighbour appeared from an adjacent villa with a small dog. Susie hailed her.

'Hello. Do you know who lives in this villa?'

'A woman lives there. Sammy, they call her.'

'Just the woman? No man?'

The neighbour shrugged. 'I see her coming and going. Never seen any man.'

Susie thanked her and passed this information onto Loveluck. 'That's handy to know. There's nobody home at the moment. Or not answering.'

They returned to the comfort of the Doghouse.

CC Mackenzie furiously strode up and down the length of his large office. He was angrily blurting out random sentences regarding Sergeant Pepper whilst Chief Inspector John Waddington sat quietly in his chair.

'What was she doing in Sherborne Abbey, for pity's sake?'

‘Perhaps she went there for a bit peace and quiet,’ said Waddington in need of a bit of peace and quiet of his own. Mackenzie had been in a fury for over an hour.

‘Are you trying to be funny?’ he said to Waddington. ‘Because I’m not in the mood for jokes. I don’t call screaming, howling and attacking members of the clergy, the public and the police as seeking peace and quiet.’ He paced several more times. ‘I don’t suppose we can keep this out of the press?’

Waddington shook his head. ‘It was witnessed by too many people. Do you think she’ll be charged?’

‘Charged? She made violent attacks on seven people. She had the poor curate on the floor and was kicking and howling at him!’

‘Howling?’

‘Howling is the description that the curate and the two members of the public who went to his aid used. I should imagine he’ll want charges pressed.’

‘I should think with her extenuating circumstances she might not be charged,’ said Waddington reasonably.

‘Oh yes,’ said CC Mackenzie softly and sarcastically. ‘Her extenuating circumstances. By which I presume you mean her anger therapy. Fat lot of good that did her. And the curate said he had seen her in a long conversation with the vicar, Rev Toby Austin.’

‘Perhaps she was seeking comfort and spiritual help.’

‘You are trying to be funny aren’t you? I would warn you very seriously about making fun of me.’

‘Of course I’m not.’ Then he added swiftly. ‘Sir.’

‘If Loveluck has got her back working as a detective after all we said about that, I’ll have that man out of the force. She is supposed to be working in the office.’ He did two more lengths of his own office. ‘And where is Detective Inspector Loveluck when all this is going on? Off on a jolly to the Costa del Sol. With Sergeant Sadie Knightly. And nice work if you can get it.’

He sat down in his chair and brooded for a while. ‘You really don’t think we can keep this out of the media?’

Waddington shook his head. ‘Olwen Evans will get onto it, and once she is onto it there’ll be no stopping her. It’ll be all over the Western Gazette.’

Mackenzie sat tight lipped then eventually said. ‘Where does that woman get her information?’ They sat in silence. Outside a church bell chimed. ‘When does Loveluck get back?’

‘Tomorrow afternoon.’

‘I want to see him as soon as possible. Any news from the doctors?’

‘The last I heard she was still under sedation. They’re worried about her. The sheer strength and violence of her reaction. They want to know what brought the attack on but only Pepper can tell them that and they want to keep her sedated and resting for a while longer.’

‘Can’t the curate tell us anything?’

‘He’s been questioned but just says he did nothing to bring it on. She just flipped from out of the blue.’

‘That’s all we need.’ Said Mackenzie. ‘A woman who flips without any cause.’

‘Inspector Anderson said he didn’t believe the curate. He thinks he’s holding something back.’

The CC thought for a spell. ‘Nothing more we can do for now.’ He stood up and Waddington followed his example. They walked to the door together. ‘What a bloody mess.’

Waddington nodded and went down the corridor to his own office. ‘What a bloody mess, indeed,’ he echoed.

Loveluck and Knightly arrived back in Sherborne in the early evening, both still dressed for the Spanish sun but greeted by an English chill. I’m going up to have a look at the funfair. Do you want to come?’

‘No thanks. Too chilly. See you tomorrow.’

She drove off up to the terraces and he walked into the Digby Tap which was fairly empty thanks to the funfair. He took his pint of Doom Bar and sat at a small table. His mind wandered on the trip they had taken to Spain. Had the game been worth the candle? Probably not. They had found Samantha Alcock and the villa owned by John Small, which was something. But of John Small himself there was no trace. What a master of evasion that man was.

But journey back had given Loveluck time to organise his thoughts and he had reached two decisions. He was going to bring Rufus Nightingale into the station for questioning. He was fairly sure he was responsible for the hanging of Winston Gale though the evidence was weak. And he was certain that he was trying to murder Jakob to protect his inheritance.

The evidence pointed to a group of people in moccasins and bare feet. The witches looked favourite for the bare feet but of the moccasins there was no trace. But Loveluck had learned that Rufus and his acolytes liked to meet at Wootton Bridge. This was a parting piece of information given him by the Hampshire police and Wootton Bridge was on his list of places to visit.

His thoughts were interrupted by the arrival of solicitor Chris Williams. 'Hello Jack.'

Loveluck nodded. The lawyer took a computer out of his case and started to fire it up. 'If you′re going to sit here playing games I′d rather you did it somewhere else.'

Williams smiled. 'Something here I think you might want to see. Hot from the press, so to speak.'

Loveluck shrugged.

'Have you seen this yet?'

Loveluck looked at the screen.

Sherborne detective in violent attacks in Sherborne Abbey.

His heart sank. Olwen Evans at her professional best. And nothing but bad news for Loveluck. He read the article through. 'How does she get this past the editor? You′re a lawyer. Is it legal to print this speculation?

'Is it true?' asked the lawyer.

Loveluck read the article again. 'I've no idea. I've been away.'

Williams smiled. 'Yes I know. To Spain. With Sergeant Knightly. How was the weather?'

At the funfair, Knightly was having a good time. She had always loved funfairs and this was a great mixture of modern rides and old fashioned ones. The scary, huge modern rides with their massive structures and not for the faint hearted.

But also old fashioned rides for younger children. The horses going round and round and up and down to whirligig music. A small helter skelter with people climbing the stairs and sitting down and entering the tunnel which when round and round the structure until the riders popped out of the bottom of the tunnel.

The ever popular waltzer with the daring young men collecting fares and spinning the cars and flirting with the girls. And the caterpillar, the young lovers favourite. Going round rapidly with the cover coming over the top and keeping prying eyes off the riders to kiss and pet and be as daring as they would until the cover suddenly was raised and all eyes were on them. And then the cover closed again until the next time.

She decided to try her hand at the rifle range. She was a crack shot, a skill learned in the police force. The rifles were all taken and she watched one young man hit the target time and time again without fail. Even with the poor sights and the fixing of the targets by the stall holders to stop too many people winning he hit everything. She was impressed.

The man put down the rifle, refused the prizes offered to him and turned into the crowds. She saw then that it was Rufus. She ran over to him. 'Hey Rufus. Great shooting. But why have you had all that lovely hair cut off?'

The man looked at her. 'You're mistaken. I don't know you.' He turned away and pushed his way rapidly through the crowds. Too rapidly for her to follow. She looked at the mass of faces blankly. Why did he deny her? Turn his back on her? What had happened to that very delightful and well mannered man she had met at his home in the New Forest.

She walked thoughtfully through the crowds. 'Something wasn't quite right. She couldn't put her finger on it but something wasn't quite right. Perhaps it wasn't Rufus after all.' But still she doubted herself.

The following morning a meeting was convened to share the information they had all gleaned over the past few days. It was soon crystal clear that the Spanish trip had yielded very little except the whereabouts of John Small's villa and the fact that Samantha Alcock was living there. Otherwise there was Stan the man's comment about it being best not to find John Small, and if they ever did find him they would know why.

General consensus was that he had some terrible terminal wasting disease and wouldn't be fit to stand trial but the decision was to keep on searching for him.

Sergeant Daly walked into Inspector Anderson's office holding a clutch of papers.

'Ah, the results of the photo appeal. Have you studied them yet?'

'Yes, sir. And I expect there will be more to come.'

‘Let’s hear it then,’ said Anderson eagerly. ‘They are bound to be better than the results from the names-only appeal which told us nothing.’

‘Yes sir. Much more informative. I think we should get the others in. Shall I fetch them?’

Anderson nodded and Daly went to find Inspector Loveluck and Sergeant Knightly. Once assembled, Daly began. ‘So what do we know already?’

Knightly said. ‘That the older woman and Lina are mother and daughter. That photo we have of them both together has them like two peas in a pod.’

Daly looked around the faces. ‘Not so. Lina is, in fact, Angela Nightingale. Sister to Rufus Nightingale.’

‘She can’t be.’

‘The response is overwhelming. Lots of people knew her. She is Angela Nightingale. Why she has no birth certificate is another matter.’

This stunned everyone. The likeness between the two women was uncanny. ‘I don’t believe it,’ said Knightly flatly. ‘They have to be mother and daughter.’

Daly shrugged. ‘I’m only giving you the evidence as it has come in. Hordes of people say she is Angela Nightingale.’ He looked at the stunned, forlorn faces before him. They had all been so convinced they were mother and daughter. ‘Next thing. The older woman is, in fact, Mrs Tregenna.’

‘Foreign?’

‘No. Cornish. She was spotted in the local Gazette by a couple on holiday in the area. They live in Cornwall and she is one of their neighbours. They say there is no doubt about it. I spoke to them this morning and they say that Mrs Tregenna has two children. A son and a daughter. The daughter certainly isn’t Lina. Doesn’t look anything like her. The daughter is a skinny, elfin like girl. He couldn’t remember her name.’

‘And the son?’

Daly paused and smiled. ‘And the son is called Jakob.’

There was a burst of relief and joy as the detectives celebrated their breakthrough. High fives and smiles were everywhere. At last they had some real facts. They had placed everyone. Everyone except John Small who remained as elusive as ever.

But one person was not celebrating. Sergeant Knightly sat staring blankly into space. The others noticed. She said when the noise had died down, 'I don't believe it. Not for a moment. It just doesn't make sense. I *know* that Mrs Tregenna and Lina are mother and daughter. All the photos show that clearly. And you all know it too.'

'We have to face the facts,' said Loveluck.

'We have to recognise the facts,' argued Knightly. 'I don't care that all those people say that Lina is, in fact, Angela Nightingale. And I don't care that I know that Mrs Tregenna and Lina are mother and daughter. Perhaps both are true.'

'She can't be two people at once,' said Anderson.

'Why not? John Small is three people at least. Check the birth certificates for Cornwall. We have a name now. Tregenna.'

Loveluck said softly. 'We also have a language as well. Cornish.'

'And we have a time scale,' said Daly proudly. 'Twenty five years.'

Chapter 29

Detective Inspector Wilson of the Hampshire Constabulary had phoned Loveluck to tell him that the search of the houses of Rufus Nightingale and John Small were to take place the next morning and would Loveluck like to attend. And so the following morning Inspector Loveluck and Sergeant Knightly arrived at Westgate Lodge at nine o'clock sharp to join the assembled police officers.

Weston, the butler, had caused a fuss and told them that Mr Rufus wasn't there and that he had no authority to let them in, but it was all to no avail. Inspector Wilson held the authority in his hand and in they went.

Some officers were detailed to search the outbuildings, paying particular attention to vehicles. Especially an old Toyota pick-up truck.

As the officers went about their search Inspector Wilson told Loveluck that the autopsy on old Mr Nightingale had shown that he had died of injuries consistent with a fall down stairs and that his body held sufficient alcohol to make such a fall likely. The verdict was accidental death and the police saw no reason to investigate further. Whether Rufus pushed him down the stairs or not we would never know for sure.

Loveluck took a tour of the house. It seemed smaller than it had looked from the outside but impressive none the less. It made Loveluck wonder just what the fortune behind the Nightingale family was.

Weston appeared carrying a tray full of small sherries. Wilson nodded Loveluck to take one and then took one himself. No such luck for the uniformed branch. They sat in the garden and sipped their sherry when Sergeant Pike came out holding a thick envelope. 'I think you should see this, sir' he said handing it to Wilson. He looked at the envelope and passed it to Loveluck. 'It's your case.'

Loveluck read the envelope. It said 'To be opened only in the event of my death.' Where did you find it?' he asked.

'Under a floorboard, under the carpet, under a wardrobe,' said Pike.

'Are you looking under all the floorboards?'

'No sir, but we moved the wardrobe and the carpet and the floorboard had clearly been fairly recently taken up. So we looked.'

Loveluck and Wilson exchanged glances. Loveluck looked again at the envelope as though this could somehow tell him more than the few written words. Wilson laughed. 'Open it.'

Loveluck tapped it on the table as if for good luck and then tore open the envelope.

'To whom it may concern.

'I, Ronald Nightingale, being of sound mind and disposition do hereby declare that the confession I am about to make is true and complete in every respect. My health is now failing and my doctor assures me that I cannot expect to live many more months. Nor do I want to since the death of my loving wife, Dorothy.

Twenty five years ago on March the second, my wife gave birth to twins. Two boys who are now known as Rufus and Jakob. It had always been my wife's dearest wish to have a son and a daughter and though happy with two sons, she had been told by the doctor at the time that she could never have more children. My dear wife would never have the daughter she craved so much.

It was then that we heard that one of the estate workers and his wife had just been delivered of a daughter. Within hours my wife came to me with a plan. It was her plan but I was fully behind it from the start and I take full responsibility for it now that my wife is no longer on this earth.

The estate workers were of Cornish origin and had spoken many times of their desire to return to Cornwall. The plan fulfilled so many dreams. The plan was this.

That my wife and I would exchange one of our twin sons for her daughter. And being fortunate enough to be in possession of a considerable fortune I was able to offer to set her and her husband up in a cottage in Cornwall and pay them a generous monthly allowance for the upbringing of their son. Our son, I should say, but soon to be their son.

The deal was struck, the midwife paid off and the exchange made as soon as was humanly possible. We had named out twins Rufus and Jakob and the estate mother chose Jakob. Within days the estate workers and Jakob were in Cornwall beginning their new life and we were at home with our son Rufus and the daughter who we christened Angela.

This deal has worked perfectly for twenty five years.

My wife died six years ago and Angela and I had a poor relationship resulting in Angela leaving home and I have not seen her for over four years. My son Rufus has proved a disappointment. He shows little interest in the estate and prefers to spend his time in the woods with strange people including, so I'm told, the witches of the New Forest. It is all nonsense to me.

One thing I did when the deal to exchange the babies was made was to involve a solicitor to ensure that the adoptions had been done as legally as possible given the secrecy of the exchange.

That solicitor is John Small. And he has been bleeding me dry with his blackmail and extortion and threats of exposure ever since.

There comes now the question of my succession. The eldest son inherits. That is the way it has always been done in the family. I have recently heard from Mrs Tregenna. She wants the boys and the girl to inherit equally. This I cannot even consider. The inheritance goes to the eldest boy and that is that.

The first born twin was Rufus. He will inherit when I die.

I discussed all these matters with John Small at the Gordleton Mill just a few days ago. It ended in a row when he suggested that the three children and he himself, John Small, should inherit twenty five percent each.

Of course that could never be and I have not spoken to him since.

Signed by my hand, Ronald Nightingale.

The document was dated and witnessed by James Weston, the butler.

Loveluck passed the document to Wilson who took it up and read it carefully. Then he tossed the paper onto the table. There's nothing there to interest the Hampshire police after all these years. The three adults involved are all dead. Ronald and Dorothy Nightingale and Mrs Tregenna. Rufus has inherited. No interest to us.

Loveluck stood up and thanked Wilson for his cooperation and help. 'Let me know if anything else turns up. Or if anything turns up at John Small's house.' The men shook hands and Loveluck left.

As he drove back to Sherborne he began to rearrange all the principal players and their role in the whole affair in his head. Bit by bit it all began to make sense. All except the initial murders. Why had Angela and her mother and John Small been murdered? And if John Small was indeed alive and pulling all the strings, who was murdered in his stead at the Poachers Inn?

'Angela and her mother,' said Loveluck to himself. Knightly had never had the slightest doubt they were mother and daughter. And how right she was.

And who were the two missing people at the meeting in the Poachers? Loveluck had no doubt now that they were Rufus and Jakob. He pulled into the True Lovers Knot in Tarrant Keynston and treated himself to a pint of beer and Mussels. And very fine they were too.

Sergeant Pepper's doctor entered the room and sat opposite Chief Inspector John Waddington. Loveluck was also in the room as was Knightly. A member of the police Human Resources was there to observe fair play even though this was not a disciplinary meeting.

'Thank you for coming doctor,' said Waddington. 'I appreciate it.'

'I am not here as a favour to you, Chief Inspector. I am here to help you understand Sergeant Pepper and her anger problems.'

'Of course.'

'I have prepared some notes for you to take away and study but I won't give them to you until I have said a few words.' He studied his audience before continuing. 'You know the details of the incident, or should I say incidents, already. I have had the advantage of speaking to Sergeant Pepper which you have not and I will tell you straight away what I have learned.'

The assembled company positioned themselves in such a way that demonstrated that they were preparing to listen carefully to the doctor.

'As you know, Sergeant Pepper had been speaking to the Vicar of Sherborne, the Rev Toby Austin for some time.'

'What about?' asked Loveluck.

The doctor gave him a stern look and continued. 'The vicar then left the abbey and shortly afterwards Pepper went to leave the abbey also. It was as she walked towards the door that the curate stood in her way and asked her what she was talking to the vicar about. She refused to tell him and he then grabbed her arm and insisted she tell him. She refused again at which point he grabbed her arm even tighter and insisted that she must tell him.'

'That isn't the story that the curate tells.'

The doctor shrugged. 'I tell you this because these are standard flash points for people who suffer from anger. For Sergeant Pepper, the use of similar violence and demands that she tell them what they want to know were used by the people who buried her alive and caused these problems in the first place. This triggered the very violent reactions we have heard about and which she doesn't deny.'

'You're suggesting that the actions of the curate were similar to the actions of those who buried her alive and the one triggered the other?' asked Knightly.

'More or less. Sergeant Pepper did tell me two other things. One was that she felt a great catharsis after the events and the sedated sleep. By that I mean she feels that she had got a lot of the anger out of her system and it has cleansed her.'

'And is that possible?' asked Loveluck.

'To a degree. It will certainly help her to recognise the trigger points and to deal with them differently, and that alone is a great step forward. The anger therapy must continue. She may think it isn't necessary but it is.'

The doctor leaned back in his chair which prompted Waddington to say. 'You said there were two things, doctor.'

'Yes. The other is more problematic. Pepper told me that she had started to drink and to miss her medication from time to time. This is typical behaviour but dangerous behaviour.'

Loveluck and Waddington exchanged concerned glances. 'Can you help with that, doctor?'

The doctor nodded. 'There are two more non-medical issues but very important nevertheless. Firstly, she has learned that a woman called Olwen Evans was responsible for her being kidnapped and, by extrapolation, for her being buried alive. There is a whole new well of anger being built up there. New triggers. New dangers.'

The doctor took a sip of water before continuing. 'Pepper also was going about detective work against the conditions of her current employment.' He looked to the HR person who nodded her agreement. 'Pepper did say that she was taking work on behind

Inspector Loveluck's back as it made her feel better. And I believe it did make her feel better, but it exposed her to triggers that she wasn't ready to handle. I also believe she has been helping other officers with their investigations with very beneficial results.'

The HR woman said. 'What exactly are your recommendations, doctor? You say that detective work has been beneficial and then you say that detective work exposes her to triggers to anger. I am not clear what you mean.'

'What I mean is that she should not go out alone on investigations. However, being part of a team working on carefully chosen lines of investigation which would not expose her to excessive risk of meeting anger triggers could be beneficial.'

Waddington tapped his fingers on the table. 'Doctor. Do you think that Sergeant Pepper should be prosecuted for the assaults?'

'That,' said the doctor firmly, 'is not for me to say. However, as the curate committed the first assault by gripping Sergeant Pepper by the arm and demanding information, perhaps he could be persuaded not to press for charges to be brought. But these are matters for you. I will just add that everything said by me today is in the strictest confidence.'

The meeting concluded and the party began to disperse. 'What do you think, Jack?'

Loveluck shook his head. 'What a bloody mess.'

Waddington smiled. 'My words exactly.'

'Doctor,' shouted Loveluck walking briskly after the medical man. 'When can I see Pepper?'

'Give her a couple of days. She's been through a lot. And she's very embarrassed about seeing anyone from the station. Except Sergeant Knightly. She is very keen to see her. Good day, everyone.'

Loveluck lounged in his darkened sitting room with eyes closed as the television played to itself. He was tired and dissatisfied. As the case neared its end the chances of bringing Rufus Nightingale and John Small to justice were small.

Rufus because there was no real evidence except moccasin marks and bare feet marks in the wood. They would be laughed out of court. And John Small because they couldn't find any evidence that he existed. Whether he was dead or alive.

But he would arrest Rufus and his clan and hope that their stories wouldn't hang together under separate and deep questioning. Pressurized people sometimes crack.

He lay back on his sofa, closed his eyes and let his mind wander over random aspects of the case, looking for subconscious links they might have overlooked. He slipped off to sleep and would doubtless have slept the night away were it not for a loud banging on the door and ringing of the bell.

He wearily got to his feet and opened the door. It was Olwen Evans.

'What time it is?'

'Time we talked,' said Olwen and pushed her way past him.

He poured drinks for them both. 'Cheers.'

'Cheers be damned. What happened to my trip to Spain?'

Loveluck sighed. 'We had to leave suddenly.'

'We? Who are we?'

'Myself and Sergeant Knightly.'

'That's a nice cosy little twosome. I hope you had a wonderful holiday, you and little Miss Cheekbones.'

'Olwen!'

'But that isn't why I'm here. It's about Pepper.'

'Pepper?'

'Yes. I think it's Pepper who is sending me those messages.'

'Really? What makes you think that?'

'She's the only real candidate. And I know that George told her that I was responsible for her burial. Or as good as.'

Loveluck sighed. 'You can understand it if it is her.'

'I know. I thought you should know. And after that attack she made on the curate in the abbey I'm starting to get worried.'

Loveluck chewed it over for a spell as Olwen poured more drinks. 'Let me have a word with her and the doctor. I understand that the attack in the abbey has had a very good side effect. Pepper seems a lot better. More in control. She understands the triggers better. But most of all, she knows that she can probably get away with it once. Another attack on a member of the public would mean the end of her police career. Together, they might be enough to really and finally calm her down.'

'Let's hope so.'

‘Another thing,’ said Loveluck. ‘That piece in the Gazette wasn’t called for. I’m surprised your editor passed it. And it isn’t going to make Pepper love you any better. Or me for that matter.’

‘Speaking of you loving me, do you fancy a meal in the Royal Oak and then bed? It’s been a while since we did that. You can show me your suntan.’

Loveluck smiled and looked long and hard at this strange, feisty but always entertaining woman. He nodded. ‘It has been a while. A meal and bed it is.’ As they walked to the Royal Oak, Loveluck and Olwen both felt that things didn’t seem so bad after all. Each for their own reasons.

Chapter 30

Loveluck and Knightly pulled into the car park at Wootton Bridge followed by two police cars from the Hampshire Constabulary. They got out of the cars and walked to the edge of the stream. 'Are we going to have to paddle?' asked Loveluck with distaste.

'Come on, sir. It's not very deep,' said Knightly hitching up her trousers. Loveluck took off his shoes and socks and pulled his trousers up to his knees.

'This is no way to arrest a multi murderer,' he grumbled.

The uniformed officers splashed through the shallow but wide stream and into a meadow on the other side. The others, including Inspector Wilson joined them and they surveyed the scene. It was picturesque and Knightly could see the attraction of regularly meeting here in some kind of occult activities.

Loveluck scanned the area around him. There was no sign of any activity.

'They're usually here around now, according to the locals,' said Wilson.

'What locals?'

'You'd be surprised how many people live in the New Forest. But I mean people who walk or drive past here regularly and see them acting out their rituals.'

No sooner had he spoken than the sound of voices floated through the trees. Singing. No one knew what they were singing but it sounded soothing. Peaceful. Knightly indicated with her finger the direction they were coming in.

And then they all saw them. 'What the hell?' muttered Loveluck.

A group of maybe twenty people were straggling through the woods and in the centre, riding on a donkey, was Rufus. Images of Jesus flashed through everyone's mind. It was eerie.

‘Make sure the backup are ready to move,’ said Inspector Wilson quietly and the uniformed officer made the call. Loveluck glanced down at his bare feet and, feeling slightly foolish, put his shoes and socks back on.

Rufus and his band came slowly towards them and Loveluck went forward to meet them. ‘We meet again Inspector,’ called Rufus cheerily. ‘And the delightful Sergeant Knightly. Come to join us?’

‘Not come to join you. Come to arrest you.’

‘How very unpleasant. What for?’

‘Rufus Nightingale,’ said Loveluck formally. ‘I have come to arrest you on suspicion of the murder of Winston Gale by hanging and further of the murders of Amy Tregenna, Angela Nightingale and someone passing under the name of John Small.’

‘Are you crazy? Do you think I would murder my own sister? And who is Amy Tregenna?’

Loveluck turned wearily away. ‘Read him his rights, Sergeant.’

Knightly did so and a uniformed officer handcuffed him. ‘I hope you have some good evidence, Inspector,’ he called out. ‘Because I have some very good lawyers.’

Loveluck turned and pointed at the feet of the group. ‘These women with bare feet are evidence. And so is that pair of moccasins’ He had pointed at the moccasins being worn by one member of the band, Bartholomew. ‘I should have listened to Kayra. Another traitor.’

‘See if he is carrying anything,’ said Loveluck and one of the officers searched him.

‘Just some money and this piece of paper, sir.’

Loveluck held his hand out for the paper. ‘Take him away.’ The officers began to lead Rufus away when Loveluck called after him. ‘Just tell me one thing, Rufus.’

Rufus shrugged. ‘What?’

Loveluck walked over and stood close to him. ‘Why did you murder them in that strange way?’

‘What strange way?’

‘By garrotting them.’

Rufus looked stunned. ‘Those people were garrotted?’ he said with a voice and eyes filled with astonishment that could not have been faked.

Loveluck stared at him blankly, and then at Knightly equally blankly. ‘Oh hell.’

‘What is it sir?’

‘We’ve got the wrong brother.’

Waiting only to give brief instructions to the uniformed police to release Rufus, he gave quick thanks to Inspector Wilson and Knightly’s car roared out of the car park and off down the forty mile per hour restricted speed limits of the New Forest.

Loveluck took the piece of paper he had taken from Rufus out of his pocket and read it. It was short but explosive.

It read; ‘Rufus. I am holding a meeting at the Poachers Inn for you, your twin brother Jakob, Mrs Amy Tregenna and her daughter whom you know as your sister Angela. I will be there too of course. The purpose of this meeting is to outline my plans for the distribution of the money left behind by your father, Ronald Nightingale. I am aware that you think that you have inherited the money, but I have documents to show that you and Jakob are twins. I also have documentary proof of who was the first born and who naturally inherits the money. Your twin brother Jakob has been sent an identical note to this one.

I will reveal who was the firstborn at the meeting at the Poachers Inn.’

There followed details of the time of the meeting.

The importance of this document was not lost on Loveluck. He ordered Knightly to pull over and park and in the sudden quiet he passed her the document.

‘Does Rufus know that he was the first born?’

‘No. Neither of them knows that.’

‘That situation is dynamite,’ said Knightly softly.

‘We shouldn’t have let Rufus go,’ she said after reading the document. ‘He stands to lose his inheritance. He stands to lose everything. He’ll murder Jakob given half the chance. To remove the threat.’

Loveluck shook his head slowly. ‘Rufus may have a lot to lose if Jakob is revealed as the first born, but Jakob has an even stronger motivation for murdering Rufus.’

‘What’s that?’

‘He has nothing to lose.’

Knightly started the engine again but didn’t move. ‘Do you think that is why someone tried to murder all the people in the know at the Poachers?’

'Yes. And either Jakob or Rufus nearly succeeded.'

'But that means that Rufus was prepared to kill his sister. And Jakob prepared to kill his mother.'

Loveluck shook his head. 'By that time Rufus knew that Angela wasn't his sister and Jakob knew that Amy Tregennan wasn't his mother. It was money, pure and simple, they were after. And they still are.'

They pulled out of their parking spot, and Knightly moved up the gears. As she did so a large and beautiful Harley Davidson came alongside matching their speed. The biker drew up his visor and smiled. It was Rufus.

'Rufus,' yelled Knightly. 'You have nothing to worry about. You are the first born. Your inheritance is safe.' But the noise of the Harley and the sports car combined blew her words to the four winds.

'You are the first born,' she screamed as she had never screamed before.'

But he pointed to his ears and shrugged. He had heard nothing.

He blew a kiss and roared his Harley to greater power and zoomed off into the distance.

'I wonder what happened to the donkey,' asked Loveluck dreamily.

'And before you ask, no I can't catch him,' said Knightly tight lipped. 'But I can have a damned good try.'

'Not with me in the car, you don't.'

Knightly smiled and watched the dot disappearing in the distance. In her thoughts she said. 'You're the man for me, Rufus Nightingale. If you can keep yourself out of trouble. And out of prison. And keep yourself from getting killed.' At this thought she pressed a little harder on the throttle. There was more at stake to her now than just keeping the peace. Keeping her man.

The call to the police station for help at the fun fair had been passed onto Anderson who glanced at it and shrugged. The funfair already had a police presence but it was packed. A haven for pick-pockets and other petty thieves with precious little the police could do about it. Every witch and psychic in the south of England was there and vast numbers of the public. Anderson passed the message back to the duty officer. 'Keep us informed if anything happens. I'll go up there and patrol the place myself.'

The duty officer smiled. 'Enjoy yourself, sir.'

Darkness had descended on Sherborne.

The town was quiet except for the distant sound of the funfair in full swing up on the terraces. The stalls had all been taken down and it seemed everyone had either gone home or were at the fair.

They approached silently.

They approached in a V- formation. Like the bow of a boat cutting through the water or the formation taken by birds as they fly at their efficient best.

At the front point of the V was Nemesis. Nemesis leading the New Forest coven with Rufus just behind her. Her hands were held out in front of her. They were holding the Hand of Glory with upright candles secured between the fingers of the grisly relic.

Slowly and silently they crossed the Church Green and approached the locked and barred door of Sherborne Abbey.

Inside the abbey Astra turned to Rev Toby Austin and said, 'They're here. They're outside.'

No one questioned how or why she knew, but they knew she was right. The abbey was cold and the tension high.

'What are they doing?' asked the vicar of Sherborne.

'We'll find out soon enough. Are you sure you daubed the entire door with the unguent which shields the door from the Hand of Glory?' asked Astra of a witch.

'You watched me do it.'

'What did you use?'

'You watched me do that as well. I used a black cat's gall, the fat of a hen'

'What colour,' interrupted Astra sternly.

'White.' Nemesis nodded. 'And the blood of a screech owl. All mixed into a paste.'

'When did you do it?'

'In the dog days, of course.'

Astra nodded again. The job had been done properly, but still she feared the power of the hand.

They stood in silence shivering. Some with cold, most with fear. Jakob stood motionless, expressionless but not fearless.

Outside Nemesis approached to within five yards of the door and stopped. 'They have daubed the door with the Hand of Glory shield.' She turned to face the witches of the New Forest. Now we need all your powers. Now we need to have the Hand of Glory work its magic.' She turned back to face the door and nodded to the man carrying two sticks to beat out time. Then she pointed the Hand of Glory with its candles burning at the abbey door.

The man beat a steady rhythm with the sticks and the chanting began.

> Now open, lock!
> To the Dead Man's knock!
> Fly, bolt, and bar, and band!
>
> Nor move, nor swerve,
> Joint, muscle, or nerve,
> At the spell of the Dead Man's hand!
>
> Sleep, all who sleep! -- Wake, all who wake!
> But be as the dead for the Dead Man's sake!'

They could be clearly heard inside Sherborne Abbey and nervous glances were exchanged all round. 'Can they really open the locked door?' someone asked the vicar who said nothing in reply.

The chanting went on and on, never ceasing to the beat of the sticks and straining the nerves of those locked inside the abbey.

The chanting was having no effect on the lock but it increased in volume and intensity, never missing a beat. Nemesis howled out loud and piercingly to the Goddess Jana to add her strength, irrespective of the fact that it was not a full moon.

'Ja-na Ja-na Ja-na.'

And still the assembled bodies chanted 'Now open lock to the dead man's knock.....' Never ceasing, never missing a beat. The two chants intermingling.

And then it moved. The sound of the lock moving a fraction. It drove the chanters to an even higher pitch. Nemesis moved closer with the Hand of Glory, walking right up to the door. The chanting was feverish and the lock moved another fraction.

They were aware of this inside the abbey. Fear began to grip them and the Reverend Toby Austin went and stood with his back to the door. 'Play and sing,' he bellowed. 'Play and sing. Sing for your lives.'

And from the shadows the Sherborne Abbey Choir walked sedately into view and the organ blasted out the tune to Onward Christian Soldiers with the choir singing for everyone's life.'

Onward, Christian soldiers!
Marching as to war,
With the cross of Jesus
Going on before.
Christ, the royal Master,
Leads against the foe;
Forward into battle,
See his banners go!

And outside the endless chant of 'Now open lock to the dead man's knock'

The noise was deafening. Inside the abbey this loose affiliation of pagans and Christians attempting to fight back against the power of the Hand of Glory.

But Toby, at the abbey door heard the unmistakable click of the lock moving.

And so the battle of hymns and chants passed back and forth as the spells worked their magic, but little by little the lock was opening.

The vicar of Sherborne signalled to the choir to stop singing and the organ fell quiet shortly afterwards. The sound of the chanting outside was very clear. The vicar went to a dark corner of the church and flicked a switch. Onward Christian Soldiers resumed on CD. He then signalled to the Sherborne coven and the choir to follow him and quickly and quietly they walked the length of the abbey leaving the hymn and the chanting behind them and slipped out through a little known exit.

'Where now?' asked Jakob.

'To the funfair. We need to get lost in the crowds.' They passed out through the Sherborne School quadrangle, the choir to disperse and the rest to walk quickly along Abbey Road, down Cheap Street and South Street, across the railway crossing at the station and up the steep, narrow path to the funfair.

'This is plan B,' said the vicar smiling. 'Always watch your back and have an escape route ready. First rule if war. And very handy for vicars at times.'

Within minutes the lock finally gave and the New Forest affiliation marched into the abbey to find the birds had flown.

The Rev Toby Austin had talked confidently about his escape route, but in truth there was nowhere to go. A large group of people would be noticed and he knew that both Nemesis and Rufus were astute enough to work it out. His only hope was that the crowds would bring safety. But Toby Austin wasn't leaving anything to chance in his efforts to keep the two factions from slipping into violence and he called Loveluck asking for help.

'We're on our way. Try and keep Jakob and Rufus apart.'

Chapter 31

At the funfair Nemesis and a few of her entourage walked through the crowds, eyes alert for the Sherborne contingent. In truth she was enjoying herself. Under that stern exterior she could be quite playful and fairs had always appealed to her.

They passed the various rides and side shows and came to the helter skelter where they stopped. 'Going to have a ride, Nemesis?' one of the girls asked.

'I don't think so.' Then she looked up to the top of the helter skelter and there smiling down at her and waving was Kayra. Kayra the traitor who had mysteriously joined Rufus' group in the New Forest but had then switched to Jakob's group in Sherborne. 'Perhaps I will have a ride.'

She swiftly climbed the steps to the top where Kayra stood a few yards away. Kayra turned to face her and the young girl looked very small and thin. No match for Nemesis. There was a skirmish as Nemesis made a grab for her then both women suddenly disappeared from view.

'Better go up and see what's happening,' said one of the girls. They hesitated for a few seconds before the girl set off up the steps. As she did so, Nemesis appeared from out of the tube which brought the riders down from the top.

She was dead. Garrotted. The thin wire still around her neck.

Loveluck and Knightly arrived at the fair. It was a quick decision to split up and go in search of Jakob and Rufus. A needle in a haystack search. But it wasn't the police who found the two men. They found each other.

By the steelwork supporting one of the very large rides they stood facing each other. Five yards apart. Rufus with his long flowing hair,

Jakob with his short cropped hair. Otherwise identical twins. Different in breeding and social graces, but from the same womb. Born minutes apart, and the agony of not knowing who was first born and thus to inherit had driven them both to this very spot with the same murderous intent burning inside them.

Neither of them spoke. There was nothing to say. One of them would live. The other die. One would inherit; the other would die in the attempt.

It was Jakob who moved first. He leapt nimbly onto one of the steelwork spars and looked down upon Rufus who also took position amongst the steelwork. Slowly, like cats, they adjusted their positions amongst the steel girders and struts, each jockeying for the best position and that vital advantage. One would climb a little higher; the other would match him, or make a different move. It was like playing three dimensional chess.

Then Rufus leapt. Taking Jakob by surprise, Rufus leapt across a gap which, had he missed, would have meant a long drop. But he clutched onto a spar and kicked out at Jakob. Jakob tried to grab the leg that kicked like a mule at him but couldn't hang on. Then Rufus lost some of the strength by hanging on too long as he kicked and now he hung by his hands. His legs too far from any girder to help.

He hung from ever weakening hands and Jakob knew he only had to wait. He descended the steelwork quickly and as he did so Rufus swung back and forth from his hands, his legs swinging in an ever increasing arc and getting nearer a steel strut. Near enough to let go with his hands and grab another strut. The manoeuvre was done well, but he didn't grab a strut cleanly and though he had broken his fall as he grabbed at struts he fell and bounced off the steelwork until he hit the ground, winded and tired.

Jakob went to make a swift and decisive grab for him, thin steel wire ready in his hands but some fairground goers were passing and offered their help. Jakob waved them away but they stayed and fussed for long enough for Rufus to get his breath and most of his strength back.

He got to his feet and the helpers went on their way. Once again they stood a few yards apart.

'I'm going to kill you,' said Jakob with a chilling certainty and Rufus knew it was true. He was weak and his adversary was fit.

Jakob held the garrotte handles in his hands. 'I'm going to kill you,' repeated Jakob with relish.

Then a voice rang out. 'You'll have to kill me first.' He turned to see Sergeant Knightly standing there in grim determination. 'And I'm a copper. Kill me and they'll hunt you 'til the ends of the universe.'

She beckoned Rufus to stand next to her. 'You'll never do it now. Together we are too strong for you.' She reached for her phone. 'And in one minute's time this area will be teeming with police.'

It didn't take Jakob more than a few seconds to realise this was true. He turned to Rufus and said. 'Don't think this is over, because it isn't. I'll be back for you. You won't live to enjoy that inheritance.'

Then he moved off quickly to disappear in the crowds.

Both Knightly and Rufus let out giant sighs of relief. 'I owe you my life,' he said.

She shrugged. 'Lucky coincidence.'

As they walked through the crowds of merry makers he asked. 'What were you shouting to me on the road earlier?'

'I was telling you that you were the first born and not to take chances.'

'Really?'

'Yes.'

'Now that's very strange,' he said with a hint of humour. 'Because I can lip read and I would have sworn that you were saying I LOVE YOU.'

'You,' she said in mock anger, 'are too cocky for your own good.'

'Am I really the first born?'

'Absolutely.'

'I see. So you are just after my money.'

'I should have let him garrotte you. I feel like garrotting you myself.' And so they wandered into the crowds to take a ride on the caterpillar. And we won't follow them there.

A council of war had hastily been organised for nine o'clock the following morning and Loveluck was surprised to find Detective Chief Inspector John Waddington in the small office waiting for him. Sergeants Pepper, Dyer and Knightly were there as was Inspector Anderson.

'All present and correct,' said Waddington. 'I won't mess about because time is of the essence. Firstly some announcements. Sergeant Daly. Your transfer to Lyme Regis has come through. Congratulations.' The congratulations were echoed all round and Daly smiled and blushed in equal measure. Anderson began to say a few words but Waddington hurried him along. There would be times for farewells later.

'The formal medical report on Sergeant Pepper is excellent. You can return to limited detective duties.' Once more congratulations were offered and once more Waddington cut them short. 'You are to return to detective duties for a three month probationary period under the supervision of an Inspector at all times. No going out alone. The position will be reviewed in three months. You will be working with Inspector Anderson.'

This raised a few eyebrows 'Inspector Anderson runs a tight ship and I think your rehabilitation will benefit from working with him.' The clear implication that Loveluck didn't run a tight ship was missed by nobody and all eyes stared at the floor.

'There will be no charges regarding the incident with the curate, Simon Peter. Neither Pepper nor the Curate will be charged. I understand the curate is leaving Sherborne Abbey to take up duties elsewhere.'

'So it's all being swept under the carpet, as usual' said Anderson. 'Suits me.'

Waddington turned his attention to Knightly. 'You witnessed a fight between Rufus Nightingale and his brother Jakob last night.'

'I witnessed the end of it. Rufus had fallen from the steel structure holding up one of the rides during the fight. He was badly shaken and hurt. Jakob was moving in for the kill. My presence scared him off. Two of us were too much for him.'

Waddington paced the floor. 'What do you think happened to bring about the murders in the Poachers which started all this off? Jack?'

'The series of events in my head is this. And I mean right from the beginning. Mr and Mrs Nightingale have twins. Two boys, Rufus and Jakob. An estate worker and his wife have just had a daughter and the plot is hatched. They swap Jakob for the girl who became Angela, pay off the estate worker and everyone is happy.'

'We know all this Jack.'

'Bear with me. At this point, Mr Nightingale gets concerned and decided to find a solicitor who can help to make it as legal as possible. And thus as problem free for him as possible.'

'Which is where John Small comes into it.'

'Yes. Mr Nightingale seeks a solicitor well away from Lymington where local lawyers know him, and goes to Sherborne to choose a solicitor at random.'

'And draws John Small out of the hat.'

'Exactly. He goes to a firm of solicitors with this strange request that he only wants to deal with one person. To keep the plot to as few people as possible. Once John Small is on the case, and he soon realises he has found his jackpot, I am sure the blackmail began.'

'Then all went well for twenty five years until?'

'Until both Mr and Mrs Nightingale were dead. Rufus automatically inherits as nobody has heard of Jakob Tregenna.'

'Nobody except John Small'

'Exactly. John Small has a copy of the confession. I don't know how. Perhaps Mr Nightingale ran it past him before adding the bits about blackmail. But now John Small really begins to plot and plan. He calls a meeting of everyone involved in the plot. Mrs Tregenna, Angela, Jakob and Rufus. He sends the letters to Rufus and Jakob saying that the firstborn will be announced at the meeting. From there I am not sure what his plans were but they doubtless involved a lot of extortion of money from the twins.'

'Then things went wildly wrong,' said Waddington.

'Yes. John Small had completely overlooked the fact that both brothers would react in exactly the same way. All Rufus had to do was to murder Jakob and everyone else involved in the plot and the inheritance was his. And similarly, all Jakob had to do was to murder Rufus and everyone else involved in the plot and the inheritance became his.'

'And what a stroke of luck it was that he decided to hire an actor or someone to play the role of John Small at the meeting. Bad luck for the actor, of course.'

'So,' said Waddington, 'who killed the three people at the Poachers? That's the big question. And who killed Winston Gale?'

Again Loveluck took over the explanations. 'I think they both set out that night to kill the other brother and all others involved. Jakob with his bare hands, Rufus by hiring a killer. Winston Gale.'

'So what happened?'

Loveluck shrugged. 'My guess is that Jakob got there first. Don't forget that his mother was there. At least, the woman who had brought him up from birth was there. His mother to all intents and purposes.

He would have a reason to be about the place even if he had taken care not to attend the meeting. He killed them. Except Rufus, of course, who also didn't attend. My next guess is that Winston Gale set off to murder them but either got cold feet or got there too late. I think he got there too late. And that's why he died. Because he didn't kill Jakob.'

Waddington said. 'So we want Rufus for the murder of Winston Gale, and Jakob for the murders of Angela, Mrs Tregenna and whoever was playing John Small for the night.'

'That's about it,' agreed Loveluck.

'So. We have a murderer on the run and no nearer catching John Small. Not a very good return for our efforts.'

'I think John Small is a lost cause. Jakob is a better bet.'

'And where do we begin to look for him? He can disappear. He can live in a tent. He is a survivor. And a murderer.'

Pepper spoke for the first time. 'Seeing as I am a detective again and well supervised, can I make a suggestion?'

'Go ahead.'

'He'll go to where he feels most comfortable. Home.'

'A good observation.'

'And home I believe is Cornwall. Gorran Haven if I remember the reports correctly. Go there. Ask around about his favourite haunts. That's where I think you'll find him'

Waddington smiled. 'And where will I find John Small?'

'You won't. He's probably living in Spain under the name of Speedy Gonzales or something. Forget John Small.'

'I'll tell you what, sergeant. Now you are reinstated as a detective, why don't you come to Cornwall?'

And so it was they all went to Cornwall except Daly who played out his last few days at Sherborne Police Station on his computer.

Enquiries at Gorran Haven soon revealed that Jakob was well known in the small fishing village as a quiet but likeable boy. He had a group of friends and was regularly seen in the Llawnroc Hotel and the Barley Sheaf pub. Besides that he was well known for his camping trips, mainly to Bodmin Moor where he liked the solitude and the wildness.

He hadn't been seen in the village for a few weeks and they assumed he was on one of his Bodmin Moor trips.

They met up with the local police. 'Bodmin Moor?' A helpful sergeant had said. 'That's a big area to look for a man and his tent.'

'How big?'

'Roughly ten miles by eight miles. Eighty square miles. How's he travelling?'

Loveuck shrugged. 'By motorbike, I suppose.'

The policeman shook his head. 'It's no place for a motorbike. There's a lot of boggy marshland on Bodmin Moor. Ride into that and you'd sink deep.'

'Even at this time of year?'

'It's just turned September. The marshes can dry out in a very long, hot summer, but our summer hasn't been that good.'

'But he knows the area well,' persisted Loveluck. 'Surely he could avoid the marshes on his bike?'

The policeman leaned forward and wagged his finger at Loveluck. 'If he knows the marshes that well, he won't be taking a motorbike on the moor.'

'Then how would he travel?'

'With just a tent and a rucksack? By horseback. It's the only way. Parts of the Moor are very steep with large granite Tors rising up. You wouldn't want to take a motorbike up Brown Willy.'

They thanked him and left. Over lunch they began to map out a plan for a low key operation. It would be impractical to try and flood such a large area with men and equally pointless to try army style helicopter raids. Not that they would get the funding for it anyway.

Police land rovers, limited helicopter flights over the area and a small horse division were their resources.

Anderson sighed wearily. 'We've had the witches, now we've got the frigging cavalry.

The weather held fine for them but with forecasts of low cloud and possible fog which would doubtless ground the helicopters and make it difficult for anyone to operate efficiently.

Waddington sat thoughtfully. He didn't do that much field work and he was beginning to wonder if he should have included himself in this operation. He didn't like to be associated with failure, but they had a triple murderer on the loose and it had to be done. He had brought two marksmen as part of the team which he hoped he wouldn't have to use. All in all he was a troubled Detective Chief Inspector.

Helicopter sweeps had provided no firm leads. People had been spotted on the moor but no lone horsemen or motorbike riders. The land rovers, with suitable local police as guides, did what they could but that too was limited by the terrain.

As a matter of course they had headed to Brown Willy, the largest Tor and probably a good vantage point to see for miles but the trip had been dogged with incidents and at the end of the sorties they were no wiser.

The horses fared better as they were well equipped to cross streams and pass over rocky ground as well as the wide open ranges. Even so, although they worked in a pattern they had really no idea what they were seeking.

The search was called off for the evening with arrangements to start again at dawn. Later that evening the team dined at the Jamaica Inn and had fun with the many memorabilia there. They slept well. Tired and contented. The Inn had that effect on them.

Rufus had mysteriously turned up at the Jamaica Inn and sat up late talking to Sergeant Knightly. It was noticed by Waddington and Loveluck. 'Do you think that's wise?' asked Waddington indicating the couple in deep conversation.

'She was arresting him yesterday,' said Loveluck.

'As I understand it she might be arresting him again. He did hang Winston Gale, didn't he?'

Loveluck nodded. 'I think so. Him or his followers.'

'Is the evidence looking any better than it was?'

'No. Circumstantial evidence at best. We'll interview everyone, of course. But a tight knit group like that will support each other.'

Waddington took one last look at them sitting at a table. 'They certainly make a handsome couple. So why do I have such misgivings?' He sighed deeply. 'See you in the morning, Jack.'

'Goodnight, sir.'

Back in Sherborne the Psychic fair and Witches exhibition had packed up and was making for home. It had been a stunning success marred only by the sad death of the head of the New Forest witches, Nemesis.

In truth, the clash between the Sherborne and the New Forest covens had given them more excitement than they had had in many a long year. The New Forest witches said that they would lobby the authorities in Lymington to host the Psychics fair and witches exhibition next year and battle could recommence. As so they went their separate ways.

Chapter 32

Dawn came to Bodmin Moor and awoke the sleeping guests rudely with hammerings on the doors and persistent voices ringing out. Breakfast was welcome and hearty and they left for another day on the Moor with a spring in their steps. They had come well prepared with hot drinks and food wrapped up for lunch. The land rovers went on their way, the early helicopters made discrete scans of the area and Anderson and Loveluck leaned against a land rover chatting.

Anderson nodded at the sky. 'Looks like the clouds are getting worse. If it rains as well it could limit the helicopters.'

Loveluck scanned the skies. 'Miserable day to be in a place like this. Have you seen Pepper and Knightly recently?'

'They went to look at the horses. Knightly is a bit of a rider by all accounts. Pepper just likes horses.'

'Is there anything that Knightly isn't good at?'

The morning ground on and the boredom set in. Lunch was taken and came as a welcome break then the afternoon began. The skies began to clear and as the clouds lifted a lone helicopter began its scanning pattern.

They moved their land rovers further onto the moor. More for something to do rather than as a cunning plan and they settled down again to wait.

And then the radio burst into life. A lone horseman carrying a rucksack and tent had been spotted. Co-ordinates of his position were given. Orders barked out. Waddington woke from his snooze in the back of the land rover.

Maps were scanned. Google was consulted.

Then a marksman said loudly. 'Lone horse rider on the horizon moving at speed. I can take him down if you give the order, sir.'

Loveluck turned to the marksman who stood still, weapon resting on the vehicle, granite face unflinching. 'No, wait.' He called for binoculars to a uniformed officer.

'Lone horseman still on the horizon moving at speed. I can take him down if you give the order, sir.'

'Wait,' said Loveluck and focussed the binoculars on the horizon. Then he had it. The rider. But there was something familiar about the rider. The proud position in the saddle. The long hair flowing behind. It could only be one person.'

'Lone horseman still on the horizon moving at speed. I can take him down if....'

'No. It's one of ours. It's Knightly. Get back-up to those co-ordinates, and get it there damned fast.' He peered through the binoculars again. 'Stupid little fool.'

But there was nothing stupid about Sergeant Sadie Knightly. Nothing little and nothing foolish. This man she was chasing was a wanted killer. She rode with determination, with fire and with cold steel in her heart. And more, he wanted to kill her man and that spurred her on to ride faster over the difficult terrain.

In front of her Jakob was well aware of her pursuit, though he had no idea who was on the horse. He had shed his tent and rucksack already to lighten his load but he wasn't a natural horseman. A decent rider but not as good as Knightly.

He was unarmed apart from his thin wire. Knightly was unarmed except for a short truncheon. He was fit. She was fit. The helicopter could be heard in the distance, getting nearer.

Jakob knew that both the horse rider and the helicopter were closing in and he decided to stand his ground and fight. He reined in the horse, leapt to the ground and positioned himself behind a rock. He knew he was better on the ground than almost anyone.

But Knightly had no intention of fighting hand to hand and run the high risk of being garrotted. She had a much more powerful weapon. The horse.

The rock he was behind was not big enough to provide any real protection and when Knightly reared the horse onto its hind legs the front legs nearly caught him.

He needed her off that horse and he made a dash to get to the horse's side and drag her off by her legs but she was too quick for him.

Again he tried but she moved and reared the horse again. And again he scrambled away. But he stumbled. And fell. And then she had the horse all over him.

The helicopter had landed and two men alighted and ran towards her. 'Leave him. Leave him.'

But she too had murder in her heart. And again and again she trampled him before the two men grabbed the rein and grabbed her. She was beside herself with fury and frustration and tried to take the reins back but they overpowered her and handcuffed a badly hurt Jakob, taking them both to the side of the helicopter.

She took one last look at Jakob, inhaled deeply, nodded to the helicopter men, walked calmly to the horse and rode off onto the moor and into the distance.

Two days later her letter of resignation arrived at the police department citing herself as not fit to be a police officer.

Chapter 33

Inspector Loveluck and Sergeant Knightly stepped out of the hire car on Calle 6, Guadalmina Baja, went through the gate and walked up to the front door of the attractive villa.

Loveluck rang the bell and waited.

It was opened by a very familiar figure. 'Hello Sammy.'

'Oh. You're back. I suppose you'd better come in. When are you going to leave me alone? I haven't done anything.'

They sat in the living room and Sammy offered them drinks, which they declined.

Knightly looked long and hard at Sammy and Sammy returned the stare. The two women's eyes were locked together as they had been in the restaurant weeks earlier. But this time Knightly knew what she had discovered and Sammy knew as well. And that knowledge was not going to desert Knightly this time.

Sammy nodded sadly. 'You know, don't you?'

Knightly nodded.

Loveluck watched this in a state of not understanding. 'Can you tell me what you both know, because I have no idea.'

Sammy looked at Loveluck. 'What have you come here for? What do you want?'

'I've come to arrest you for aiding and abetting John Small in extortion and blackmail. I have an international warrant for your arrest.'

Sammy laughed out loud. 'He really doesn't know, does he?'

Knightly smiled.

'Put him out of his misery, sergeant.' And she laughed again.

Knightly stood up. 'Sammy, meet Inspector Loveluck.'

'We've met many times before,' said Loveluck feeling that he was becoming the butt of a joke.

'Inspector Loveluck. Meet........John Small.'

Sammy took a bow and then removed her wig. 'John Small at your service.' She replaced the wig.

Loveluck glanced from Sammy/John Small to Knightly and back again. 'How long have you known this?' asked Loveluck angrily.

'For certain, about as long as you. A minute.'

John Small sat down again and said to Knightly. 'What made you first suspect?'

'The photographs. On the beach and on the bikes.'

'Those photos were lousy quality.'

'Yes, they were. But there was something about them that just rang a faint bell in my head. I didn't know or suspect anything then. There was just something vaguely familiar about the face. I never for a moment thought of you, even though you were there at the time. What I actually thought was that I might have seen John Small somewhere and that was exciting. Little did I realise I was talking to him.'

Loveluck shook his head in disbelief. 'Sitting there you are Sammy Alcock to me. I still don't know what John Small looks like.'

Sammy smiled and took the wig off again. The light make up remained on her face and all Loveluck could see was Sammy Alcock with a bald head. 'You'll always be Sammy to me. I remember thinking that you could be as elusive as John Small. You are a master.'

'I'm sorry I led you such a merry path, but you wouldn't go away. I thought if I identified that corpse in the morgue as John Small you might leave me alone.' She shook her head sadly. 'No such luck. Now. I have a busy day so if I can just show you out? And thanks again for looking me up.'

Loveluck smiled. 'I'm afraid you don't quite understand, Sammy. Or should I say, Mr Small.'

'What don't I understand Inspector?

'I have an international arrest warrant in my pocket.' He took it out and waved it at her.

'I'm sorry, Inspector. I thought I heard you say that you had an arrest warrant for Samantha Alcock for aiding and abetting.' She went and stood very close to him. 'Inspector. There is no such person as Samantha Alcock. Your warrant is worthless.'

She ushered them to the door and they began to walk down the path when Knightly suddenly turned round again and looked long and hard at Sammy.

'Something else I can do for you?'

Knightly smiled and shook her head. 'No. I just want to take one last look at you. I have this feeling I'll never see you again.'

Sammy nodded. 'You won't. Goodbye Inspector. Sergeant.'

'Goodbye, Sammy. I really can't call you Mr Small. I hope you don't mind. Take care.'

And with that Loveluck and Knightly turned and left, both thinking of Sammy with admiration.

'I suppose the name Alcock should have been a clue.' said Loveluck. 'And it's a good job they didn't accept your resignation or you'd have missed Mr John Small.'

They climbed into the car, Knightly driving as usual. 'Well, boss. Where to? Or can I guess?'

'I think you can guess.'

And together they said.

'The Doghouse.'